DYING BAD

Recent Titles from Maureen Carter

The Bev Morriss Mysteries

WORKING GIRLS
DEAD OLD
BABY LOVE
HARD TIME
BAD PRESS
BLOOD MONEY
DEATH LINE

The Sarah Quinn Mysteries

A QUESTION OF DESPAIR *
MOTHER LOVE *
DYING BAD *

available from Severn House

DYING BAD

A Sarah Quinn Mystery

Maureen Carter

CRÈME de la CRIME

This first world edition published 2012
in Great Britain and the USA by
Crème de la Crime, an imprint of
SEVERN HOUSE PUBLISHERS LTD of
Salatin House, 19 Cedar Road, Sutton, Surrey SM2 5DA

British Library Cataloguing in Publication Data

Carter, Maureen.
Dying bad.
1. Quinn, Sarah (Fictitious character)–Fiction. 2. Women
detectives–England–Birmingham–Fiction. 3. Women
journalists–England–Birmingham–Fiction. 4. Assault
and battery–Fiction. 5. Detective and mystery stories.
I. Title
823.9'2-dc23

ISBN-13: 978-1-78029-036-2 (cased)

All Severn House titles are printed on acid-free paper.

Severn House Publishers support The Forest Stewardship Council [FSC],
the leading international forest certification organisation. All our titles that
are printed on Greenpeace-approved FSC-certified paper carry the FSC logo.

Typeset by Palimpsest Book Production Ltd.,
Falkirk, Stirlingshire, Scotland.
Printed and bound in Great Britain by
MPG Books Ltd., Bodmin, Cornwall.

Four Years Earlier

The moon's soft glow, just perceptible behind the cotton blind, barely penetrated the stark space. The girl lay on her back, stick-thin arms clamped tight to the sides of her slight body. Though her eyes were open, she saw little in the near darkness, and too much when they were closed. Picturing her surroundings was no problem anyway: the cheap wardrobe, flimsy three-drawer chest, worn carpet, blank walls.

For nine months her bedroom at Heath House had passed for what some people called home. It was the longest she'd stayed under one roof since being taken into care. Care. What a laugh. Hysterical, that was. There'd been countless short-term placements. As for foster families – was it three? No, four. Heath House was no better, no worse than any other second-best substitute. The windows weren't barred, the doors weren't locked 24/7, most of the staff were indifferent and as for the other kids? Who cared? Precisely. The girl had one or two mates, but mostly everyone kept to themselves. Maybe she was sick of running, too cowed to escape. Difficult anyway, with clipped wings.

Wincing, she shifted slightly, turned her head to one side. She could just make out the familiar silhouette of a teddy bear sprawled on the floor under the window. Alfie was one of the few belongings she'd hung on to from her mum's place. BC, she thought of it. Before she lost her childhood; before Christ had it in for her. She gave a resigned sigh. She adored Alfie, treasured his thinning fur; knew every inch of his squashy old body. Like the bloke now pinning her down, the cold hand pawing her boob, the mean fingers probing between her thighs. Her shudder was involuntary.

He'd been doing her more or less since she got here. The shit-for-brains probably thought she didn't know who he was. Strangers in the night. Like hell. Sneaking in while she was in the bathroom, taking the bulb from the bedside lamp was as good as an early warning system. The girl knew what would happen when she got into bed. She'd lie waiting, listening out for the soft footfalls that stopped at her door, the creak as he turned the handle. She knew who it was even in the dark. The reek of BO laced with onions was pretty distinctive. At least he didn't hurt her as bad as the others.

'Hey, girlie, what's up?' A whisper; warm breath against her neck. 'You know you like it, don't you?' Menacing now. 'Tell me you like it.' It wasn't a request.

'I like it.' Listless. Experience had taught her it was easier and usually quicker to comply. She'd heard the threats before, knew them by heart. If she didn't do what he said, he'd feed her piece by piece to his dogs.

'Course you do, babe.' He forced open her thighs. She clamped her mouth shut, just wanted it over. In her mind's eye, she was drinking cocktails in a bar in New York. In her mind's eye she was swimming with dolphins in clear warm water. In her mind's eye, she was an A-lister swanning down the red carpet, pausing now and then to let the snappers get a decent pic. It was anytime, anyplace, anywhere in her mind's eye. Frigging Martini girl, she was.

When he thrust into her, shuddering, rasping her name, she tensed, terrified her spine would snap, scared it would never end. Last time, she'd sworn she'd never cry again, only realised she'd broken the promise when cooling tears trickled into her ears. She counted thirty, forty seconds until he got his breath back. Then, as usual, he straddled her, forced her hands over her head and hissed the same old question.

'Why'd you make me do it, babe?'

She knew her line. ''Cause I'm bad.'

Sweat dripped off his face, stung her eyes, tasted salty on her lips. She flinched as he stroked a finger along her jaw. 'How bad?'

'Dead bad.'

ONE

'Cheer up, love. It may never 'appen.' The landlord of the Queen's Head gave a cheesy wink as he pulled a pint, blissfully unaware how close he was to getting it in the neck. DI Sarah Quinn tapped a tetchy index finger on the tacky bar, itching to lash out with the verbal equivalent of a good slapping. As far as she was concerned *it* had happened, and as for the *love* – not even her nearest and dearest got away with the endearment let alone some nerd who happened to run the squad's local.

'Play nicely now, Quinn.' A bulky presence had sidled over and mouthed a gentle warning in her ear with all the subtlety of a ventriloquist's dummy. Without looking she knew who it was. Though the chief was more accustomed to throwing his weight than his basso profundo. Detective Chief Superintendent Fred Baker was the only officer at Lloyd House nick – senior or not – with the brass neck to address her habitually as Quinn. The aftershave was a clue, too. The chief doused himself during the day with Paco Rabanne, even now it was coming off him in waves. Glimpsing that butter-wouldn't-melt big face in the mottled mirror at the back of the bar was the clincher.

The DI's finger stalled. 'I never opened—'

'You were about to bite, Quinn.' Talking out of the corner of his mouth was not a good look. He could've walked a gurning contest.

'With you in a tick, Mr B.' Len shuffled off ferrying two pint glasses, grey slacks straining across his bum.

Baker toasted the landlord's back with what was left of his bitter. 'No sense taking it out on other bods, Quinn. Besides . . .' He drained the dregs, then wiped a meaty hand across moist lips. '. . . pissing off Laughing Len is not a good move.'

He had a point: the pub was less than a five-minute walk from the nick and the saloon bar was second home to some cops. Len was a more than genial host. Lock-ins being a speciality. Shrugging, the DI muttered 'my mouth' desultorily under her breath. Just as well. Baker wasn't listening, he was finger-combing his hair in the mirror. After six years working under him, so to speak, she was inured to his idiosyncrasies. His default mode was sexist git and ordinarily it was water off a duck's back. Ordinarily.

Stifling a sigh, she caught sight of her reflection alongside his, surprised in a way that the afternoon's debacle didn't show in her face. *Come on, woman. Don't play the drama queen.* Any impact, if or when it hit, would harden her attitude, not her appearance. And she had enough cynicism, thanks. Station clowns called her the Snow Queen, the Ice Maiden, the Arctic Cop, you get the drift. The names weren't entirely down to her Nordic colouring, tight bun, piercing grey eyes. They were more indicative of an emotional detachment that bordered on aloof, the cool exterior designed to keep feelings – and people – at arm's length. It was a persona she was happy to play on.

So how come she was so frigging worked up?

And what was taking Len so long? She was gasping for a drink though she'd only dropped by in the hope company would be a distraction. Like that was happening. The chief was currently fiddling with his phone, checking emails, messages, whatever. He'd been spitting razor blades along with everyone else earlier. But Baker didn't seem to dwell long on anything, especially cock-ups. Clocking him in the mirror again, she had a bird's-eye view of the top of his head. Apart from a white streak down one side – like a badger with an off-centre parting – the hair was too dark for a man pushing sixty. Not that he'd own up to it. Six-four and chunky, the chief must've shed around a stone since his wife took off. Mind there were still several boulders to shift. Sarah gave the ghost of a smile then pursed her lips. Had to admit, he wasn't a bad looking guy.

Ramming the phone in his pocket, his glance met hers in the glass. 'Admiring the view, Quinn?'

'Oh, how they laughed.' She overdid the simper. As for laugh, it was more than the squad had. 'I just can't believe—'

'No sense harping on.' Baker was signalling for a refill with an imaginary glass. 'We'll nail the bastard.'

The DI's jaw slackened. For an insensitive sod, the chief could be amazingly intuitive. He read her mind so well she reckoned he'd mentored Derren Brown.

'It may have escaped your attention . . . we'd already nailed the bastard. How the hell they could—'

'Life's too short. Let it go, Quinn.' Jingling coins in his pocket, he was more interested in trying to catch Len's eye.

'For fuck's sake.' The expletive was rare. She felt a flush rise on her cheeks. 'Just for once, will you let me finish a—?'

'Sod this for a game of soldiers – I need to turn the bike round. Get the drinks in, will you, lass?'

Lass? Still open-mouthed, she watched him wander off to take a leak, wishing she could move on so easily. She'd been about to say the word 'sentence' – and of course that word resurrected *it*.

Earlier that afternoon, she and Baker had been in court to observe sentences being handed down on a pair of scumbags. The men, both in their late-thirties, were given fifteen months apiece for relieving four schoolgirls of what was left of their childhood, and leaving emotional scars that would stay with the teenagers and their loved ones for the rest of their lives.

She pictured the pinched features, pale faces, haunted eyes, sensed the girls' hurt, the betrayal they must have felt, twice over. Amy, Dawn, Laura and Natasha – the eldest, just fifteen – were the latest victims of a criminal growth area: older men preying on young white girls from comfortable homes, good families. Sarah wasn't the only cop shocked by the lack of official statistics; equally disturbing was the fact the media generally pointed the finger at Asians, more specifically Pakistani men. Racial stereotyping was a cop-out; the issue went deeper, was far more complex than colour.

'Not on your own are you, ma'am?' Paul Wood paused en passant carrying a tray full of drinks for some of the lads. He was the longest serving detective sergeant in the squad, usually kept a paternal eye out for her.

'No. I'm good thanks, Woodie.' Her fleeting smile belied her thoughts. Grooming, the media called it. Pimping with knobs on, Sarah called it. Not that the girls were on the game. Only in the sense the men regarded them as sex toys.

And when the big boys had had their fill, they passed the goods on to their playmates. Emotive phrases like 'easy meat' and 'white trash' were bandied about in the press, spouted by people who should know better, or choose words more wisely.

The issue wasn't just complex – it was explosive.

She cast her mind back to the afternoon's bombshell, the vocal fireworks in the court when a third defendant was unexpectedly released. Insufficient evidence, dodgy statements, flaky performances in the box from shit-scared witnesses, the judge dismissed the case and Jas Ram walked. Running a gauntlet of death threats from the public gallery.

Sarah's verdict? Whoever said two out of three ain't bad was talking bollocks: Ram was the biggest scumbag of the lot, head groom in a stable of terrified and vulnerable young girls. And he was out there now probably adding to his livestock.

'Ditch the scowl, Quinn. You'll frighten the horses.' Baker grinning ear-to-ear.

Her expression was glacial. 'Why don't you—?'

'Here you go, Mr B. Sorry to keep you waiting.' Len's interruption was timely. She might have said something she wouldn't regret. The landlord handed over a glass as if it contained holy water. *What was it with blokes and beer?*

Baker ran an admiring glance over the contents before taking a slurp. 'Liquid gold, Len. Liquid gold, my son.' He smacked his lips. Sarah would happily have done it for him.

'What about you, love?' Forget pints, the landlord's grin revealed a couple of teeth that needed pulling. 'The usual, is it? Or you livin' dangerously tonight?'

'Listen, sunshine . . .' Narrowing her eyes, she beckoned him closer, vaguely aware Baker was having trouble swallowing.

'What you drinking, boss?' Good timing again, or what? DC Dave Harries, back from a bit of legwork, had materialised on her other side. Maybe there was a conspiracy to keep Len sweet. Either way, it was her young sidekick's lucky day.

'Large gin and tonic, ice, no lemon.' She treated Baker to a tight smile. 'And it's the chief's shout, Dave.'

'Ta, very much, sir.' Harries loosened his scarf, smoothed his hair. 'Pint of Guinness, cheers.'

'Don't drink it all at once, lad.' Was Baker's parting shot. Hand in pocket, he wandered off to join the blokes watching soccer on the telly. The big screen didn't exactly blend in with the low ceiling and dark panelling. Glancing further round, Sarah clocked Christmas lights flashing from smoke-blackened beams; copper bed pans still trailed garish green tinsel. It was more than a week since Twelfth Night. She frowned. Supposed to be bad luck, that. *Could explain a lot.*

'Cheers, Dave.' She raised her glass, took a sip. Harries sank an inch or two of his stout. 'I heard what happened in court, boss. It's a real downer.'

'Got that right.' Leaning back against the bar, she ran her gaze over a squad that should be celebrating not drowning sorrows. By now, tables were strewn with glasses, and cops with a bevy or two inside them were maybe slightly less pissed off than a few hours back. But the derisory prison terms and Ram's shock release had been a kick in the teeth for every officer who'd built the case and helped get it to court. Making an effort, she moved on. 'How about you, Dave? Any joy?'

He'd been out knocking doors, trying to trace witnesses to a street attack. He wasn't the only detective landed with a short straw, half the squad was working on Operation Steel. The incident – two days ago – had been particularly vicious. It had similarities with a mugging a week earlier and the fear was it wouldn't be the last.

'Joy?' He snorted. 'I wish.' As if working the streets of Stirchley wasn't bad enough, he clearly hadn't thawed out yet. She could almost smell the cold wafting off the black wool of his coat. Dave had taken to wearing dark gear all the time recently. He probably reckoned it bolstered his passing resemblance to a pre-raddled Keith Richards. Maybe she shouldn't have mentioned the likeness. He'd be getting ideas above his station next. She twitched a lip. The Boy Wonder, as Baker called him, had only made detective eighteen months back.

'Nothing doing, then?' she prompted.

'On a scale of one to ten?' Harries took another drink. She cut him a stop-faffing-around glance which he clearly didn't catch. 'Twenty. Tell you this, boss, I'd have got more chat out of Tommy.'

'Tommy?'

'Deaf, dumb, blind kid. The Who? Y'know.'

'I know I shouldn't have asked,' she muttered. A quick glance at her watch coincided with the News at Ten bongs blaring from the box.

'We'll have to go back any road.' Harries turned his mouth down. 'Loads of people were out. Again.'

Friday night. Course they were. On the splurge: wages, benefits, ill-gotten gains. Getting hammered on cheap booze. As opposed to just getting hammered – like the victim of Wednesday's assault. She grimaced. 'Having the guy's ID would help, of course.'

'Difficult that.' Harries scratched his chin, probably thinking along similar lines. The body had been stripped of any clue and even the poor sod's mother would struggle to recognise him. Maybe when the swelling went down and the stitches came out, they could issue a mug shot that wouldn't give kids nightmares.

'Still nothing on misper, boss?'

She shook her head. Asked herself if it was significant that no one in the late-thirties/early-forties age group had been reported missing? Dossers and druggies often don't have anyone looking out for them but the victim didn't have the appearance of a vagrant or a user. He might just live on his own and his absence hadn't yet been noticed. Mind, it had taken three days for the mother of the first victim to come forward. Thank God she had, he'd been beaten so badly he could barely remember his own name.

Loud jeers went up from the crowd congregated around the TV and for a second Sarah assumed there'd been a foul or a missed penalty. No, couldn't be that. The game had finished. Curious, she turned her head to look at the screen.

Foul and missed penalty were both spot on.

Surrounded by cameras, Jas Ram was centre-frame kicking off in front of Birmingham Crown Court. The words were inaudible under the reporter's voice-over. The body language and face were vocal enough; both said relaxed, confident, confiding even. It struck Sarah again how physical attraction could mask the basest behaviour, that good looking men – and women – often came across as more plausible, that so-called lookers generally got an easier ride in life. Like high cheekbones meant high morals. Regular features denoted a regular guy. She sniffed. Bring on the fleet of Ferraris. Ram was one of the best looking men she'd ever seen. As a person – one of the ugliest.

'. . . vilified, spat at, I've been to hell and back.' There was instant silence in the bar – Ram now had a speaking role. 'No one should get away with treating people like that.'

'No one' meant the police, of course. And for 'people' he meant himself. *Unless, he was playing the race card.* Glancing round, she guessed colleagues had the same idea. Heads shook, expressions were incredulous, there were a couple of low whistles. Harries was on the phone.

'Naturally, I'll be seeking compensation for wrongful arrest.'

Naturally. Christ, even the guy's voice was seductive: smooth, honeyed, accent free. Lowering his gaze an artful touch, he bit his bottom lip, paused as though weighing up whether to continue. Like there was ever any doubt. 'But this isn't all about me.' Humble murmur. Decision apparently made, he raised his head, swept a blue-black fringe out of dark treacle eyes and talked into the nearest lens. 'I'll be seeking legal advice with a view to taking action against the police. Innocent citizens like me need protecting from suffering the same ordeal.'

Paul Wood played an imaginary violin. Other cops were more vocal.

'My heart bleeds.'

'Arsehole.'

'What about the victims, you twat.'

'Shush.' Baker's raised palm quelled the squad's running commentary. Saint Jas no longer held the stage. Cameras were trained on a middle-aged man striding into shot with his fist raised. Even distorted with rage, the face rang a bell with the DI. She cut Harries a querying glance but he still had the mobile clamped to his ear. *Come on, Dave, you're missing the best bits.*

The man barged his way through the media scrum. 'You evil effing bastard. Prison's too good for your kind of scum.' A second or two more and he'd have landed the punch he was swinging, but a police sergeant had sprinted across and now held the man's arm out of harm's way.

'Shame,' Baker murmured.

'Hear this, shit head,' the man snarled. 'I'll see you rot in hell.' He was a relative of one of the girls, but Sarah still couldn't put a name to the face. Suddenly the guy threw his head back and spat. Ram ducked but not fast enough. He was wiping gob off his cheek when the picture cut to the reporter's piece to camera.

That, and the accompanying cheers from the squad, was probably why it took a few seconds for the DI to clock who the hack was. The fur hat was a distraction, too. When, by popular request Len switched channels, Sarah turned away, lips still curved. Christ on a bike. It must have been brass monkeys for Caroline King to go out looking like that. And why was a journo of her calibre covering a Birmingham court case? Surely there had to be richer pickings?

'Earth to Major Quinn.' Baker's hand played windscreen-wiper perilously close to her face. 'A few of us are buggering off to the Taj. Fancy a bite?'

A naan finger if you don't back off. Mind, there was very little food at home, as per – and none of it appealed. 'Yeah, OK, why not?'

'Maybe not, boss.' Harries shoved the phone in his coat pocket. 'Uniform are requesting back-up. A man's body's been found off Newton Road.' Not a million miles from the law courts.

'And.' Reaching for her coat.

'He's Asian. And the death's suspicious.'

TWO

Jas Ram – recent recipient of a bunch of death threats – taken out? A stone's throw from the court where he'd been released? No way. Mouth turned down, Sarah tapped the wheel. There were coincidences and there was wishful thinking. Hers. And the notion put a novel slant on the term death wish.

'Sure you're OK, boss?' Harries was scoffing a late supper grabbed on the way out of the pub: salt and vinegar crisps with Mars bar chaser. If he didn't watch the crumbs, it'd be his last supper as well. They were in her new Audi. They'd toyed with walking it, the crime scene was barely half a mile from the Queen's Head, but depending what panned out, they'd need wheels later, if only to deliver the death knock. Traffic was light in the heart of the city, biggest hazard was jaywalkers tanked up on jolly juice.

'I'm fine, Dave.' She definitely wasn't over the limit. Not on half a G&T. Baker's levels had been borderline and turning up half-cut at a crime scene was probably the best way to get your hands on a P45 and wave goodbye to a pension. Besides, suspicious deaths don't ordinarily warrant the presence of a DCS. He'd waved off the DI instead, cracking some limp line about who shot JR?

So not funny. Besides, as far as they knew, and detail was skimpy, the death wasn't gun-related. But Sarah's humour bypass was down to more than that. She was battling with the uncomfortable knowledge that if Jas Ram had been wasted, she wouldn't give a rat's ass.

'D'you reckon it's Ram, then?' Harries was still stuffing his face.

'I don't do predictions, Dave.' They'd find out soon enough. What she did reckon was that Ram was a worthless piece of shit who'd inflicted untold damage – physical, emotional, psychological – on naïve and vulnerable school-girls; innocent kids approached on the street and turned into lucrative sex slaves. Sarah had spent countless hours interviewing the victims, drawing out the detail, pulling together the picture. She rarely let cases get under her skin, never this badly.

Idling at a red in Temple Way, she felt a shiver down her spine. Either someone had walked over her grave or the temperature had taken a dive. She leaned forward, peered up through the windscreen, pinpricks of starlight glittered in a clear indigo sky, but the star turn was the moon, a perfect disc of white light. She blamed her goosebumps on the falling mercury, aware it wasn't the only cause.

Harries had been watching. 'Penny for 'em boss?' He was licking his fingers.

'Cost you more than that.' The light changed and she eased the car forward. Right now her thoughts weren't for sale, or to share. Still the front runner was how the world would be a better place minus Ram. For Sarah, professionally and personally, the judgement was questionable. She was a cop, for Christ's sake. Wanting some thug's premature demise wasn't exactly on the job description.

'Actually, DC Harries.' She jabbed a finger towards the foot-well. 'I'm wondering how many more sodding crisps are going to end up on my carpet.'

'Whoops.' He swept a hand across his lap. Bad move.

'Just because your motor doubles as a trash cart . . .' The corollary was tacit. Harries drove a red two-seater MG that Highgate clowns called the babe magnet. Sniffing – mock offended – he turned ostensibly to window-gaze. Catching his yada-yada face in the wing mirror, she masked a smile. The affectionate irreverence was good, stopped her taking herself too seriously, as long as he didn't cross the line.

She got a whiff of vinegar fumes as he leaned across to stuff the empty packet in his pocket. 'Should be coming up on the left, boss.'

'You don't say?' she muttered. Biggest clue was the burly cop in a high vis vest stopping traffic. He recognised Sarah, turned his salute into a hand signal, waved the car through. Three police vehicles, blues still flashing, were in situ and a forensics team stood round the open doors of a white transit. Towards the end on the right, blue and white tape cordoned off the pavement and a wide section of road. Duckboards had been laid and led into a gap between two properties. The architecture on both sides of the street was a mishmash: mock-Gothic stood cheek by jowl with Georgian, Victorian, Edwardian – you name it. It looked as if a load of hyperactive kids had been let loose with the Lego.

'Still, it's good to know you've got your priorities right, DI Quinn.' Harries' delivery had an arch you could drive through.

'Meaning?' She was cruising, eyes peeled for a parking place out of forensics harm's way. As well as registering a shed-load of black doors and brass knockers, the glint from discreet wall plaques caught her eye. They'd be advertising professional services, mostly law firms, given the proximity of the courts and the coroner's office.

'Well, there's you stressing about the state of your interior while me, I'm sweating the hard stuff. The case? The victim?' He released the belt as she cut the engine. 'How we're going to crack it.'

'Great.' Opening the door. 'Don't let me stop you.' She was reaching into the boot by the time he joined her. 'Those great thoughts, then? Are you sharing, or what?' Handing him a sealed plastic bag.

'Sure am. Numero uno: if someone's bumped off Ram it'd do us all a bloody favour.'

Great minds. 'And?'

'Two: we'd be swimming in suspects.'

She managed a nod. Even with one hand on the car for support, she was struggling to get into the bunny suit. She was pretty sure Harries was on the money though. Who had better motive to see Ram dead than the girls' families? What if a father, say, had taken a pound of the proverbial? He'd get sent down for life and a family already suffering would be ripped further apart.

Nothing like getting ahead of yourself, Sarah.

As they headed in step to the action, her keen gaze raked the surroundings. 'Any more in that crystal ball of yours, Dave?' The query was casual, she was concentrating on possible exit and entry routes, clocking hidden cameras.

'I see you and—' he was hamming it up, fingers massaging temples – 'a tall dark guy who's dead fit and going places. Initials are DH.'

She twitched a lip. *Yeah right.* That's definitely what she called wishful thinking.

THREE

I t was far too good to be true. A cursory glance, even from a distance, had told Sarah the victim wasn't Jas Ram. The body was too short, too fat, and what little flesh was exposed, too white. Besides, knowing Ram, he wouldn't be seen dead in cheap shoes and an ill-fitting shiny black suit.

After liaising briefly with the crime scene manager and the first attending officers, the DI now hunkered down by the body; the pathologist Richard Patten squatted across from her. Space was limited and cross-contamination the last thing they needed. Harries was down the road picking the duty inspector's brain.

Sarah cast a curious glance over her shoulder. 'How come you thought he was Asian, Phil?'

The ruined face could've been any ethnicity, but a trouser leg had ridden up and the few inches of skin on show was definitely pale. The black shirt had a Nehru collar but sartorial preference hardly counted as a pointer to race.

'My mistake, ma'am.' Helmet under arm, PC Ryan stood the other side of the tape studying a pair of hastily borrowed Doc Martens. His own boots, bagged and tagged, were with forensics. Not many cops come across a body by chance. Phil Ryan had been on foot patrol and virtually tripped over the bloody thing. His partner, Linda Fellows had been tasked with keeping the attendance log and was currently working the street, recording anything with a pulse.

Not something troubling Mr Shiny Suit.

'I'm sorry, like.' Beads of sweat glistened over Ryan's top lip. Surely, he wasn't hot? Every time anyone opened their mouth, Sarah thought a new pope had been elected. 'It was a lot darker then, ma'am, couldn't really see much of anything.'

So, why speculate? She let it go. The guy might as well have 'newbie' tattooed on his forehead. At least he was upfront about the slip and probably still freaked out from the shock.

Once he got over it, he'd likely dine out on the story. From what she'd gleaned so far, everything else had been done by the book. Which the experienced uniformed inspector who'd turned out could have written: an outer perimeter had been established, the inner forensic corridor laid and the crime scene secured. The actions were built into a cop's DNA: if it was too late to save a life, top priority was preserving the evidence.

That the victim was a goner was as plain as the nose . . . Sarah sniffed. It wasn't the best analogy, given the state of his face. Death had been formally pronounced by the divisional surgeon before Sarah arrived. A doctor had to declare life extinct even when a body had no head, let alone heartbeat. At least the medico hadn't hung around, the fewer live bodies trampling the scene the better.

Uniformed officers posted at both ends of the street were keeping out any passing punters. Chambers Row was neither rat run, nor pedestrian cut through, but police activity was like a magnet. Sarah had encountered grandstanders at previous crime scenes totally convinced a cop show was being shot. Mind, these days, savvy types hefted their own cameras with an eye to flogging the footage. That's if the media weren't already out in force. Which, a quick scout round confirmed, they still weren't.

She had to shield her eyes for a few seconds when the auxiliary lighting kicked in. They'd been making do with torches and strategically-directed full beams from a cop car. Enough light had been cast to see the victim was Caucasian, middle-aged and, as far as Sarah could tell, had no distinguishing features. Swallowing, she tasted bile. Now it was more like no distinguishable features. And where had all the blood come from? The jacket and shirt were slick with the stuff.

She glanced up at the pathologist. 'OK if I leave you to it, Rich?' He didn't need an audience and she'd seen enough. Actually, not. The body had no ID.

Patten raised his head, dark irises visible between mask and hood. 'No worries. I'll find you when I'm done.'

She gave a fleeting smile. He was probably the best pathologist she worked with. His willingness to voice an opinion at the scene was worth its weight. Doctors generally kept their cards so close to their chest she was surprised it didn't stop circulation.

Standing now, she snapped off the latex gloves while making eye contact with Ryan. 'You're sure you didn't touch anything?' Not likely but the young PC had already put his foot in it, literally.

'No ma'am. I could see he was dead. I'd no reason to check. That's exactly how I found him.' Stuffing the gloves in a pocket, she followed his gaze. The body was slumped against a red-brick wall in the cobbled passageway between two buildings, a law firm and offices of the probation service. When Ryan came across it, it had been wedged between a brace of wheelie bins. 'I shouted Linda to keep away, had a quick shufti, then kept a watching brief with her out here until Inspector Wilding and the others arrived. One of the forensic people said it'd be OK to move the bins to gain access but that's it.'

Gain access? She frowned. Couldn't be doing with manual speak. Why not just say, get closer? Was Ryan one of those people who adopted formal language to distance ugly reality? She hoped not for his sake.

Hearing rustling, Sarah turned to see two FSI photographers return for more shots. They'd already reeled off a load of stills and video but the more the better. The inquiry needed pictures of every inch, every angle and, as Baker invariably put it, every orifice. A full accurate record showing the location both with and without the body was vital. Not just for evidence but every squad member needed a feel for the scene even though most would never set foot in it. *Unlike Ryan.*

The cameramen were clearly ready for their close-ups. Holding the tape for them, she nodded a greeting. Given the stink of blood and piss and whatever was rotting in the bins, thank God it wasn't smelly-vision.

Ducking under the tape herself, she signalled Ryan to follow. Right now he was both police officer and prime witness and, in her experience, neither was infallible. No one recalled facts immediately, fully or accurately. More intelligence invariably emerged during retelling or under questioning. Halting under a street light, she asked him to talk her through it again. Studying his face closely she was also on aural alert for any discrepancy, deviation. Ryan had no difficulty holding her gaze and his second account was virtually verbatim. He and PC Fellows had been nearing the end of their beat. She was on police radio so stayed out front while he went to check the rear of the premises, primarily because there'd been an attempted break-in at the chambers the week before. He didn't make it that far because the victim's legs were protruding and Ryan almost went arse over tit.

'Sorry, ma'am, I meant I nearly—'

'I've heard worse, Phil.' She scratched her cheek. 'And it was nine fifteen, nine thirty when you realised what you were dealing with?' Establishing a timeline early on was vital. The real question was how long had the body been there. She and Harries had arrived at 10.54. It was getting on for half-eleven now. Ryan fumbled in a tunic pocket. Did he really need a notebook?

No. He wiped a tissue round his mouth. 'I put the call in to control at 21.45, ma'am.'

'And there was no one else around? You didn't see or hear anything? Before, during, after?'

'No, ma'am, not here, anyway.' Noise, he told her, had filtered through from surrounding streets, traffic passing, people laughing, footsteps. It was Friday night in the city, go figure. So why didn't he look too convinced. Was it possible he'd been so fazed he was scared something or someone had slipped the net?

'OK, Phil. If anything comes back . . .' It didn't need spelling out and he'd give a formal statement later. Thank God for CCTV though, they'd chase the footage soon as. There was half decent coverage round these parts. In theory, there should be something on tape. But what had they got on their hands? Random attack, premeditated murder, booze-fuelled fight or another mugging gone belly-up? The injuries here weren't dissimilar to the previous incidents but that meant little without corroborating evidence.

She watched Ryan join the end of a slow-moving line of officers in dark overalls. Seven or eight men and women head down, shoulder-to-shoulder, heavy duty torches trained on the ground. It put Sarah in mind of a Spielberg movie. All they needed was an alien or two, maybe a bit of dry ice. She shivered again. If it got much colder, they'd soon have the real thing. She suspected the current search grid was too wide. The street was full of the usual crap: butt ends, bus tickets, chewing gum, chips. There'd be a fingertip search at first light and they'd need to get a move on, the road couldn't stay closed indefinitely. Once the body was removed and the FSI guys moved in, hopefully the chances of turning up something more significant would increase. She blew her cheeks out on a sigh. Wouldn't say no to the murder weapon.

'Blimey. That was from the depths, DI Quinn.' Richard Patten was walking towards her, medical case in hand, glint in eye. 'I thought you were happy in your work. Freezing your butt off all hours of the day and night. Keeping our streets safe.'

'Happy? I'm delirious.'

'I could probably give you something for that?' Deadpan.

Her wide smile was the first for a while. She found Patten attractive and sensitive, a rare combination in her cop circle. Tall and lean with dark hair that fell into a floppy fringe, he invariably dressed casually, usually wore T-shirts you could read. She respected him and was pretty sure the feeling was mutual.

'I'll tell you what you can give me, Rich.' Mental cringe. God, that came out wrong.

'You'll be after an early steer?' *Was his lip curved?* She walked him to his beat-up old Land Rover where a grizzled black Labrador stared mournfully through the back window. Opening the driver's door, Patten said he'd try and schedule the post-mortem for mid-morning. *Good man.* He knew she'd have to attend and any earlier would be a pain.

'I'll tell you this though, Sarah: the killer doesn't do half measures. That's a hell of a savage attack back there.' He slid his case across, climbed in effortlessly after it. 'The facial injuries were caused by some sort of blunt instrument. And there are stab wounds to the chest and neck. The knife'll have a serrated blade.' *Make that two murder weapons.* 'As to cause of death? Take your pick. Trauma injury? Blood loss? Shock?

Could even be cardiac arrest.' Winking, he clicked on the
ignition. 'Catch you in the morning.'

Arms crossed, she watched the tail lights disappear,
murmuring, 'There y'go . . . I said I was delirious—'

'You will be, boss.' Harries joined the farewell party rocking
on his heels, looking like a kid in a sweet shop. 'Rumour has
it Jas Ram's just been nicked.'

FOUR

J as Ram, in rude good health, was laying down the law in
the custody suite at Lloyd House. 'I'm not being fobbed
off with some fucking drongo – I want my own brief.'
Maybe he thought thwacking the booking-in desk added weight
to the argument.

The custody sergeant gave a one-shoulder shrug and what
might have been a tight smile. Dick Klein was as inscrutable
as a Chinese poker player. 'Beggars, Choosers, Mr Ram.'
Easing back into the chair, Klein folded beefy arms over barrel
chest. He had a blond crew cut and light blue eyes. Other cops
called him Fritz.

'You saying I'm a beggar, fatso?' Ram cut a contemptuous
glance which extended to a traffic cop at each shoulder
currently cramping his style. Neither officer possessed Klein's
sphinx-like countenance. In their case, it was more Cheshire
cat grin. When they'd run the Porsche number plate through
the PNC and Ram's details popped out, it was like hitting pay
dirt. Well, dirt.

'Would I do that, Mr Ram?' Klein asked equably. 'But if
Mr Blunt chooses not to represent you . . .' His opened arms,
one with a rose tattoo, asked: What can I do? Vincent Blunt
had already made up his mind. He'd been Ram's tame lawyer
during the grooming trial, but clearly had a feral streak. Or
maybe it was easier on the end of a phone to tell your client
to sling his hook. That was Klein's interpretation; he'd only
heard Ram's side.

'The offer's still there, Mr Ram. If you want legal representation, I can get the duty solicitor here in half an hour.' Klein checked the Tag Heuer on his wrist. 'That'd bring us up to midnight. Calling in your own – sorry, *another* of your own – could take a while. And as we know, the clock's ticking.'

'Tick-tock. Tick-tock.' One of the traffic cops provided helpful sound effects. 'Tick—'

'Shut it, dipstick,' Ram snarled. He didn't need the distraction, not when he was desperately trying to think it through. Pulled over on suspicion of drink driving, he'd refused a breath test so Arsy and Butch here had hauled him in to the station. Ram wasn't convinced he was over the limit so he'd applied delaying tactics. But, as fat pig hadn't long pointed out, if he refused to blow in the bag a second time, they'd charge him with failing to produce a sample. Either way he'd lose his licence: banned if he was, banned if he wasn't. Vinnie could've tried pulling a Mr Loophole, but the bastard had sounded pissed as a fart. Like Ram, he'd probably been celebrating the victory in court. And that's what this little performance was all about. Ram wasn't stupid: he knew full well it had nothing to do with his driving. Everything to do with his walking.

'I know your game.' The sullen scowl said he wasn't happy to play. 'You're a bunch of vindictive tossers.'

Unmoved, Klein lifted a pen from the desk. 'If you'd like more time to consider, Mr Ram?'

'Tick-tock.' The helpful cop.

Klein consulted a list like it was a hotel register. 'I'm sure I must have *one* cell free.'

'All the sea views gone, Fritz?' Helpful cop number two.

'Why don't you shut it?' The pig had a point though. Ram glanced round. The Ritz it was not. Décor was grunge-grey shot through with snot green. The dive heaved with lowlife scum, losers stinking of piss and BO, shouting their mouths off, throwing their guts up, fucking health hazard wasn't in it. Sooner he was out the better.

'I'll have the duty solicitor.'

Klein reached for a phone, didn't miss a beat. 'Needs must when the devil drives, Mr Ram.'

*   *   *

The offence wasn't serious enough to keep Ram in overnight, he was being detained in an interview room pending the lawyer's arrival. Sprawled in a chair, sipping machine coffee, he leafed through the copy of PACE he'd told Klein to provide. Ram knew the Police and Criminal Evidence Act better than his bank statements, requesting it was a pointed gesture to keep the pigs on their toes. PC Troglodyte seated opposite, didn't bat an eyelash when Ram slammed the tome shut and chucked it across the table. *Moron looked brain dead anyway.*

There was only so long Ram could admire his nails. He shot to his feet and started circling the small overheated room, hands jammed in pockets of black denim drainpipes. The brown leather jacket draped carelessly over the back of his chair displayed an Armani label.

The cop – he'd told Ram his name was Graves – had less animation than a posthumous slug. Ram suspected he was only there to intimidate. A minder wasn't required by law, Ram wasn't going anywhere and he sure as hell wasn't on suicide watch. His room mate would be Klein's idea of a joke. The cop was built like a tank and ugly as sin. 'How much longer are you lot keeping me here?'

'Pass.' Graves gave a jaw cracking yawn, hairy arms already stretched over close-cropped scalp.

'Says in there, you lot have to treat me with respect.' Ram jabbed a thumb at the regulations.

He tugged an imaginary forelock. 'Pass . . . sir.'

'Fucking comedian.' Ram continued the circular tour, trying not to breathe in the stale air and stench of despair a host of previous occupants had bequeathed. Their visible legacy was sepia stains and stripes on the walls and floors. Ram didn't bother trying to pin down the exact source, sidestepped the worst patches. The silence was broken by the chiming bells of a church clock. He was well aware of the time without counting.

More pacing. This was all about mind games, who was in control. Ram knew that but his patience, like the carpet, was wearing thin. Planting both palms on the table, he leaned into Graves' space. 'It's gone midnight. The cop out there said . . .' He heard the door open and spun his head around, eyes narrowed, mouth flecked with saliva. 'Where the fuck've—'

'Sorry to keep you waiting, Mr Ram.'

You been all my life? 'No harm done, babe. Take a seat. Let's have a little chat.' Ram smiled, licked his lips. Oh, yes. He'd definitely have the duty solicitor.

Ruby Wells had been patronised – and hit on – by bigger men than Jas Ram. And women come to that. It was one of the downsides of striking good looks. In London, where she'd studied Law, she'd been approached twice in the street by scouts for modelling agencies. Reasoning that a decent brain had a longer shelf life she'd said no. Only occasionally did she regret turning her back on the big money offers. Stepping forward to take Jas Ram's extended hand could be one of them. Not that she had any call in the matter: duty solicitors had to take the rough with the smooth and from what she knew of Ram, he was a shoo-in for the roughest category of all.

At six feet tall in kitten heels, Ruby looked down on the man in more ways than one.

Not only had lawyer colleagues acted for a couple of his victims, but until a few months back Ruby had lived next door to one of the families and still kept in touch with Alice Hemming and her daughter. The conflict of interest here wasn't legal, but – morally – they were worlds' apart. Flashing a fleeting smile, she lightly touched his fingertips with hers. 'Mr Ram. My name's Ruby. Ruby Wells.' Shrugging off a taupe suede jacket she strode to the table, cut a glance at Graves. 'Perhaps . . . officer?'

'You got it.' Consultation time alone with her client. The cop hauled his bulk from the chair, paused at the door. 'If you need anything, Miss Wells?'

Smiling her thanks, she slid out a legal pad from a black leather attaché case, placed the case on the floor. She crossed her legs, aware Ram was studying her like a degree. Ruby was taking things in, too. The calculating look on her client's face was at odds with the predictably laboured laid-back pose, ankles casually crossed, laced fingers held a few inches from his chest, head tilted knowingly.

Having spent ten minutes with Klein, Ruby was up to speed. Toying a slim gold pen between her fingers she said, 'OK, Mr Ram, I need you to—'

'Anyone ever told you, you look like Lily—'

'Savage? All the time.' Sighing, adept at the game by now, her aim was to deflect the pass. She wasn't blind, she appreciated Ram was a pretty boy but seriously doubted there was much going on between the ears however streetwise he came across. Besides, Ram could be fitter than Brad Pitt's kid brother and pure as virgin snow, Ruby never mixed business with pleasure. She masked a smile. However simple the pleasure.

'Not just a pretty face, eh, Ruby?' He raised what he probably imagined was a cool eyebrow. 'I was about to say Cole, cause of the hair.' Lustrous warm-red locks that flowed halfway down her back. 'Nah.' Ram flapped a hand. 'On second thoughts . . . you're hotter than her.'

Surely to God the cheesy pun wasn't deliberate? She ducked her head, bit her bottom lip.

'Cole. Hotter. Get it?' Ram looked pleased as punch. And if he didn't button it . . .

Suppressing another sigh she said, 'I suggest we concentrate on what you're likely to get if this incident isn't sorted.'

'Come on, love, it's the filth trying to stitch me up.' He leaned forward, legs spread, elbows on knees. 'You're a lawyer. You must know who I am, what happened in court today.'

Yesterday actually. She nodded. Given the saturation press coverage, even without a legal background, you'd have to have been living on a different planet not to know about the trial, events leading up to it, and have a vague idea who the main players were. 'I'm aware of the case, Mr Ram. But it has nothing to do with why I'm here.' Easing back in the chair, she smoothed her skirt, watched Ram ogle. When he resumed eye contact, she continued, 'Sergeant Klein tells me you were arrested on suspicion of drink-driving and you refused a breath test. Is that correct?'

'Yeah.' He slumped back, legs still wide, crotch now centre stage. Macho body language that said, So what?

Her gaze was still on his face. 'Is it possible you were over the limit?'

Dismissive sniff. 'I'd had a couple a drinks.'

She tapped the pen against perfect white teeth. 'My advice to you is to supply a blood or urine sample as soon as the

police can organise it. More than likely you'll then be released
without charge pending analysis of the results.' She'd known
suspects drink water from the toilet bowl in the vain hope it
would dilute their sample. Ram didn't look as if he'd stoop
that low. And it certainly wasn't advice she'd pass on.

'They'll let me go straight away?'

'Almost certainly.' She could see the clogs going round in
Ram's head. Ruby reckoned it was a no-brainer – and she
didn't mean Ram's decision. The thought brought a slight
curve to her full red lips. Bad move. Wrong message.

'OK, Ruby. I'll do what you say.' The crooked smile oozed
confidence. 'On one condition.'

'I hardly think—'

'I need a lift home. How you fixed?'

It was nearly one a.m. when Sarah called it a day and headed
back to her place. She could probably have made it a fraction
earlier had the urge to see Jas Ram in custody not outweighed
the desire to get home. As it was, she'd only caught a glimpse
as he left the station looking dead pally with Ruby Wells.
From what little she knew about Ruby, he'd have more chance
with the Bishop of Wells. Doubtless Sarah would pick up
the low-down tomorrow but whatever Ram had been nicked
for, it wasn't a capital offence. Shame.

As she walked the short distance from her garage, Broad
Street was still buzzing with bright lights, busy bars, revellers
reluctant to return to sober reality. The only sign of life when
she reached her apartment in Brindley Place was a lamp left
burning in the hall – a habit she'd started since the split from
lawyer boyfriend Adam. More than twelve months on, the habit
was pretty ingrained.

Yawning, she dropped her bag and keys on the console
table, half shucked off a long camel coat, then thought better
of it. Hugging the material round her, she made a mental
note to adjust the heating, timing and thermostat. Even after
three years in residence the canal side pad didn't feel like
home, probably because she treated it as a hotel. Ordinarily
she blamed work but thinking on, maybe the single life was
a factor, too. Or maybe work was also the reason she could

give Bridget Jones a run for her money. Chicken and egg scenario?

God, it was all too complicated and she was too knackered and starving to think straight. Shame it wasn't a half decent hotel though. It'd be a damn sight warmer and room service would be on tap. Passing through the sitting room, her glance took in the pale woods, ivory sofas, white walls and not for the first time, she wondered if it wasn't a touch sterile. The room used to please her but she'd hardly stamped her personality on it and nowadays, thanks to a cleaner, it looked so damn pristine.

The kitchen where she spent most of her down time more than compensated. Hands jammed in coat pockets, she stood in the doorway and surveyed the wreckage: crumb trails, open boxes, sink full of unwashed crockery, surfaces ring-stained with tea, dried up milk. Was it because every other aspect of her life was so precise and well-ordered that she needed a space to slob out, let down her hair? Nice try, Sarah. She knew the theory was bollocks. She just couldn't be arsed. The place was a tip because she had zilch interest in cooking. Her skills lay in walking a grid, not handling a griddle.

Which was a pain; right now she could eat her own hand. She gave a lopsided smile, loosened her bun, felt the hair fall almost to her waist. The notion had brought to mind one of her mother's favourite sayings. How did it go? Something like, I'm so hungry my stomach thinks my throat's cut. The smile vanished. Given the night's events, it wasn't a thought to hold. Every time Sarah closed her eyes, the victim was in her head. And the uneasy thought that his murder had been a disappointment.

Right place, right time. Wrong man.

FIVE

*A*lways get your man, don't you, Caz? You're a regular Canadian Mountie.' Caroline King lay back full length on top of her king-size bed and gave a lazy grin. The observation on her powers of persuasion had been made years back by one of the reporter's first editors. Recalling it now, she wished someone had mentioned it to Jas Ram. She'd just asked him for an interview and was getting short shrift. Even holding her smart phone at arm's length, she could hear the guy pissing himself. No worries. At least he hadn't hung up on her. She raised a leg in the air, admired the calf muscle, waited patiently for the guffaws to abate.

'You have so got to be joking, love,' he eventually responded. 'Why'd I talk to a reporter? You're all devious shits.'

'That's hardly fair, Mr Ram. You don't know me from Adam.' She pursed her lips, reckoned the red polish on a couple of toenails needed a retouch.

'You're a journo, aren't you?' Loud sniff. Like that said it all.

'Meaning?' Like she hadn't heard it all before. Punter opinion was bad enough before the phone hacking scandal but the whole *News of the World*/Leveson debacle had turned press-bashing into an Olympic sport. No sweat. She was at the top of her game; Ram wouldn't know what hit him. Assuming she could persuade him to play. Obviously he wasn't aware of her ground rules yet.

'Meaning you'd sell your granny to screw some poor sod over.'

An ethics lecture from a fucking pimp? The snort erupted before she could stem it. She quickly turned it into a cough, swung her legs over the side of the bed and sat up straight. It might be wiser to give the guy her full attention. 'I assure you I don't deal in dirt, Mr Ram. And for the record . . .' She forced an ingratiating smile into her voice. 'I don't have a granny.'

'Yeah yeah. Hold on a tick, love. I've got a call on the other line.'

Take your time, mate. Still in her short scarlet nightdress, she pulled the duvet over her shoulders. No sense freezing her butt off. She was happy to wait if she got what she wanted and that was something rare, rarer than veal at a vegan barbecue: an in-depth chat with an on-street groomer. The missing component of her work-in-progress. She already had interviews in the bag with a couple of London victims; cops and social services were usually happy to put their case. Caroline had feelers out, and few worries about gaining similar access. But no one had nailed the elusive exclusive: the perp's viewpoint.

She pursed her lips; no one in her league anyway.

So where was he? If this was a wind-up, she'd hit the sodding . . . Ears pricked, she pressed the phone closer, relieved to hear noises off. *Thank you, God.* Bastard was probably doing business with a grooming crony.

Catching sight of her reflection in the cheval glass, she grimaced. The dark circles looked like she'd missed the lids with her eye shadow. The late night drinks sessions with lodger Nathan weren't doing her any favours. Strictly speaking Nat Hardy was lodger-stroke-tenant, depending whether Caroline was in Birmingham. She'd inherited the Selly Oak terrace after her mother died two years ago. On the market ever since, there'd been no takers, little interest. The reporter's main base was her flat in Fulham, so when Nat had said he needed a place to rent, she'd jumped at the deal. It suited her to have someone she knew, as opposed to putative squatters, living in a property that would otherwise be mostly empty. The fact that Nat was easy on the eye, knew his way around a kitchen and was a fellow journo, had nothing to do with the arrangement. Well, not much.

'Right where were we, love? Oh yeah. The screw bit.' Ram's snigger made her flesh creep. 'You never mentioned if you were into screwing?'

'I'll pretend I didn't hear that.' She curled a lip. Thank God she hadn't showered yet. She itched to puncture the sleaze ball's bubble, but provoking him would get her nowhere. 'As I say, Mr Ram, I'd really like to help. I think you have the makings of a case against the police.'

Like hell she did. King had no doubt the guy was guilty as sin. She'd followed the case, talked to some of the players, watched him swagger out of court yesterday, and registered the shock on Sarah Quinn's face. Why the hell Caroline hadn't grabbed him then she'd never know. Except she did. First off, she'd been so keen on delivering her perfectly staged piece to camera, by the time she'd finished, Ram was getting into the back of a black cab. And second, she wanted to keep a discreet distance from the guy until her time of choosing.

'And I'd care what you think because . . .?' She pictured him nail gazing. Arrogant twat. She shed the duvet, rose from the bed, padded to the sash window that looked out onto the street. If she wanted to secure the scoop, she needed to sharpen her act.

'Because I know what I'm doing.' Authoritative, unequiv-ocal. 'What you said about suing the police makes sense. And I have experience in the field.' Not. Her only motive was to elicit from Ram what made him tick, what drove him – apart from great wads of cash – to isolate, alienate and rape girls young enough to be his daughter, then pass them round like slabs of meat. What did he see when he looked in the mirror?

As for the cops, it wasn't often Caroline felt sorry for the Ice Queen – way too much bad blood under the bridge for that – but Sarah Quinn had clearly been gutted when Ram walked.

'I didn't say I'd sue, dumbo. I said I'd be seeking legal advice.'

Don't split hairs, dipshit. 'It's a fine line, Mr Ram.'

'Yeah and you're crossing it. Christ, if you cock up simple facts like that, you'll probably get your own name wrong, never mind mine.'

Future tense there. Crap grammar or good sign? At least he might be thinking about it. She hoped so; Ram was clearly no Einstein but neither was he thick as pig-shit. It augured well. Caroline wasn't in the market for a meaningless quote or a twenty-second sound bite. Not when she'd signed a lucrative book deal. Doodling distractedly in the condensation on the window, she focussed on her quarry, went in for the metaphorical kill. 'I'm a professional, Mr Ram. I don't make mistakes. Why don't we meet for an off-the-record chat? No strings. No commitment. If you like what you hear, you can decide then about going ahead with the interview.' Up-beat, engaging. Like it was an offer he couldn't refuse.

'Or not.' Intransigent. The guy was no pushover.

She tightened her mouth, so regretted making the move on the phone. The reporter had no problem using body language and sex appeal to get what she wanted, if you had the looks and the nous it was stupid not to. She had both in abundance and had heard that when Ram wasn't molesting under-age kids, he fancied himself as a ladies' man. She'd be right down his street, as it were. Except she was on the end of a line. On the other hand, never say die. 'How about we—?'

'What's in it for me?'

The genuine opportunity to put his side of the story, however unpalatable. 'Lunch? Dinner?' She smiled. *And that's just for starters, mate.*

'Look, love. I don't know who you are.' Shit. She was losing him. 'And I don't know what two-bit rag you work for—'

'I don't.' This approach was off her own bat and she'd almost certainly keep the material under wraps until she needed it to promote the book. Ram so didn't need to know that. 'I'm a TV journalist.'

'Really?' Upward inflection, then a telling pause. 'Why didn't you say so before, love?'

Two minutes later, she ended the call, ran her tongue over her top lip. Lunch it was then.

Registering the doodle, she turned her mouth down. It looked like a ram with horns, cloven hooves. And a knife through its neck. 'Whoops,' she murmured. But then, her aim had been to make a killing.

'Bitch must think I was born yesterday.' Snarling, Ram tucked his iPhone into a breast pocket. His wife's pocket as it happened; she'd just crossed his path on the way to the kitchen. 'Put it on charge, will you, love.'

Nadia nodded. 'Which bitch is that, Jas?' As if he ran kennels as a sideline.

'Mind it.' He tapped his nose with a finger. Shrugging, she walked out, careful to ensure her back was to him before pulling a face. 'And keep the bloody kids quiet, will you?' His petulant shout was almost an afterthought. Ram's thinking was on more pressing matters than his six-year-old twin daughters bickering somewhere overhead. The noise and clutter was a reminder why he spent so little time at the two-up-two-down in Small Heath.

He snatched a pack of Marlboro from the coffee table, lit one and released smoke trails through flared nostrils. Pacing in front of the tiled fireplace, his black silk dressing gown flapped open revealing black satin boxer shorts. Seething didn't come close. To think some white slag imagined she could play him. Jas Ram didn't do fiddle.

He'd realised early on it was Caroline King on the phone, recognised the stuck-up vowels as much as registering the name. What he didn't know was what the cheeky bint wanted. His eyes creased as he took a deep drag, flicked ash in the direction of an open fire.

All that guff about the cops? Ram didn't believe a word of it. He'd only told her to hang on so he could check her out on Wikipedia. Know thine enemy and all that. Having read the entry, he was sure as eggs the reporter would have an – as yet – unwritten agenda. He'd agreed to meet because he needed to know what it was, where she intended going with it, and if he could allow it. Not that Ram didn't have a damn good idea. Pound to a penny she was after dirt on his so-called grooming activities. He'd been good to those girls, bunch of ingrates, if you asked him. The judge had released him fair and square – Ram had no intention of going back or of being hounded by a hack.

He chucked the butt into the flames, then sank down into a brown leather settee, tapped a mouse on the table alongside his laptop. The page reappeared on the screen and he reread it. 'Caroline King, born in Birmingham, moved to London after graduating from Warwick with a 2:1 in English. King entered the industry in 2002, and after stints on national newspapers and radio, has worked variously for the BBC, ITV, Channel 4 and Sky News.' *Media tart.* Ram scowled. 'King made her name covering a string of high-profile crime stories and has won a clutch of awards including three Sonys. Now an investigative journalist, King is thirty-two and single.'

Investigative journalist? He stroked his chin. Didn't like the job title. Sounded more like posh for nosy bastard. Mind, if she still looked anything like her picture, she was serious tottie. He liked women with dark hair and the jaw-length bob framed a classy heart-shaped face. What with the big eyes and full lips, Ram reckoned he could quite fancy doing a bit of journalist investigating himself. However it panned out, he'd be gaining an Italian and she'd be picking up the bill.

Who said there's no such thing as a free lunch?

Ram blew an ironic kiss at the screen before closing the lid. Either way he was bound to get more mileage out of King than he had last night with Ruby Wells. He'd left the station with Ruby after giving the filth a urine sample. She'd refused him a lift and – he could see her now – threw back her head and laughed in his face when he asked for a date. Fists unwittingly clenched, he took a deep calming breath. Next time she'd show a bit of respect, or she'd be laughing the other side of her face.

Four Years Earlier

The girl studied her face in the mirror on the dressing table. Small-ish brown eyes, mousy hair, snub nose, OK mouth, nothing striking. She saw little to write home about. Not that she had a home. Glancing round, she dropped the knee-jerk scowl but, really, you could hardly call this place home. Her reflection grew as she leaned in, took a closer look. OK, she'd taken a pair of kitchen scissors to her hair, hacked most of it off. But even so, she couldn't see why her dad used to call her a pretty little thing. And it wasn't as though she could ask him. He'd been knocked down by a bus, died two weeks later in hospital – on her ninth birthday. That was six years ago. Her ma had struggled on for eighteen months or so. The girl liked to think the overdose that killed her wasn't deliberate. If she'd done it on purpose, the pain would be almost too much for the girl to bear, given the back-breaking baggage already bowing her thin frame. The bottom line either way was that nothing would bring them back.

She opened a drawer, took out a creased and dog-eared photograph. Her smile was unwitting and mirrored her parents'. She'd kissed their faces so often some of the colour had leeched

but it was all she had left of a life that had once been happy
and normal. It wasn't as though she wanted the world – she'd
settle for average. Not the foster home from hell. The last
placement had been bad, but this . . .

Last term, she'd had to read a poem at school. Something
along the lines: 'it was better to have loved and lost than never
to have loved at all.' Utter crap. Even now the sentiment made
her spit.

Knowing what love was really like made her current life
intolerable. The woman was bad enough but at least she didn't
expect to be called mum. No way was the girl going to call the
man dad. Over her dead body. Dads ruffled your hair, chucked
your chin, tucked you up in bed. Not got in with you and . . .

She squeezed her eyes tight. Then wiped another tear off
the photograph.

SIX

Perched on a desk at the side of the incident room,
Detective Chief Superintendent Fred Baker, wearing
a dark charcoal Boss designer suit, stuffed a hand in a
jacket pocket and nodded at the whiteboard. Dominating it
were three colour photographs in a spectrum of shades of soft
fruit. The third victim's so-called likeness had been added to
the earlier line-up of two just in time for the eight thirty
briefing. DC Harries, who'd done the artwork, now sat at the
front, hunched forward, notebook and pen in hand.

'Not chinless wonders – faceless,' the chief mused. 'Three
mugs left looking like raw mince, and we're the suckers left
wondering why.'

Features impassive, Sarah stood centre stage forcing herself
not to tap a foot. Through the picture window, she glimpsed
a watery sun seeping into a leaden sky. The DI hoped the al
fresco gloom partly accounted for the sluggishness on show
inside. Motivating officers on a complex and fragmented
inquiry like this was never easy. Of the dozen or so detectives

seated on or at desks arranged around the open-plan room, only a couple appeared even vaguely keen. Too many sprawled legs and slumped shoulders were evident. Paul Wood and John Hunt propped up facing walls like novelty bookends, the detective sergeants' folded arms and crossed ankles said they'd seen it all before, and then some. And now Baker, who'd not only turned up unexpectedly but had missed the start, was chucking in what Sarah considered fatuous observations. Thank God for small mercies: there was no overpowering reek of aftershave but the day-old stubble would account for that.

Holding his gaze, she said evenly, 'Not helpful, chief.'

Dead silence; telling eye contact. In her periphery vision, she caught squad members exchanging shifty glances. One of Baker's well-deserved names round the nick was Bruiser. Not that Sarah was known for backing off easily. Still staring at the chief, she rolled the sleeves of her jacket. The grey wool trouser suit was proving too warm, but it was the first outfit to hand that morning. Given she'd not got to bed until two, time had been pressing.

'Get off the high horse, Quinn.' He jabbed a finger at the board, clearly itching for a fight. 'Take a proper butcher's at them.'

Like she hadn't? The images were imprinted on her brain. Three white males, two still unidentified and – given the extent of the injuries – damn near unrecognisable. Other similarities between the three existed, the big difference was that last night's victim hadn't survived. As for Baker, she didn't know where he was coming from and could live without the less than constructive commentary. 'And?'

'Think about it.' Eyes creased, he was still scrutinising the lurid montage. 'Why would anyone batter some poor sod that badly?'

Why batter anyone, period? Even as the notion crossed her mind, she dismissed it as unrealistic, simplistic even. Cops – more than most people – dealt with the darker side of life, came up daily against crims and bad guys, sorted out the crap no one else could be arsed with. Baker had even coined his own classification system: in CID it was known as the four Ss: sadists, sad-sacks, sickos and shits.

Clearly Baker thought he held the answer, but Sarah was sick of playing twenty questions. 'What exactly are you saying, chief?'

She watched him shuffle off the desk, join her at the front and run his gaze over the squad. 'Is anybody on the same page as me?' The challenge went unanswered. They'd tossed ideas around at previous briefs. Given drug addicts would batter their own mother for a few quid, Wood reckoned the attacks were down to smack heads desperate for a fix. On the basis no one could dish out that level of violence sober, Harries had opted for yobs on the lash. Unless – and this theory had been mooted since the first incident – it was down to youths hunting in a pack, a gang initially out for kicks as much as nicking a few quid. They'd got sketchy descriptions of three or four teenagers spotted near the scene of what – if they were dealing with a series – was probably the first mugging. Baker was as up to speed as anyone in the room with what was on the inquiry table. Why the hell didn't he just get on with it?

'OK.' Sighing, he loosened an already slack silk tie. 'What if it's personal?' He paused, but again no one ran with it. 'Surely to God, beating the shit out of someone so viciously—'

'Could mean the attackers know their victims? They're targeting them?' Sarah narrowed her eyes. 'Is that your thinking?'

'Give the girl a gold star. To do that –' he tilted his head at the board – 'it strikes me you'd need to hate someone big time.'

Girl? Her mouth was a tight line. And Sarah wasn't convinced. You only had to skim the red tops to see how often people were attacked by strangers. Innocent passers-by who made the wrong sort of eye contact or didn't shift out of the way quickly enough were regarded as target practice, yobs treated them as human punchbags and/or footballs. And if an assailant was armed, a fist in the face or a kick in the head was infinitely preferable to a knife in the neck.

Even so, had Baker got a point? Until now, the squad's premise had been that the attacks were random mindless acts carried out by perps on the rob. Could there be more significant links? Was it possible the chief's theory stacked up? Or was

it a big fat red and damson herring? The savagery had undoubtedly escalated, but any cop could testify to the fact that once
someone committed violence, he or she found it easier to
inflict next time. And the next. Literally, near as damn it, a
vicious circle. Villains got a taste for it: bloodlust it was called.
Sarah could see nothing human in it, let alone personal.

'OK.' She pursed pensive lips. 'With the chief's point in
mind, let's take another look from the top.' It couldn't do any
harm. Catching Hunt's eye, she mimed writing, nodded her
thanks as he dragged a flip chart closer. With one hand aloft,
Baker trudged back to the desk. The gesture was open to
interpretation, but right now it wasn't top of her priorities. She
flipped to a new page, headed it Operation Steel in thick black
marker pen, then sectioned out three columns and gave each
a date: Wednesday 4 January, Wednesday 11 January, Friday
13 January.

'As you know,' she said, 'we've been able to identify only
one victim.' She wrote Duncan Agnew in the first column.
Agnew was still in hospital, mainly down to an underlying
medical problem exacerbated by his injuries. An epileptic,
the twenty-six year old had suffered several fits since being
admitted. Doctors were keen to keep an eye on what looked
like a deteriorating condition. One of the squad's sharpest
interviewers had spoken to Agnew briefly on two occasions,
but the man's mother, as well as the medicos, were ultra
protective. Given the new urgency, DC Shona Bruce had been
despatched back to the Queen Elizabeth to push for a third
session. On the off-chance the second victim had regained
consciousness Shona would drop by the intensive care unit
as well. Kill two birds . . . *Best not go there.* Sarah asked
officers to call out observations as she quickly added times
and locations to the chart: 23.00, Kings Road, Selly Oak;
22.30, York Road, Stirchley; 21.45 Chambers Row.

'None of the victims had ID.'

'Nor wallets.'

'No valuables full stop.' Harries was right. No watches, rings,
mobiles, not so much as a gold filling had been recovered at
any of the scenes.

'Attacks are getting worse.'

'And more frequent.'

Various members of the squad chipped in further, but none
of it was new. Nodding, she hid her disappointment. Fact was,
they couldn't really be certain the attacks were down to the
same offenders. They couldn't even be sure it was offenders,
plural. The line of inquiry was being followed only because
an elderly couple who'd discovered Duncan Agnew lying
injured in Kings Road told the first attending officers a gang
of youths had been hanging round. In Selly Oak at that time
of night, it'd be a first if dodgy juveniles hadn't been in the
vicinity. Even so, the couple would have to be re-interviewed
and Sarah would send detectives to canvas the neighbourhood
again.

She cut the chief a glance. Ominously quiet, he was staring
at the whiteboard, pulling on his bottom lip.

'We're piss . . . whistling in the dark without IDs on the
other two, ma'am.' Wood sniffed.

'Pisswhistling?' Hunt gave a lopsided smile. 'That's a new
one on me, Twig.' The name alluded to the sergeant's build:
sumo wrestler meets brick shithouse. The big guy's grip
on small detail was formidable though, which made him a
first-rate IRM: Incident Room Manager. Hunt's piss-take had
prompted a few sniggers but Twig was right. Without knowing
who the men were, it was difficult to establish possible
connections. And without those, they'd no way of knowing
if – and more importantly, why – the victims might have
been singled out.

'OK Woodie, can you get on to Rose Atherton?' Police
artist. 'Ask if she's prepared to draw up a couple of likenesses
we can actually use.' With one subject dead, the other on life
support, the woman would need a vivid imagination and strong
stomach – and still have her work cut out. Worth a try though.
The press was more likely to bite if Sarah had visuals as bait.

Wood tapped a temple.

Given the dearth of information on victims two and three,
the Agnew incident was clearly the inquiry's richest seam to
mine. Sarah reckoned it was a shame she hadn't recognised
its full potential before. Details had been released to the media
and the attack had been covered initially by both the

Birmingham News and Radio WM, but more exposure might have prompted more intelligence. And hindsight was a wonderful thing. She sighed, made a mental note to have a word with the press bureau. Actually, stuff the mental bit.

'Dave, will you liaise with Ted White? Ask him to set up—'

'A news conference? Leave it with me, boss.'

She laid down the pen, checked her watch. With a bit of luck there'd be time to drop by Chambers Row on the way to the post-mortem. With a bit more, the forensic guys – who'd been digging since first light – might have unearthed some solid evidence, and with a shed-load more she'd scoop a few squillions on the lottery and stroll off into the sunset.

Yeah right. Masking a wry smile, she tasked teams of officers to revisit the crime scenes, knock more doors, stop and question pedestrians and drivers. Other detectives were already viewing Christ knows how many hours of CCTV footage. Still more would soon be making contact with CHIS: Covert Human Intelligence Sources – long for snouts. They needed to gather more gen on street gangs. Squad members were already liaising closely with opposite numbers in the Gangs Unit, but crews sprang up so fast these days even specialist officers couldn't keep on top of them all.

'Are you finished then, miss?' Baker was back on his feet, a hand jangling keys in his trouser pocket. She'd almost forgotten he was there, still wasn't sure why he'd bothered to put in an appearance and certainly didn't appreciate the school ma'am crack.

She gave a brisk nod. 'If you've something *useful* to add, chief—'

'Don't come the lip with me, Quinn.'

Come the lip? That was a new one on her. But what was Baker's beef? Whatever was bugging him, she didn't do whipping woman. Slipping papers into her briefcase, she muttered, 'Class dismissed.'

'I heard that, Quinn.' *Good.* 'And I'm not through here. Has it occurred to you if I'm right there'll be more victims? That, to coin a phrase, we ain't seen nothing yet?'

'Why are we standing round gabbing then?' Whoops. Bad move. She was knackered – the DCS was being arsy, but there were lines you shouldn't cross. She almost stepped back when the Baker finger was jabbed again.

'I'll give you twenty-four hours to put names to those two faces, Quinn.'

'Or what?' Arms tightly crossed, she watched as he shrugged and walked away.

At the door, he turned his head. 'You're the clever dick. You tell me.'

Forty minutes later and Sarah still wanted to tell the fat bastard to go fuck himself. In a twelve-year career, she'd never felt more like slapping a face or sticking in a complaint. Not that she would, but that wasn't the point. Her knuckles were tight and white round the steering wheel, the air in the Audi blue.

'Shit, boss. That was a red.' Harries swivelled his head to glance through the rear window, presumably checking for road kill. Staring implacably ahead, she sensed a glare in her direction as he turned back adding, 'If I were you, I'd chill.'

'You're not,' she snapped. Her female Stig impersonation on the way to the path lab wasn't down to the fact they were cutting it fine, she was as fired up as the engine. Smarting didn't even come close. 'Anyway, we're late.'

He muttered what sounded like 'we soon will be' but she could live without asking for a repeat; Baker's words still echoed in her head. The chief's dig had gone deep, the attempt to undermine her had gone too far. Ridiculing her in front of the squad was out of order and unprofessional. They'd had their run-ins over the years but had lately reached a reasonable working relationship. At least that's what she'd thought.

Harries had his head down, checking his phone. She cut him a glance and sniffed. He could please himself. The wintry sun had beefed up its act a fraction; she pulled down the visor, nudged up the heating, ran through a mental to-do list. The in-car silence was shattered when she ran another red and a blaring horn competed with Harries' sharp intake of breath. 'We only have to attend the post-mortem, boss. The rate you're going, we'll end up on his and hers slabs.'

'You can walk if you like.'

He shoved his phone in a pocket, stretched his legs and

crossed his arms. 'What I'd like is for you *not* to let the chief wind you up.'

Was it so obvious? She took a deep breath and loosened her grip on the wheel. She'd deliberately not bad-mouthed Baker, never denigrated colleagues in front of Dave. Either her DC had honed his already enviable empathy or her famous cool was on the slide. Mind, there was a first for everything. 'That wasn't a wind up, that was a sodding great put down. Me. In front of junior ranks.'

'Come on, boss. You're bigger than that. Besides you were—'

'Enough, constable. In my book, slagging off colleagues in public is out of line.'

'Better than shit bagging behind your back.'

'Who's frigging side are you on?' She whacked the wheel with a palm.

'Yours.' Talk about rapid response. No arguing with that. She closed her mouth, verbal incontinence – like emotional – was no good to anyone. She counted ten then asked if he'd sorted the news conference. He told her it was set for mid-afternoon in the hope Rose Atherton would have time by then to come up with the goods. She made a mental note to assign extra officers to phone duties. The press coverage would almost certainly lead to a load of incoming calls, hopefully a handful would lead somewhere worth going.

'You heard the latest on Ram, boss?'

'Drink-drive, wasn't it?' Not that charges had been brought, he'd been released on bail pending results. 'Let's hope he pissed absinthe.'

Harries laughed. She thought he was about to say something but nothing emerged for several seconds, then: '*Boss* . . .' He stretched the word to two syllables. 'Back to Baker. Did anything strike you?'

Apart from a load of verbals? 'Give us a clue.'

'The loose tie? The crumpled suit?'

'I was holding a brief. Not checking his gear.'

'The whites of his eyes were like road maps.'

She turned her mouth down, tried to recall. That Baker-thy-name-is-vanity was well turned out was something you took

for granted. And she had. *No. Hold on.* She'd spotted the day
old stubble.

'You didn't notice, did you?' Harries gloating was not a
good look. 'Call yourself a detective?' His grin froze when
he clocked her arctic glare. 'Boss – it was a joke.'

'Could've fooled me, Harries.' For a few seconds she thought
on what he'd said, then gave a one-shouldered shrug. 'So the
guy was hung-over. It's not my problem.' Her bag was nailing
the bad guys. Baker was a big boy now, if he'd overdone the
booze, he'd only himself to blame. Besides, cop nursing sore
head was hardly going to make the front page. Harries was
staring ahead, ostentatiously shtum. Sarah sighed. 'Don't keep
it to yourself, Dave.' She sensed his gaze as he weighed up
whether to wade in.

'Grapevine has it it's more than that, boss.'

'Go on.' And why hadn't she heard any murmurings? 'Car
park next left, isn't it?'

He nodded. 'Yeah, if you're going via the back. As I say,
a few of the guys think he's drinking on the job. You know
his missus legged it?' She nodded. 'Word is, he's taking it
hard. He's been seen mooching round the nick on his days
off, like he's at a loose end or something.' Was that why he
was in today, she wondered? 'Apparently he keeps a bottle or
three in his drawer, tops up when—'

She raised a hand. 'Thanks, Harries.' Too much ill-informed
information. She'd had her say, but gossiping about a senior
detective wasn't on. She'd keep tabs on it though. If the rumour
held a grain of *veritas* and the alleged drinking got worse, it
could be everyone's problem. She opted for a diplomatic
change of tack. 'How'd you know I was hacked off, Dave?'
The question was casual as she reversed the motor into a tight
space between Richard's beat-up Land Rover and a gleaming
black BMW.

'Where shall I stop, boss?'

She matched his smile as she locked the motor, grimaced
when she spotted Richard's dog. She was beginning to suspect
it was stuffed until it perked up and pressed its nose against
the grimy window. Snotty saliva trails. Nice.

'As I was saying . . .' Harries – complete with hand signals

– listed her giveaways as they walked to the back entrance. He majored on body language and repeated the expletives. 'Plus you called me constable twice and Harries three times. No worries though, boss.' He strode ahead to get the door. 'It means we're a good team.'

The Victorian redbrick, innocuous on the outside, never failed to give her the shivers. The sickly sweet odours permeated even here to the threshold, they'd stick in her nose, cling to her clothes and the image of last night's victim would shortly be added to the macabre picture gallery in her brain. She recognised Harries' banter as a diversion from what lay ahead, thought displacement in action. Each to their own. 'How'd you work that one out, Dave?'

'I reckon you're getting more chilled, you feel you can open up to me.'

The raised eyebrow was sceptical. 'And what's in it for you?'

'I'm learning from a great . . .' *Don't say teacher.* He was clearly struggling to avoid the T word. '. . . master . . . mistress . . . no . . . I mean . . .'

Mistress? You should be so lucky. She curved a lip. 'Dave. Quit while you're not ahead, eh?'

SEVEN

I t was a potential opening, or at least the glimmer of a crack. Caroline was itching to home in on the topic she wanted under debate, but she held fire while the waiter delivered a solo dessert. The strawberry tart was pricey, like everything else Jas Ram had selected in one of Birmingham's most expensive eateries. The reporter was happy to pick up the bill: it would be dirt cheap if the sweet-talking paid off. If her instinct was right, he was almost there, the interview not a million miles from the Mulberry.

Playing her fingers round the stem of a wine glass, she met Ram's gaze across the table. Her red sheath dress and Ralph

Lauren jacket said serious player, but subtle flirting was virtually second nature when she was working a source and/ or found a guy tasty. Ram, though she was loath to admit it, fell into both categories. He reminded her of the lead in the Twilight movies. Robert Pattinson, wasn't it? OK, the skin tone was way out, but the chiselled features, the piercing eyes, the mobile mouth . . .

Skin deep, Caroline, skin deep.

'La Signorina is sure she wants nothing?' The whip-thin waiter's eyebrows disappeared under a glossy black fringe. With a white napkin draped over his forearm, the guy was straight out of central casting – complete with dodgy accent.

I want you to sod off, pronto. 'No, *grazie*.' Smiling sweetly, Caroline patted a stomach she strived to keep looking good. The gesture ensured she wasn't the only one watching her figure. As well as Ram's gaze, the restaurant was packed with diners giving her the eye – men in suits, ladies who lunch, yummy mummies with offspring in tow. San Luigi's was one of those places to be seen. Décor was monochrome with checked floor tiles, striped walls, blowsy lilies in huge black vases, mirrors everywhere. Tasty and tasteful. And clientele classy enough not to gawp or ask for a signed picture.

'You revel in it, don't you?' It was Ram's first conversational gambit. After initial small talk she'd steered the bigger issues in his direction, ushered in the so-called victory in court, the shabby treatment dished out by both police and press, how she could help repair the damage. *Any reporter will tell you people like talking about themselves* – Ram loved it. She wasn't a fan herself. 'You've gone quiet all of a sudden, Miss King.'

Her celebrity, such as it was, wasn't a topic she wanted to pursue. She ran an index finger over her phone to play for time, toyed briefly with feigning ignorance but as she was discovering, Ram was sharper than a sharpened tack, acting the ingénue would only delay resuming where they'd left off.

'Being on the telly? Getting recognised? What's not to like?' She raised her glass, took a sip of by now tepid Prosecco. 'It's better than scrubbing floors for a living. But let's—'

'My wife's a toilet attendant.'

Shit. That was a couple of turn ups for the yet to be written book: a) there's a Mrs Ram and b) she shovels other people's shit. Caroline swiftly calculated how she could work it into the story, it should make a few lines at least. Ram was staring, still waiting for a response.

'No offence. I didn't mean . . .' *Damn.* She'd walked straight into that one. The crooked smile told her he was taking the piss. And boy, had she fallen big time. The designer-clad, Porsche-driving Ram – letting his wife scrub loos? Not good for his public persona that. But what was the public persona? The more she tried, the harder it was to get a handle on the guy. Greased eels had more traction. She reached for the bottle. 'Top up?'

He shook his head, poked the tart with his fork. 'Seems to me, Miss King, that for an investigative journalist – sorry, an *award winning* investigative journalist – you're pretty easily taken in.'

She tipped the glass again. 'First time for everything, Mr Ram.' Clearly he was a better liar than she gave him credit for. And despite all her years in the people business, she found the guy harder to read than a Stephen Hawking book. She watched his strong white teeth sink into the soft flesh of a strawberry. 'And you're a very convincing man.' Her lips parted in what might have been a smile. And how come he was au fait with her CV?

'Regular boy scout me. As in, I do my homework.' He was no mind reader, he was warning her how smart he was. Or thought he was.

'Makes two of us, Mr Ram.' She tilted her head, thinking of the meeting she had lined up that afternoon at the home of one of his victims. And she'd heard about the spot of bother with the law last night. 'A little bird tells me you might be getting yourself a bus pass soon?' Given his predilection, there were probably better ways to voice that. Pavarotti's dulcet tones on tape covered what could have been an awkward silence. As for fellow journo Nat Hardy who'd tipped her the drink-drive wink, he certainly wouldn't appreciate being likened to a—

'Little bird?' Ram's full lips were stained red with juice.

Boring. She flapped an impatient hand. 'No matter. The point is . . . it appears the police are out to get you.' As if she wasn't. And once she got what she wanted, she'd happily lend the cops a hand.

Chewing slowly, he stared into her eyes. Surely he'd have to blink soon? What was going on under that blank exterior? She'd no idea what he was thinking and the fleeting emotions in those cold dark irises were impossible to identify. She fought hard not to shift in the seat, felt a frisson that could be fear, or – God forbid – arousal. Possibly both. Either way the intense scrutiny was unnerving, unsettling. Seemed to her, he looked at, and through her, simultaneously. Was he onto her not-so-little game?

He dabbed his lips with a napkin then treated her to a lazy smile. 'May I call you Caroline?'

Phew. Mental wipe of brow. 'Sure.'

'Try telling me something I don't know . . . Caroline.'

She turned her mouth down as if giving it serious thought. 'The cost of a travel card?' *Please, Lord, let him have a sense of humour.* It took a second for the penny to drop. His laugh seemed genuine. Hallelujah. The quip had lightened an increasingly tense atmosphere. Disclosing she knew about the drink-drive incident wasn't clever, she'd allowed herself to be diverted by his cocky arrogance. But there was no mileage in point-scoring, she needed to get the chat back on line. She opened her mouth but he spoke first.

'Go on then, tell me.' Pushing the plate to one side. 'What's it cost?'

Christ knows. She wouldn't be seen dead on a bus. 'Got me there. Google it, shall I?' Half-joking she reached for her phone but Ram laid a restraining hand on hers, and pressed hard. His flesh was warm and soft. She registered a rise in her pulse, didn't yet question why.

'Caroline, Caroline, Caroline.' Smiling, he shook his head, kept the tone calm, almost amused. 'There you go, taken in again. Gullible, or what? I don't give a rat's arse about bus fares.' There was nothing vaguely jocular in the eyes. 'I want your price. What's my story worth to you, Miss Award Winning Journalist?'

The pressure grew when she tried sliding away her hand.

'Are you trying to intimidate me, Mr Ram?' She looked down, pointedly. He didn't need telling. When he released his grip, the faintest outline on her skin was just visible. Lightly, he traced the mark with his fingers. She said nothing, both knew his upper hand had been metaphoric as well as literal.

'I'm not *trying* anything, Caroline.' There was an ostentatious straightening of a pristine white cuff, then: 'You've still not answered the question.'

Ram wasn't the sort of guy who'd give anything away. Caroline had already budgeted in a fee, what you might call a sweetener. Equally she was sick of playing games, being taken for a fool's ride; it was rare for her to feel wrong-footed. 'I'm prepared to go to five grand. Take it or leave it.'

He nodded. 'I'll let you know.'

'You do that.' Indifferent bordering on curt. She'd blown it. Ram was more likely to open in a test match than come to the interview wicket now. Unsmiling she signalled to the waiter, reckoned it was time to cut her losses. 'Go Dutch, shall we?' Her tongue was in both cheeks but it was worth a try.

'Yeah, you can take it out of my five grand.' For a split second she thought it was another joke. 'No kidding, Caroline.'

Owzat! By the time she'd settled the bill, they'd more or less sorted time and location for the first session. The reporter was certainly banking on more. Ram rose first, walked round to do the chivalrous bit with her chair. She caught a hint of lime when he lowered his head close to hers. 'You never did tell me.'

'Tell you what?' Hoisting her shoulder bag.

'The little bird? The one with the big mouth?'

She reached for her car keys. More than her life was worth, revealing a source. In this case that was overblown bollocks, but Ram could go whistle. Mind, tossing the fob in the air, was pretty tactless and given the look on his face, offering a lift wouldn't go down well either. 'Sorry, Mr Ram. First law of journalism.'

'No worries.'

She led the way across the chequered floor that put her in mind of a giant chess board. Her lip curved as she toyed with the notion. If she was King, what would that make Ram? The King was the most powerful piece in the game, wasn't it? The smile faded as the rules came back to her. The piece with the most clout was the Queen. And that reminded her, she needed a word with Sarah Quinn.

EIGHT

'**D**I Quinn, here.' Sarah had the phone nestled under her chin, hands occupied with an egg mayo roll and the initial forensic report from last night's crime scene. At gone three p.m. the working lunch was late, nothing new there. Nothing earth-shattering from Chambers Row either, though fibres and samples were en route to the labs. Sarah hadn't fancied eating earlier anyway. She'd been on the PMD: otherwise known as the post-mortem diet. As an appetite suppressant, blood and guts won hands down, though a body covered in grotesque tattoos like John Doe's came a close second. She shuddered. Either way, the multiple injuries meant cause of death had been too close to call.

'Someone in reception I think you should see, ma'am.'

Swift flick through her mental Rolodex came up with Dennis Law on the front desk as the owner of the voice. The veteran sergeant rarely gave his name, the West Country accent spoke for him. Plus he'd been a fixture for so long, everyone in the nick knew him as Laydown. Old time cop he might be, but he'd also been around long enough not to waste anyone's. Even so. She cast a glance at twin piles of leaning paperwork on her desk. Snowed under wasn't in it. Pass the ice axe.

'Who is it, Laydown? I'm really pushed.'

'Wouldn't say, ma'am.'

Lips pursed, she dragged closer one of the artist's portraits Twig had left on her desk: victim number two, airbrushed within an inch. Rose Atherton hadn't done a bad job. 'Can you get—?' *Tom, Dick or Harries to do the needful?*

'I could.' Laydown's pauses were usually telling. 'She asked for you by name.'

The sigh blew out her cheeks. By the time they'd finished arguing the toss, she could have dealt with whoever/whatever was down there. 'On the way.' Laying the egg roll back in its wrapper, she cast it a longing look before heading for the door. *Sod it.* A swift about turn and she crammed in another couple of inches, dashed into the corridor, clocked Baker sauntering the other way, hands deep in pockets.

'Good way to get IBS that.' *Yeah, well you'd know, chief.* 'I want to see you later in my office, Quinn.' She watched agape as he strolled past finger pressed to his lip. 'No talking with your mouth full. Bad manners that.'

She narrowed her eyes. The man must have eyes in the back of his bloody head.

Sarah was biting her tongue now. Laydown had informed her the proverbial bird hadn't flown so much as legged it. 'So what did she look like?'

'Just a slip of a thing, ma'am.' Simian brow furrowed, the barrel-chested sergeant scratched an armpit. Christ. He'd be swinging through the trees next. 'One minute she was here, the next—'

'You're a trained observer, sergeant.' Her foot tapped the lino. Loud and clear.

'Right. I'd say five-foot-nothing, seven stone or thereabout. In old money that is.' His smile was short-lived. 'Sorry, ma'am. Dark hair down to here.' His hand went to a breast pocket. 'Blue eyes, pasty-faced.'

It wasn't ringing any bells. 'Age?'

'Not my strength, ma'am, but I'd say in her teens.' She was beginning to wonder if he had a strength. He knew she'd not been sitting round twiddling her thumbs. Why summon her down to deal with a kid who wouldn't even give her name?

'She must've got cold feet, ma'am.' He picked up a pen, started writing, as if he'd decided it was a wrap.

Sarah had other ideas. 'And why would she do that, Sigmund?'

Still scribbling, he said, 'She told me she was here about

Jas Ram.' Handing her the note. 'That's the number I got out of her.' His shrug said for what it's worth.

Could be genuine. You never know. She gave it a quick glance before slipping it in a jacket pocket. 'Thanks Laydown, can you—?'

'Get on to the you've been framed boys? No worries.'

Police HQ had more cameras than Rupert Murdoch. The anonymous girl who'd given them the slip would have been captured in at least a couple of shots.

'Hey, boss! We could be cooking on gas.' Tie over shoulder, a slightly flushed Harries burst into Sarah's office, Boy Wonder energy barely contained.

Cooking on gas? God, he had a way with words. She looked up, fingers poised over a hot keyboard. 'Go on then.'

'Two names on the hotline.' Tie straightened, he smoothed his hair.

Unsubs? Mispers? Flashers? Could be all three given the revelations so far.

'From the top, eh, Dave? And do me a favour. Either sit down or keep still.' The fidgeting was getting on her nerves. It wasn't as if there was a shedload on, of course the Policy Book could wait. Like hell. Operation Steel's PB needed updating, like yesterday. A detailed written log had to be available to every squad member at all times, and as senior investigating officer the task fell to her. If anything slipped the net or went tits up, her neck would be on the block. As for the Action Book? *Don't get me started.*

Perched on the seat edge, Harries looked ready to spring into action any second. *He'd learn.* Leaning back in her swivel chair, she sipped from a can of Red Bull, as he told her that in the last half hour two separate callers had left messages on the Crimestoppers' line naming two individuals allegedly involved in the Stirchley attack – the second the squad was investigating.

'These names,' she asked, 'are they known to us?'

'Since they were kids.' In their late teens now, Zach Wilde and Leroy Brody had been in and out of cop shops as often as they'd been in and out of care. Checks had revealed cautions

– and later, convictions – for a string of offences including criminal damage, nicking cars, burglary, antisocial behaviour. *No violence though.*

'Current addresses?'

'Soon – with a bit of luck.' Two squad members were tracking down whereabouts now. Luck shouldn't come into it – it was hardly Smith and Jones territory.

'Anyone checked Facebook?'

'They're both on it.'

Straightening, she tapped a few keys, ran her gaze over the screen. Zach Wilde held two thumbs up to the camera. He had tattoos across both sets of knuckles – 'bad' and 'boy'. Looked as if he'd done them himself. She pointed it out. 'Not quite got the hang of it, has he?'

Harries grinned. 'I know a wom . . . mate who reckons his girlfriend's got sweet and sour tats on her t—'

'Thank you, constable.' Frowning, her gaze was still on the screen. Wilde's ink work, shaven head, missing front tooth were visual clichés for stock yob. *But they didn't equal sadistic bully.* Maybe her reservations showed.

'Problem, boss?'

'Curious about timing.' She slung the can at the bin. 'Like – why now?'

'Bull's eye. Why not?' His frown said, why ask?

Leroy Brody's tight curls were dusted with blue dye, a crucifix dangled from an ear lobe.

'We've got someone working on this, I take it?'

'Course.' Harries scratched his chin. 'I thought you'd be chuffed. Gift horse, mouth and all that.'

Gift, yes. Booby prize not. Intelligence without evidence wouldn't get them far. Dave might be on the right lines though. She'd skimmed today's local rag. Last night's attack had made page five with a sidebar summing-up previous incidents. The coverage could've prompted witnesses to come forward.

She sat back. 'Two sources, you said?'

'Affirmative.'

'Christ, Dave. Spare me the police speak. Male? Female?' *One of each?*

'One's a bloke, I think.'

'Think?' The raised eyebrow said it all.

'The line wasn't brilliant, boss.'

There's a surprise. 'Accents? Ages?'

'Young . . . ish?'

'OK.' *If you want a thing doing.* 'I'll listen to the tape. And I'd like to speak to them both.' Despite what parts of the media would like the public to believe, cops don't just drag people in off the streets. Certainly not on the say so of a couple of disembodied voices. She laced her fingers. 'Reckon they'll come in?'

'Ah.'

'And "ah" means?' As if she didn't know. She raised a don't-bother palm. Anonymous calls were a pain in a cop's bum. They didn't always mean duff info, informants were often too scared to give their name. But it made things a damn sight easier when the police knew who they were dealing with.

'I'll get the tape, boss.' He was on his feet when the landline rang. She took the call, caught his eye, mouthed 'hold on'. While hovering he spotted the artist's impression, picked it up for a closer look. As she hung up, he slipped the image back on the desk with a murmured, 'Poor bugger.'

'Not quite, Dave.' Sarah nodded at the phone. 'That was Shona at the hospital. And that –' pointing at the likeness – 'is Sean William Foster.' Who'd come round long enough to give his name to one of the nurses. It wasn't a lot, but it was better than nada.

'Top notch, boss. You telling Baker?'

The old boy wanted two names, didn't he? She gathered a few files ready for the news conference. 'No hurry, is there?'

NINE

The black BMW roadster was going so slow there were parts of the city where the driver would be pulled over for kerb crawling. Tudor Rise was in Harborne and Caroline King was on the look out for house names not street girls. Her eyes lit up when she spotted Hawthorn Villa. After parking a couple of detached houses down, she checked her face in the rear-view mirror. No make-up and the sleek black bob pulled back tauter than a Croydon facelift. The horn-rimmed glasses held clear lenses and – like her vision – were perfect. The sober image they fostered was just the ticket, entrance ticket. Her own mother wouldn't recognise her. Fiona King was dead but that was beside the point.

The long hot shower after lunching with Ram, though not strictly necessary, had helped the reporter feel less . . . contaminated. The main reason for the detour home had been to change her outfit, alter the look. It was more than possible the Hemmings had seen her before, either on TV or in the press gallery in court yesterday. But she wanted to create a first impression – and it had to be convincing. Caroline had arranged the meeting on the phone and may have been a tad stingy on the *veritas*. She'd not mentioned her profession – as a journalist.

As she aimed the fob at the motor, the sun struggled through a bank of cloud the colour of suds; the rays had no heat, the temperature below freezing. Tightening the belt on a beige raincoat, she headed towards the double-fronted Victorian red-brick. Come summer the façade would be covered in ivy; brittle tendrils clung now, dotted with what looked like desiccated confetti. *Hawthorn* Villa? Someone had a sense of humour. Glancing up, she saw smoke drifting from one of the chimneys. Cosy. She could but hope. Despite the chill, her palms were clammy, heart rate up a touch.

Deep breath, lick lips, press bell. Big Ben chimed even louder when the heavy wooden door swung open. Alice Hemming looked older than forty-two, nearer fifty would be Caroline's guess. The greying pageboy wasn't flattering and the deep lines etched into a gaunt sallow face couldn't all be down to laughter. 'You must be Mrs Hunter? Isobel?'

'That's right.' Suitably unassuming Caroline shook hands, made eye contact, took in the woman's black slacks, grey fleece, pearl earrings. 'Thank you for seeing me, Mrs Hemming.' The reporter had flattened her vowels a tad and once she'd caught more of the woman's delivery, she'd aim to match that too.

'Come through. I was about to make tea.' Slim and slight, Alice Hemming could pass as a teenager from the back. Over her shoulder, she called out with an over-bright comment, 'You'll have to take us as you find us.' Why did people always feel the need to say that kind of stuff? Caroline didn't care if houses were dives as long she came up with something. That said, from what she saw the place did need a little TLC. Décor was tired, paintwork chipped, skirting boards scuffed. Money could be tight, she supposed. Or interior design not a priority. A piano was being played downstairs somewhere, thick hardbacks lined two of the hall's walls and baking smells wafting from the kitchen were to die for.

'You look younger than I expected.' Mrs Hemming flashed a polite smile as she indicated one of six high stools round a breakfast bar. 'I'll pop the kettle on then just finish off here if you don't mind?'

'Of course.' Caroline had a quick nose round while the woman busied herself at one of the work surfaces. 'It's good of you to give me your time.' The L-shaped room was red tiles and terracotta, old pine and copper pans, light glinted off nine or ten serious looking knives clinging to a magnet on the far wall. Two loaves cooled on a tray, Mrs Hemming walked to the Aga carrying tins with two more. 'Wow!' Caroline gushed. 'You make your own bread?'

'Well spotted.' The barb was deserved, but her half smile softened the sting.

'Sorry. That wasn't the brightest remark.' Caroline gave a sheepish grin. The dumb question had been deliberate, a delaying tactic and a diversion.

Straightening from the range, Mrs Hemming leaned against the rail, arms folded. 'How old did you say your daughter is?'

Glad that worked. Caroline would've preferred a bit of bonding before getting down to business. 'Fifteen . . . the same as Amy.' Though Mrs Hemming's only daughter was just thirteen when Ram took her on what could be called her first ride. After nine months' forced unprotected sex with numerous strangers, Amy had her first abortion. A tame social worker had helped Caroline with the homework: apparently the

Hemmings' marriage was in trouble; he'd now moved out, lived in a bedsit; three sons were away at uni.

'Is this her?' Caroline asked. The school photograph on the fridge showed a little girl with blonde pigtails, blue eyes, shy smile. 'So pretty.'

'It's an old photo.' Mrs Hemming ran fingers through her bob. 'She's . . . grown since then.'

'Is Amy here, Mrs Hemming?'

She paused a few seconds, head tilted. 'That's her on the piano.' It sounded like a Beatles' song to Caroline. Odd choice for a teenager, Amy was a mean player though. 'It's the first time she's touched it . . .' *Since Ram got his hands on her?* Whatever was on Mrs Hemming's mind, she didn't voice it. 'I'll get that drink.' With her back to Caroline she said, 'I'd rather we talk first before seeing if Amy wants to meet you. She's been through . . . a lot.' That was one way of putting it. Hell and back another.

'Of course. I understand.'

'Do you?' She cast a withering glance over her shoulder. 'I doubt that, Mrs Hunter. You said your daughter was playing with fire. Not that she'd been burned.' Burned was a weird kind of euphemism. Amy had been raped, abused, buggered, psychologically and emotionally scarred. And the man who'd orchestrated it was still on the streets.

Of course Caroline couldn't comprehend it. No one could, unless they'd been there. It was why she'd inveigled herself in here. Why she'd cooked up a sob story featuring a fictional child and putative groomer. Why she'd told Mrs Hemming on the phone she desperately needed to talk to a family who'd gone through the experience in the hope of saving her non-existent daughter from the same awful fate. The last part was true, except it was other people's flesh and blood the reporter wanted to help. If writing a book exposing the crime, describing the sort of people who got caught up in it, stopped one child from stepping into a groomer's car then Caroline would spin any number of lies. And not apologise for it.

'Forgive me. It was a crass remark.'

'Yes it was.' Unsmiling, she passed tea to Caroline, nodded at milk and sugar on the bar, then sat on the stool opposite.

Small hands cupped round a thick red mug with gold lettering, she fixed the reporter in her sights. Fighting the urge to squirm, Caroline could just make out the words: Keep Calm And Carry On. She swallowed. *Easy for you to say.*

Saying nothing, Mrs Hemming sipped her tea, studied Caroline over the mug's rim. Piano chords drifted into the silence. It *was* a Beatles' number, but Caroline couldn't name it just now. Not that she was trying, her mind on more pressing matters. The reporter had no doubt she was being measured up, feared she was falling short. Suspected her cover was blown.

'OK. Let's talk.' The woman drained the mug, pushed it to one side. Caroline breathed a huge mental sigh of relief. 'What do you want to know, Mrs Hunter?'

Everything. Shuffling forward she rested open hands on the bar, keen to bridge any gap between them. 'Whatever you can tell me. Anything that might help.'

The woman talked for twenty-five minutes. At some stage the piano music must've stopped. Caroline may have interrupted once. It was as if a verbal floodgate had opened, pent up grief, fury, fears, frustration narrated in a dry monotone. Every word of it was on tape, Caroline was still covertly recording. She'd probably pick up nuances when she transcribed it. Either way, the material was stark, detail graphic. Amy's story was truly shocking, profoundly moving. The flat delivery only underlined its heart-shattering content. It was rare the reporter welled up.

Mrs Hemming's apparent lack of emotion during the telling would be her way of distancing the appalling events. The automaton mode was a coping mechanism Caroline had seen many times before. But the woman's emotional armour had chinks: the tic in her right eyelid had become difficult to ignore, the compulsive worrying at loose skin round badly bitten nails had drawn blood.

Caroline reached out a tentative hand. 'I'm so terribly sorry, Mrs Hemming.' The sympathy was real and the need to talk to Amy greater than ever. The story had everything, but was nowhere near complete. 'Is there anything I can do?'

'Yes there is.' The woman sat back out of arm's reach.

'Drop this ridiculous pretence.' She raised a hand. 'Please. The injured look cuts no ice. I know who you are, knew almost from the word go.' Slipping down from the stool, she rescued the bread from the Aga. Caroline opened her mouth to speak, but Mrs Hemming hadn't finished. 'I won't report you to the police, don't worry on that score. It was my decision to let you stay, my decision to talk to you. I know you have clout in the media and I want people out there to know what can happen if . . .' Biting her lip, she dropped her gaze.

'Mrs Hem—'

'Please. No.' Shaking her head. 'Just write your story or whatever it is you're working on. Tell the world 'the truth, Miss King. That's what you can do. And now . . .' Pointing to the door. 'I'd like you to go.'

'What about talking to Amy?' She was pushing her luck. 'Is there any chance—?'

'You heard her.' A slender youth slouched in the doorway. He had close-cropped hair and a skinny roll-up clenched between white teeth. Eyes creased, he struck a match, released twin smoke trails through pierced nostrils. 'Now bog off.'

'Ask her yourself, Miss King. But I think that's a no.'

TEN

'No comment. Sorry.' Sarah took a sip of water, aware of rustling sounds as she crossed legs under the conference desk. The noise might have emanated from her, could easily have come from the audience shuffling in front. Eight or nine hacks had deigned to show, none appeared overwhelmed, one had barely glanced up from her phone, another was already stowing notebook in jacket pocket. She'd even glimpsed Ted White, the press officer next to her, stifling a yawn. You didn't have to own a Pulitzer to know a bog standard witness appeal wasn't sexy in news terms. But the DI wasn't yet prepared to go the whole hog and confirm press speculation. Why is it, she wondered, reporters want to insert 'serial' in front of every crime?

Stupid question.

'So you're saying there's no link, DI Quinn?' Nathan Hardy, *Birmingham News*. She'd come across him before on stories. Sharp operator, dark good looks, bit of a charmer for someone who could be full of himself.

Suppressing the latest in a series of sighs, she said evenly, 'I'm saying we're keeping an open mind. I'm also saying we need help identifying the man on the right.' She turned her head briefly at the screen behind. Three faces stared back, enlarged images of Duncan Agnew, Sean William Foster, John Doe. 'And it's important we speak to anyone who was in the relevant places at the specified times. We want people to come forward. You have numbers they can call.' Details were in a news release handed to everyone at the start. At least that information was kosher.

Hardy propped casual ankle on knee inadvertently showing a Superman sock. Least she assumed the revelation was unwitting. The dark suit, tie and glasses had more than a touch of the Clark Kent about them. 'And you don't reckon the attacks are down to one gang?'

Dog. Bone. 'I think I'd have mentioned it, don't you, Mr Hardy?'

He turned his mouth down. Good as saying no. Hardy was a big fish in this particular hack pool, the free-sheeters and stringers seemed happy to sit back. 'So you're not issuing a warning then?' Must be a flying fish – with a kite. 'There isn't a gang on the loose, mugging people on the streets?'

Had the guy been to rhetorical question school? Tapping a pen on the desk, she said, 'At this stage we've no—'

'How many attacks qualify then, inspector?'

'Qualify?' *And for God's sake stop saying 'then'.*

'Till you admit they're serial.'

How many times . . . ? 'I've already made it clear, we need proof—'

'How many men have to end up like that before you tell the public the truth. Four? Five?' A stroppy journo was hardly new but Hardy was running out of toys.

Holding his gaze, she heard her watch tick in the silence. Counted ten. 'The truth, Mr Hardy? What is it you're getting at exactly?'

Mouth tight, he shrugged off the question, smoothed his hair. His peers seemed a mix of amused and bemused. Sarah gazed at faces as she finished her water, questions had apparently dried up. 'If that's it, ladies and gentlemen?' It was. Chairs were scraped back, reporters wandered out, she started gathering papers.

Ted slid an envelope across the desk. 'We're not issuing these then?' '*Then*' again. Must be catching.

'Maybe later.' She knew what was inside, didn't need to take another look at the 'after' shots of Foster and the murder victim. Unlike the artist's sanitised 'before' versions on the screen, they showed the men's injuries in stark close-up. Doubtless the newspapers would make space: if it bleeds, it leads and all that. She hoped the case would be featured without making readers feel sick. 'See how it goes, eh?'

'Can I run something past you, DI Quinn?' It wasn't technically an ambush: Nathan Hardy hadn't stuck a leg out to trip her, but he was propping up the wall outside the conference room.

'Why now, Mr Hardy?' She made a show of checking the time.

'It'll only take a second.' The smile was tentative. Not surprising given his recent angry-thirty-something-man performance.

'That's no answer.' Not that she needed one. He hadn't run it past her earlier because clearly whatever juicy titbit Hardy had, he certainly wouldn't share it with the pack.

'What I have isn't for general release, inspector.'

'Get on with it, Mr Hardy.' Arms folded, she watched as he peeled himself off the wall and retrieved a notebook from his back pocket.

'Mean anything to you?' He showed her two names, the same names left on the police hotline.

Sensing his hawk-eyed gaze, she'd shown no reaction, thoughts were whirring though. 'Should they?'

'You tell me.' Hardy matched her apparent insouciance.

'Who gave them to you?' The intelligence had only come in to HQ a couple of hours ago. God and/or Baker forbid, it was a cop on the take. Like Hardy would give away his source.

'Tip-off.' Tapping the side of his nose. 'Call to the news desk.'

'Saying?' She pursed her lips.

'This isn't a one-way street, inspector.'

'Off the record?' She waited for what was patently a grudging nod. 'Follow me.'

'Not trying to bribe me are you, DI Quinn?' Arch delivery, crooked smile. Hardy was in sock-showing stance again, leaning back in a window seat in the canteen. Sarah played it safe, tightened her lips, as she placed a tray on the table. It would cost a lot more than a mug of canteen coffee to buy the reporter's silence, or loosen his tongue. Not that she was in the market for either. Dangerous territory these days. Post the Filkin Report, most cops had lost count of the latest guidelines on cosying up to the media. To Sarah's way of thinking, the most condescending on an overlong list were: keep a note of every conversation with a reporter and try to avoid joint drinking sessions. As for no flirting. *What a frigging cheek.*

Soon as she sat down opposite, Hardy raised a toast and another knowing smile crossed his face. 'Are we sure this isn't a case of "inappropriate hospitality," inspector?'

So Superman had read Filkin too. Big deal. 'It's not spiked, Mr Hardy. No worries.'

He flapped a hand. 'Nat, please.' The charmer returns.

'So . . .' Stirring Earl Grey tea. 'This call? Tell me more.'

A woman had been put through to the news desk, he said. Claimed she had information about the attack in Stirchley on the eleventh. Insisted she'd actually witnessed it and recognised two of the 'bastard toe rags' responsible.

'Two of?' Sarah frowned. *Did that mean there were more?*

Hardy shrugged. 'It's what was said apparently.'

Apparently because Hardy hadn't spoken to the woman, a colleague had picked up the phone. She'd taken down the names, even got the caller to spell them. It was as far as they got, the woman rang off without giving her own.

Playing the spoon between her fingers. 'Are calls recorded as a matter of course at the *News*?'

Slight hesitation? 'I think so.' Hedging his bets most likely. 'I'd like a copy.'

He tapped a salute. 'I'll see what I can do.'

The big question was what Hardy – make that his editor – intended doing with the information. Without corroboration, they'd be mugs to run anything. Not yet anyway. Apart from risking a legal suit, it was meagre fare, it needed fleshing out, they'd want to put faces to names. If they hadn't already. She'd be amazed if they confined the digging to Facebook. Which meant hacks sniffing around, rooting into backgrounds, attracting the wrong kind of attention. If Zach Wilde and Leroy Brody were culpable, there was only one way quicker to signal they were under suspicion. The police at the door. Uniform had despatched unmarked cars to various addresses in south Birmingham, she'd not heard feedback yet.

She spotted Hunt and Twig at the counter grabbing coffees before the brief. She acknowledged the waves with an absent nod. Hardy, she knew, hadn't taken his gaze off her.

'You recognised the names, didn't you, inspector? I saw it in your face.'

Like hell. Even if he had X-ray vision that was a bluff. 'How long have you had the information?'

Another shrug said he didn't like the brush off.

'What are you doing with it, Mr Hardy?'

'Nothing far as I know. I don't call the shots.' No. But he knew a man who did. 'What are you doing with it, inspector?'

Bullshit or bluster? She'd go for both, bolstered with police-speak. 'I'm not going to lie to you, Mr Hardy.' Just lay it on a bit thick. 'We're in possession of the same intelligence.' Leaning across the table, she lowered her voice. 'In strictest confidence . . . as we speak, a high level operation's under way. Any interference from the press or anyone else for that matter could jeopardise its entire outcome . . . and more importantly endanger officers' lives.' She let that sink in. 'So, if your paper has anyone out there . . .' The warning was tacit. What she'd said and not said had clearly shaken him.

Playing for time perhaps, he was cleaning his glasses with his tie.

She added weight by spelling out the warning. 'As much as anything, it's for your own and your colleagues' safety.' On the assumption Wilde and Brody had morphed into knife-wielding nutters, a press card wasn't going to cut the Colman's wholegrain. Over-egging the pudding? Yes.

'Meaning?'

'Think about it, Mr Hardy.' Her chair scraped tiles as she got to her feet. 'I need to get back.'

'Hold on.' The outstretched hand was withdrawn sharpish when he saw her face. 'Quid pro quo, inspector. There must be something I can use?' *Your head?* 'Two-way street, remember?'

'Every word was off the record . . . remember?' She treated him to a warm smile. 'If that changes, you'll be the first to know. Come on. I'll see you down.'

The apparent concession seemed to do the trick, as they made their way to reception the small talk was amiable enough. He offered a hand at the door. 'Well, inspector . . . thanks for . . .?' The twinkle in his eye was quite attractive. 'The coffee?'

'You're welcome, Mr Hardy.' She wondered vaguely if there was a Lois Lane on the scene.

'I know Filkin wouldn't like me saying this, but you have a lovely smile, DI Quinn.' Her lips were still curved when he turned back. 'Oh, and I nearly forgot, an old mate of yours asked to be remembered to you.'

'Old mate?'

'Yeah. I'm living with her at the moment – Caroline King.'

ELEVEN

Caroline King? The name rang a distant bell. Pensive, Ruby Wells tapped the business card against her perfect white teeth. She'd found it lying on the doormat when she dashed downstairs, a scribbled request on the back for

Ruby to phone. Why hadn't King rung Ruby? If she knew the address, surely she must have a number? She wouldn't be surprised if the request had something to do with the Hemming family. Amy had already called Ruby to ask how she could get the press off her back. The timing was too close to be a coincidence. Either way, the card hadn't been there when she arrived home around six which meant she must have been in the shower when King, or whoever, delivered it. Tough tees. Ruby had a date with her mates and if she didn't get a move on . . .

She slung the card on the bottom stair, grabbed a leopard print coat off the banister, shook out her long red hair and drew the fur collar round her neck. Still, she shivered, as the cold night air hit her face. Pulling the door to, she glanced up, saw fingers of indigo cloud trailing across a full cream moon. Gasped when something brushed against her legs. Instinctively she kicked out, a scrawny cat went flying. *Fucking stupid animal.* Biting her lip, she took a deep breath. 'Sorry, puss.'

Hardly the cat's fault it had spooked her. She'd almost forgotten how it felt. Depending which of her friends or colleagues were asked, Ruby was ballsy, bold or badass. Ruby would claim all three. A nervy nature would make a difficult job twice as tough. The sort of people she dealt with could smell fear, sense weakness; the occasional threat went with the criminal territory.

Squaring her shoulders, head high, she made for the car. Weekend spaces were at a premium in Sandstone Row, so she'd parked in the next street. Stilettos clacked on concrete as she strode past 1960s semis that housed a smattering of students and mostly young families. Through cracks in curtains she glimpsed kids gawping at the TV, heard muffled laughter from both sets of audiences.

Recalling the brush with the cat, she shuddered again. *Get over it, girl.* Ruby Wells didn't do wimp.

'What the . . .?'

A couple of feet from the Mazda, she froze, brain struggling to process what her narrowed eyes saw. For a split second she thought it was down to the frigging cat. Ludicrous notion. No creature was capable of a sick show like that. A mangy black bird – crow, maybe – was splayed against the windscreen: blood, feathers, innards smeared against the glass. She stepped closer. Definitely a crow. Its curved black bill was agape and one dead eye seemed to stare accusingly at her. Had it crashed? Taken a nose dive? *Get real.*

No matter how disoriented, a bird doesn't fly backwards, and no way could it pin its own wings under the wipers.

So who, why, when?

It took a while to clear the carcass, wipe the gore, go home, wash her hands. It wasn't until she was in the driving seat, Ruby noticed the note.

TWELVE

Places to see, people to go.
Sorry about earlier.
Catch you later.

T he post-it hadn't been there an hour ago which meant he'd sneaked in while Sarah was holding the brief. Unsmiling, she peeled the note from her screen, read it standing. No prizes for guessing the author. The scrawl was unmistakable. Though why Baker hadn't deigned to sign it, God alone knew. Like the mix up in the opening line, was that deliberate or a cack-handed stab at humour? It *so* didn't work. Shaking her head, she screwed the paper into a ball, tossed it in the bin. Surely he could have had the guts to see her, apologise in person? The old boy needed to get a grip. The line wasn't that fine between lovable eccentric and erratic oddball. If not already crossed, he was damn close.

Still on her feet, her glance lit on a new arrival in the in-tray: a colour print grabbed from one of reception's security cameras. Laydown or one of the video techs must've nipped it in while she was out. She took it from the top of the pile, ran her gaze over the image of the girl, the desk sergeant's so-called slip of a thing. Slip girl had certainly eluded the cops with her alleged phone number. Sarah had checked earlier, called what turned out to be a Birmingham undertaker's – in Quinton of all places. After establishing the number was pukka, she'd found herself at the end of a sales pitch. Guess you had to admire the guy's cheek. Not sure about the girl's though, there wasn't enough on show to judge. Sarah pursed her lips. Was the scarf and hoodie combo deliberate? If this was the best Laydown could come up with. And if she didn't sit down soon . . . ouch.

She sank into the chair, winced as she eased off a shoe, eyes closed in bliss she massaged a throbbing foot. Thinking on, it was probably for the best Baker hadn't shown his face at the brief. None of the squad had been in the mood for taking prisoners. Wilde and Brody were still AWOL and it seemed like every line of inquiry officers had taken that day, led down a blind alley.

She swapped feet, dished out the same treatment, swore the heels would never see the light of day again. *Talk about seeing the light.* What was the saying about counting chickens? She'd been convinced CCTV – especially given the battery of cameras in Chambers Row – would furnish a few decent leads. Four detectives had scrutinised footage for nine hours. Not a dickie bird so far. Nothing earth shattering from snouts either. As for moving on with ID-ing the vics, late editions had carried pics, but there'd not been enough punter feedback to justify extra officers on the phones. House-to-house and street interviews round the crime scenes were ongoing. She'd put in a couple of hours' foot slog herself that afternoon, an SIO in the field was good for morale and – better yet – meant a break from the desk. She twisted her mouth. Next time, she'd remember to change shoes.

Knock off or crack on? Quick glance at the desk was answer enough. The in-tray was on its way out the door, and the logs wouldn't write themselves. Given tomorrow was a scheduled day off, best bite the paperwork bullet now. Not just paper. Harries had left the recording from the Crimestoppers' hotline on her desk. Twice she listened to the tape and was still no wiser to the callers' ages or even gender. Presumably the voices had been deliberately disguised. OK. Move on. Forty minutes later and she found the hunger pangs difficult to ignore, like the extraneous tick of the radiator, low hum from a strip light. Mind the rumbling stomach took the biscuit, as it were. Her mouth watered at the prospect of a bacon sandwich. Perish the thought. No way was she being seen in the canteen on a Saturday night. A quick rifle of the bottom drawer came up with four polos and a pack of smoky bacon crisps past its sell by. *Tell me about it.*

As she tackled another report, niggling thoughts along the line of all work no play wormed their way into her head. Home truths she could live without. She glanced at the clock on the screen, another half-hour and she'd call it a day. After a final scroll through latest witness statements, she sat back, arms stretched high. *Job done.* The smile faded. Like hell. They'd yet to make an arrest, let alone secure a conviction. No point dwelling on negatives though.

The Brody bunch, as Twig had christened the youths, could still come good. Or bad, depending on one's standpoint. They were definitely the best hope for a potential break. Course the squad had to track them down first. She took a few sips of water. None of the addresses checked out, and family appeared thin on the ground. Detectives had been talking to friends, known associates, fair few to get through yet. Was the fact the two youths weren't around significant? Could be an innocent explanation, or they'd got wind of police interest and made themselves scarce. Either way, they couldn't lie low for ever and with every officer in the West Midlands on the lookout, it was just a matter of time till the teenagers were traced, questioned, charged or eliminated.

Come on, Sarah. Time to knock off. Her eyelids drooped as she mentally totted up the edible contents of her fridge. The list wasn't long, the office warm, the chair cosy. She gave a wide-mouthed yawn. When she could bear putting on the shoes again, she'd shake a leg. Plan of action first. Blitz Tesco? Fish and chips? Push the boat out and drop by Pizza Express? Yeah, yeah. In a min. Her head slumped onto her chest. Eeny meeny miny . . .

'Did you know you talk in your sleep, boss?' Harries in the doorway, arms out either side, hands flat against the frame.

Eyebrow cocked, she straightened deliberately slowly, smoothed down her skirt. 'I know you're going to regret not knocking, constable.'

'I did knock. You couldn't've heard.' He dropped his voice. 'Not when you were—'

'I was *not* asleep.' Subtle shuffle of feet to locate the damn shoes.

'Course not.' Nodding at the floor. 'Three inches to your right.'

'Thanks.' Christ he'd be down on one knee calling her Cinderella next. That's if she could get the bloody thing on.

'The other one's back a bit to the left.'

Easing her foot in gingerly, she bent her head to mask a smile. 'Are you here for a reason?'

'The snoring was keeping me awake.' The grin was back, an arm raised to ward off imaginary blows. 'Who's this, then, boss?' Diplomatic change of tack? He'd picked up and was studying reception girl's picture. She told him what she knew – not a lot.

'Nice eyes.' Turquoise almost. He dropped the print back on the desk. 'We bringing the press in on it?'

Her thoughts and hand wavered. A police appeal asking the teenager to come forward had crossed Sarah's mind. But if Blue Eyes had inside gen on the groomer, putting her image out there was tantamount to feeding her to the lions-slash-Ram. Sarah tended to agree with Laydown that the girl had legged it because she got ice-cold feet. On the up-side, she'd called at the nick on her own volition. Who could say it wouldn't happen again? On balance, Sarah would rather hang fire. Seated now, legs sprawled, Harries' downturned mouth said dubious.

'You don't see it that way, Dave?'

'We don't have to say *why* we need to speak to her. We could come up with a plausible excuse. Something bland. Nothing to do with Ram.'

'OK.' Rising, she walked to the window, perched on the sill. 'Say, she's one of his girls, or he's just got his eye on her?' She waited for a nod to say he was on board. 'Right. He sees her on screen, in the papers. And there's us asking her to come forward as a witness to a street robbery say, or an RTA, whatever. You really think Ram's gonna buy that?'

'And if she's got dirt that'd take the bastard off the streets, put him behind bars . . .'

'Risk's not worth taking.' She folded her arms. 'Ram's not just a bastard. He's evil, depraved. You know what he's capable of. You've seen the results.' She frowned, wondered why he'd cocked his head. 'Problem?'

'Nah. Can't argue with that.' He straightened, smiling. 'I'm just trying to think who you remind me of.'

'I'm so glad to hear the serious debate's hitting home.' She rolled her eyes. 'And?'

Lips pursed, he shook his head. 'No. I'm not getting it. I'm sure it'll come.'

'Remind me, Dave.' She wandered back to the desk. 'Why did you drop by? Something I should know about?'

'Nah, squad room's like a morgue. Anyway, I'm off-duty now. A few of us are heading for a bite to eat, wonder if you'd like to join the party.'

What, with George Clooney pining for her at home, peeled grapes and oiled pecs at the ready?

'Yeah, why not?' He helped her into the camel coat. 'So where's everyone going, Dave?'

Jamie's Italian in the Bullring as it turned out. Small party. After a couple of drinks, she realised it was just two-strong: her and Dave. After a couple more drinks, she didn't care. No one was counting.

THIRTEEN

Ruby Wells was making the most of the only settee in the house. Lying on her side, wine glass in hand, she twitched an indulgent lip. 'Have you lot quite finished?' As soon as she'd arrived, she'd told the girls about the dead bird. A few drinks had diluted the initial shock and genuine simpatico. By now, tea and sympathy had gradually given way to a cheeky-vodka-fuelled scoff-fest. One-liners were coming thick and fast.

'Must be what they call a special delivery, Rube.' Charlotte. Who shortened every name in the book.

'As the crow flies,' Shannon added with sage nod.

'Might be pigeon post next time.' Lily.

'Is that cheaper?' Michelle. The only comic in the room who couldn't keep a straight face or stem the giggle. 'Geddit, Ruby?'

'You'll get something if you're not careful. You muppets.' Ruby shook her head. The slight wasn't serious. She appreciated the girls' gags were well intentioned. In their own way, they were trying to protect her; gee her up, make light of a sick stunt. If push came to shove, they'd do anything for her.

Besides, she'd failed to mention the note.

On the can't-beat-join-basis, Ruby threw in her own line: 'No more crowing – or the pizza'll get cold.'

Sitting cross-legged on the floor round two family-sized Sicilians, all four started flapping imaginary wings, the routine could've been synchronized. Ruby rolled her eyes. Happy sipping wine she watched them swoop on the food, listened to the easy banter; Adele providing backing vocals. The girls weren't blood-related but the bond so strong most people would take them for sisters. Not in looks. Ruby gave a crooked smile, ran her gaze over the motley crew.

Wraith-like Lily with long curtains of almost white hair; shaven-headed Charlie who struggled – not hard enough – with her weight; people-pleaser Shannon, mousy, plain, average-everything; Michelle a busty blue-eyed blonde who, Ruby was convinced, fostered the ditzy image. An airhead, she was not.

'Top up, Ruby?' Lily proffered the bottle, giving an unwitting Alice in Wonderland impersonation.

'Yeah, go on then.' She could sleep over need be, the girls would be happy enough. Stop thinking of them as girls, she told herself. They were young women, late teens, Michelle the eldest at nearly twenty.

'Hey, babe, put something decent on for a change.' Michelle was eyeing Shannon who'd got up to change the music.

'You can talk,' she sneered, flipped the bird.

Michelle stuck her tongue out, yanked down her pink spandex boob tube another inch.

'Children, children,' drawled Ruby. God. Only twelve years older, she sounded like a bloody mother hen. Then again, she was the nearest thing they had. Not one parent was on the scene, a couple were dead, the rest good as damn it.

'Choice, Shan.' Michelle gave the thumb's up to Birdy's *Shelter.* Had Shannon chosen it deliberately? Maybe subconsciously, though Ruby doubted it; joined up thinking wasn't Shan's forte. Ruby toyed with mental connections though. Birdy was pretty obvious: despite the joshing, the crow incident was playing on Shannon's mind. As for shelter: if it wasn't for Ruby, likely the girls would be on the streets, sleeping rough, among other things.

Ruby had come across the group last summer, literally bumped into Michelle in a pub one night, accidentally slopped cider down her Stones' T-shirt. Superficially they had zilch in common. Then they got chatting . . . Michelle mainly. Episodes in her life gradually emerged, related without guile or self-pity. With a crack-addict single mother who could barely keep herself, Michelle had been taken into care. The system spat her out when she hit sixteen. By the time Ruby met her she lived in a squat with three mates who were in similarly homeless boats. They looked out for each other, just about got by, but life wasn't exactly rosy. Gutsy Michelle had a mouth on her and had Ruby in stitches most of the night. For some inexplicable reason, despite the differences, they'd clicked. Intrigued, Ruby had asked to meet the others.

A few months later, she'd helped find a place where they could stay without the threat of being turfed out. The scruffy end-terrace in Sparkbrook wasn't much to write home about, furniture was mostly skip-chic, other people's cast-offs. Make-do wallpaper came courtesy of *Heat, OK, Closer*: colour spreads of royals, soap stars, boy bands, C-list slebs. The day-glo display was enough to give Ruby a headache, but better than plaster and brickwork.

She helped with the rent, pointed out jobs they could go for without Masters' degrees. Lucky, given they didn't boast a GCSE between them. For Ruby, the learning curve was steep, she'd never fended for herself, felt it was only right to put something back, helping the girls sort their lives for a start.

Hauling herself up from the settee, Ruby joined the party on the floor.

'Last slice going spare, Rube?' Charlotte's tiny eyes were almost lost in the doughy flesh of her face. She was patently hoping for a no. The morbid obesity saddened Ruby. Strip away the blubber and Charlie would be drop-dead gorgeous. She raised a palm to turn the offer down.

'Hey, look! It's got my name on it.' Lily made a grab for the box. ''Sides, Charlie's watching her weight.'

'Someone's got to,' Michelle quipped.

'Come on, give it a rest.' Ruby reached for the bottle, wished niggling thoughts would take a break, too. The note was in her breast pocket, cheap lined paper rustled when she moved, now and then she felt it scratch against her skin. The words she knew by heart.

> ***should of been a canary***
> ***next time, eh?***

Dead subtle. She'd bet bird man thought he was up there with Einstein, pity the grammar was shite. The message was clear though: he was accusing her of singing. Road kill crows were presumably easier to land than canaries. She'd assumed, too, the writer was a bloke. Had to be, didn't it?'

'Any idea who done it then?' Gaze firmly fixed on Ruby, Charlotte casually popped in the last bite of pizza. Fat she might be, but not much got past her.

Ruby had two ex-clients in mind and in the running. Maybe she'd put out feelers come Monday. 'Tell you if I had, Charlie.'

Pause, weighing it up. 'Straight up?'

'For sure.' She smiled. 'No worries.' *Except.* The note per se wouldn't lose Ruby any sleep. What bugged her now was the knowledge bird man had her address and had made himself at home in her car. And, if his sign-off was meant to be taken literally, was confident of doing it again. She changed the subject, asked about boyfriends, night life, what they'd been getting up to. After ten minutes' light chat, she drained her glass, got to her feet.

Charlie glanced up. 'Not off are you, Rube?'

'Yeah, sorry chaps.' The prospect should've hit her before: if the bastard had gained access to her motor . . . 'I'd best get back.'

Michelle rose. 'I'll see you out.' In the narrow hall, she laid a hand on Ruby's arm. 'Sure you're OK?'

'You bet.' She shucked into her coat, turned at the door. 'I almost forgot. Amy's keen to pop round again. Likes the company.' Ruby winked. 'God knows why.' She'd introduced Amy Hemming to the group a few weeks back on the basis Michelle and the others could make decent role models. If they were turning their lives round, getting back on track, maybe Amy post-Jas Ram's brutality would see a light at the end of the tunnel, too.

'Sure, any time. She's an OK kid. Been through a lot of shit.'

'Not through it yet.' She mentioned Amy's tearful phone call, how she felt hounded by the press. 'Bit of light relief with you lot'd do her the world.' She hoisted her bag on her shoulder. 'I'd best fly. Listen, if you guys need anything? Just let me know.'

'I reckon it's you who needs something, Ruby?' She smiled. 'A scarecrow, maybe?'

FOURTEEN

It doesn't start with fear, you see. It starts with love. It starts with rides in flash cars, nice gifts, lots of compliments. The men are older, good-looking, charismatic, even. The girls are made to feel like princesses. They fall for it, of course. [MRS H's FINGER TAPPING] *They're children really. They fall for the men – later they get hooked on the drink, the drugs. The really unlucky ones fall pregnant.* [PIANO PLAYING IN BACKGROUND] *It's only later the fear kicks-in.* [LONG PAUSE]

Amy was scared, you see. Scared she'd lied to us. Scared she'd get found out. Scared she'd get into trouble. Trouble? [SNORT] *But more than that, more than anything in the world, she was scared of that . . . man . . . that piece of . . . scum.*

Scared doesn't cover it . . . doesn't begin to really.
She was petrified. Paralysed. Not eating. Not sleeping. She'd
have night terrors. Wet the bed. Throw up. Have panic attacks.
Wouldn't you be scared? [PAUSE]
If the man you were convinced loved you – and who you were
besotted with – forced you into having sex with six, seven
strangers a night, or day. Whenever, wherever, whatever he
said. If he told you to jump, you wouldn't say how high: you'd
roll over on your back and . . . [PIANO STOPS]
If Amy cried, or heaven forbid, refused. Or maybe threaten to
confide in someone. Shall I tell you what happened then?
[LONG PAUSE] *This big brave man would thrust a bottle of*
acid in her face, threaten to blind her, disfigure her for life.
Or kill her. Bury her alive in a crate with rats, cockroaches.
Another favourite was to say he'd make her watch while
he and his friends raped me. Oh, yes, and a few times, he
threatened to set fire to this place while we were asleep.
So you see . . . it wasn't easy to . . . stop.
Amy was too scared to tell a soul. She'd always been such a
good girl, model pupil, perfect daughter. Never lied. No backchat.
Never hid anything from us. We always knew where she was.
She was naïve, I suppose. Certainly not streetwise. Easy meat,
as these monsters see it. It's how they get away with the evil
for so long. He isolated her from us, from most of her friends,
her teachers. Amy felt she had no one to turn to. That she'd
failed us. That we'd judge her. Do you see . . . ?

Caroline saw. Even through smarting eyes. Saw too much. Swallowing a lump in her throat, she pressed the pause button, shoved keyboard, pens and pad to one side. She slumped back in the chair, her hands pushing back her fringe and resting, fingers entwined on her head. She sighed. She'd had enough, though the transcription was nowhere near complete. Way past midnight, she was at her desk in the makeshift home office. She'd fancied an early night but sleep proved elusive and she'd finally padded downstairs in her dressing gown. Maybe subconsciously the tape had been burning a hole in her mental pocket. The Gordon's had gone some way to quenching it. Not far enough.

Caroline drained the remains, wandered into the kitchen for a refill. Glass in hand she leaned on the sink, gazed sightlessly through the window. Still saw it all: Amy alone, frightened, abused. Alice Hemming recounting every word in that robotic drone, the tic in her eyelid, the ragged skin round her nails. And she saw wicked bastards getting away with murder. OK. Not murder. No bodies. Journalistic licence. But when a child's psyche was destroyed? A personality shattered? In the reporter's book, it amounted to the same thing.

Sure as hell, the Amy she'd exchanged a few snatched words with bore little relation to the girl described by her mother. And absolutely nothing with the grinning child in the school photograph. What was it Alice had said? *She's grown a lot since then.*

She sure has. Eyes narrowed, Caroline sucked gin through her teeth, recalled the not so touching scene when she'd left the Hemming house . . .

Sitting in the BMW, smoking, making notes, marshalling thoughts. Always better to mentally digest interviews soon as. Impressions, observations, interpretations fade, go astray if not jotted down. Caroline's unwritten agenda was the notion that Alice Hemming didn't like anyone smoking in the house. Including her daughter.

Mind, with the evening gloom growing, temperature falling, Caroline had been on the point of driving off when a door banged, footsteps crunched gravel. She counted seven before the girl emerged into view and – thank you, God – turned right out of the drive. Five seconds later Caroline, minus the glasses and back with the bob, leaned against the motor, legs casually crossed at the ankle. Amy trudged on unaware, head down, one hand buried in the pocket of a bulky donkey jacket. The red dot at hip height put Caroline in mind of a telescopic sight, except she knew it was a ciggie.

'Got a light, Amy?' Friendly smile, warm voice. Last thing she wanted was to startle the girl.

Drawing alongside, staring at Caroline, she took a deep drag. 'What part of bog off don't you get? *Mrs Hunter.*' Make her jump? She'd clearly marked Caroline's card a while back.

'Let's think . . . bog . . . and . . .' – mouth down, one finger up – '. . . off.' Two fingers in the air now. Caroline caught a twitch of Amy's lip. The reaction was likely involuntary but, hey, strike while the iron might be hotting up. 'Thing is, when it's important, I don't let go. Dogged, that's me.'

'As in bitch?' Red sparks flew as she flicked the stub towards the gutter.

She bit back a comeback in kind. 'No call for that, Amy.' No point talking down to her either, treating her like a child. She wasn't. Not any more. And she'd see through smarm or bollocks sooner than you could say jackshit. 'As I say, if it's important . . . another?' She offered a pack of Marlboro.

Swatting it away. 'Cut the crap. What d'you want?'

This is going well. 'You shouldn't anyway.' Sparking up. 'It's against the law.'

'What?' The unintended irony must have appealed. 'You mean – at *my* age?'

Under the amber street light, Amy looked a sickly fifteen going on fifty. Arms folded, legs spread, the girl was aiming for stroppy sod, not quite pulling it off. Caroline reckoned it must be hard work keeping a more or less permanent scowl in situ. Fact the girl hadn't flounced off was telling. A second later, she turned on her heel. Caroline performed the pavement equivalent of a foot in the door, stepped in front, both palms held out. 'Amy. Listen. I can't begin to imagine—'

'Got that right. Go on then.' Smirking, she snatched the pack from Caroline's hand. 'You twisted my arm.'

Ring your neck in a minute. She smiled. 'Keep it. I've got—'

'A bloody nerve.' The pack disappeared in a pocket of her jeans.

Caroline was beginning to understand why one of Amy's front teeth was chipped. *Cut the girl some slack for Christ's sake.* 'So can we talk?'

Amy jabbed a thumb over her shoulder. 'After Mrs Blabbermouth just spilled her guts out? What more do you want?' Her eyes creased as she lit a baccy.

'I want to help.'

'Bit late for that, innit?' Toeing the ground with a scuffed Converse trainer, patches of white scalp were just visible under the brutally short hair. Beneath the prickly veneer Amy was pitiably vulnerable. Caroline resisted an uncharacteristic urge to offer comfort; she doubted Amy wanted another stranger pawing at her. She paused while an old man ambled past with what sounded like an asthmatic bulldog.

'Help girls *like* you then. Stop other kids going through the same shit.'

Amy played air violin, smoke wafted along with virtual bow. It could explain the glistening eyes – again, Caroline doubted it. 'What are you?' Amy sneered. 'Some kinda fairy godmother?'

'I wish.' Grinding the half-smoked cigarette underfoot. She wished she could turn the clock back, wished she could get a better handle on the girl. As bonding sessions go, this hadn't.

'Yeah, but you're not. And if you think there's a happy ever after, you're even stupider than you look.' She flapped a hand. 'People like you haven't got a frigging clue.' Hard face. Big talk.

'No. But you have, Amy.' She reached out, voice velvet-soft. 'You could make a difference.' A single tear ran down Amy's cheek, difficult for Caroline to ignore.

'Leave me be. I can't do this now.' Abrupt turn then she stomped off, digging in a pocket presumably for a tissue.

Now? Just about on the cards then? Caroline took a few steps, before calling out, 'We can stop him, Amy. Walk away – and he wins.'

Her boot already covered the white card she'd seen fall when the girl pulled out the tissue. Scooping it from the pavement, she glanced at the lettering, slipped it in her bag. Amy was nowhere in sight or – naturally – Caroline would have returned it.

Next time.

Back in real time, Caroline tapped a finger against her lip. She peeled herself off the sink still curious why Amy had been carrying round a solicitor's card. And why it had a home address and phone number scrawled on the back. Finger combing her hair, she headed for the stairs. Far as she knew, Ruby Wells hadn't acted for the girl, so what was it all about? There'd been one way to find out, and she more or less passed the street on her way back. The little detour hadn't done any harm. Made sense to drop by, suss it out. But Ms Ruby Wells had neither been in – nor called back.

Which meant Ruby was near the top of the reporter's to-do list.

She tapped lightly on her lodger's bedroom door, sure she'd heard him come in earlier. 'You awake, Nat?'

She pricked her ears, Nada. Probably just as well. Business, pleasure, all that.

FIFTEEN

L ying flat on her back in bed, Sarah held two fingers in front of her face. She screwed her eyes, held a recount, just to make sure. When she'd tried the same trick an hour ago there'd been four there, at least. Groaning, she dragged the duvet over her head, made an oath to sign the pledge, soon as the pounding stopped. The church bell accompaniment didn't help either. She didn't normally get hangovers. Mind, she didn't normally neck that much booze. Maybe drink more in future? Develop a tolerance for the stuff? *Do me a frigging favour.*

OK, Sarah. Two fingers good. Gingerly she rolled on her side, slowly lifted the cover. Thank the Lord. No spinning, no churning, no gagging, no splitting head, no sleeping policeman. She smiled. Knew she hadn't been *that* hammered. Had she said the word, Dave Harries would have been in like a shot. Probably see it as a career move. No, that was below the belt. Had she been tempted? Is the pope celibate? Debatable then. Fact was, fit, good-looking guys who made her laugh didn't fall in her lap every day. Smiling, she cocked an eyebrow. If memory served, that was the point she'd poured him into a cab. Damn good job he was off duty today as well.

Swinging bare legs out of bed, she grabbed a fleecy dressing gown off a hook on the door. Bedroom felt like an ice box.

A smile still in situ as she entered the bathroom, faded a touch when she examined her face in the mirror. Actually, not bad, considering . . . The panda eyes weren't down to a night on the lash. She reached for a couple of wet wipes. Christ, she was only thirty-two, a few late nights wouldn't do any harm. Maybe she should take a few more? Lighten up? Live a little?

Sighing, she loosened the bun then perched on the edge of the bath, added bubbles to the water. Would it really have been such a bad thing to wake and find Dave beside her? Shoot, woman, are you mad?

Even ignoring the age gap and different rank – which no one at the nick would – she'd been there, done that, got the bite marks. Years back, she'd been involved with a DI in the Met. More than involved – lived with him, wedding planned, the works. He was stabbed when a reporter panicked and inadvertently blew an undercover operation. Jack died in her arms on a London street. Turned out, he'd been screwing the journo, too. The fallout had damn near destroyed Sarah and her then fledgling career. Never again . . .

Letting the gown drop, she lowered herself into the water, lay back as far as five and a half feet of bath allowed. With the hair trailing she could've posed as a blonde Ophelia. Was she supposed to live like a nun as well? Given how much time she spent working and the gender ratio in the force, declaring cops off-limits had to be blinkered. Talk about restricting the market. If she wasn't careful she'd end up married to the bloody job. No way. Besides, she didn't want marriage, someone to share a bit of down time with would be good, regular sex with a decent bloke wasn't a lot to ask.

Jack had been dead ten years. She'd not mixed business with pleasure since. Maybe time she did. The journo involved back then hadn't let it stop her. But when had Caroline King ever let anything stop her?

Enough already. Let it go.

Maybe she'd nip into the nick later, just see if anything was kicking off?

* * *

'So, Davy, how's it going?' Caroline King sounded like she was chatting to an old mate, then listened to four seconds' dead air before a groggy, 'Sorry, who is this?'

Colombo was still on the ball then. The reporter twisted her mouth. Maybe the call had broken his beauty sleep. Stirring brown sugar into black coffee, she injected her voice with a lazy smile. 'Come on, sweetie – it's not been that long.' Since she and DC Harries had been very good mates indeed. A quick fling is all, but Dave had been a damn good . . . 'Don't say you haven't missed me?'

'What do you want, Caroline?'

Sounded a lot perkier now. And prickly. She pictured him sitting up, hair tousled, chest bare, stay-in-bed eyes. Hadn't needed to draw on imagination. 'Want?' Verbal pout. 'Can't I phone a mate for a little chat these days? Since when's that been *against* the law?'

'Oh, let's think.' Rustling noises. Black satin sheets getting the elbow? 'Since you almost got me the boot?'

She arched an eyebrow, traced an index finger round the mug. Strictly speaking, that wasn't down to her. It was Sarah Quinn who'd pole-vaulted to the wrong conclusion, accused Harries of leaking intelligence during pillow talk. Body fluids may have been swapped, but not sensitive information. No point arguing the toss. Truth be told, she regretted alienating him now. 'Come on, Dave – water, bridge.'

'Under? Jump?'

'Fun-nee.' She gave a lopsided smile. The laughing policeman he was not. She sauntered to the sink, swilled the mug. Nat's breakfast bowl sat there flecked with soggy corn-flakes. She didn't clear anyone's mess, not even hers if she could get away with it. 'I need a favour.'

'Well I never.' Was that water running? Surely he wasn't having a pee?

'Get the boss lady to contact me?' She'd left loads of messages for Sarah Quinn, but nada in return. Short of door-stepping the DI, the delectable detective was Caroline's best bet. Anyway, it was about time she and Dave kissed and made up. Life's too short. She wished Sarah would chill, too. The Snow Queen hadn't always been so high and bloody mighty.

'It's urgent, Dave. I might have something for her. To do with Jas Ram.' And vice versa, naturally. Give it enough spin, and she could probably convince Quinn the upcoming interview with Ram would benefit the cops, too. In the back-scratching stakes, the reporter wanted Sarah's help with the police take on the issue. 'Have a word, eh?'

'I'll mention it . . . but don't call this number again. I'm not your—' Harries narrowed his eyes, heard static. Great. Always loved talking to himself. Mouth tight, he wandered back to the bedroom, slung his mobile on the side table, absently scratched his chest. A glance in the mirror registered just how hacked off he was. Apart from the cocky attitude, King was congenitally incapable of letting anyone else have the last word.

Make that two. He'd been about to add 'errand boy'.

Errand boy, go-between. Shrugging, he sank onto the edge of the mattress. It boiled down to the same thing. Everyone knows what happens to the messenger. In his mind's eye he saw Sarah holding a gun, blowing down the barrel. Pissing her off was the last thing he wanted. Through a hangover the size of a planet, he seemed to recall making great strides last night, hoped to God he'd not put his foot in it, had an in vino adidas moment.

Too late now, Prosecco under the ponte and all that. He checked his watch: twenty to eleven. Half the day, down the pan as well. OK. Shave, shower, bite to eat then maybe make the call. Groaning he ran a hand down his face. The prospect of telling the DI he'd had his ear bent by her favourite hack . . .

The ring tone blared a snatch of 'Teenage Kicks' before his clammy hand reached the phone. The nerve of the bloody woman. 'I told you not to phone again. How difficult is that?'

'Frigging tricky, Harries. I'm not into telepathy.' A terse-sounding uncharacteristically uptight Paul Wood. The DS wouldn't be calling an off-duty officer to inquire about his health. 'You at home?'

'Yes, sir.' Sparkbrook bedsit. All he could afford.

'We've got an ongoing incident, Jubilee Way. Stand-off involving a bunch of youths. How soon can you get there?'

Twig always did his homework, he'd know the street was a stone's throw. 'Ten minutes, sarge.'

'Make it five.'

His hand froze en route to the shower control. 'The DI, is she . . .?'

'Get your ass in gear, lad. An officer's down.'

SIXTEEN

No shower, no shave, hastily garbed in last night's crumpled gear, Harries pounded down a narrow pavement slick with rain, dotted with dog turds. Almost oblivious to his surroundings, he dodged stinking bin liners, hurdled a rusty bike frame. A mental mantra kept pace with his thudding footfalls: not her, not her, not her. God knows why but gut instinct, sixth sense, call it what you will told him Paul Wood had held back. Harries expected to see Sarah lying injured or, God forbid, worse.

Fists clenched, he upped the pace. Thirty or forty gawpers milled round at the Jubilee Way turn. Scowling, he assumed telly must be crap this morning, nothing like a bit of street entertainment. No audience participation, thank Christ. The cordon slung across the top of the road saw to that, plus the thin line of constables and community support officers posted just beyond. Elbowing his way to the front, it looked like a few idiots were auditioning for Strictly Come Cop Baiting – especially the girls. Talk about playing to the cameras. And the radio mics. Great. The media was out in force as well.

Ducking under a sodden Do Not Cross tape failing to dodge droplets, he ignored an ironic desultory round of applause, tried doing the same with the sharp stitch in his side. A hand he used to brush hair from stinging eyes came away wet with sweat and drizzle. He wiped the palm down damp black denims, fumbled in a leather jacket pocket for ID, headed for a police constable he vaguely knew.

Doug Fraser had already stepped out of line, now raised a gauntleted arm. 'That's far enough, sunshine.' Stocky and swarthy, Fraser carried too much weight, had a reputation for throwing it. Late-forties, intellectually challenged, his career had long since stalled.

Harries flashed a warrant card. 'Piss off, Dougie.' Still trying to catch his breath, he winced as the stitch kicked in again.

'Sorry Dave, didn't recognise you for a sec.' Maybe needed an eye test or better fitting hat. He lifted the peak. 'Are you OK, old son? Looking a bit rough there.'

Harries nodded absently, total focus on the view over Fraser's shoulder: a narrow street of grey pebbledash two-up two-downs, no gardens, no groundcover. Several appeared uninhabited: grimy uncurtained windows, rotting frames, warped doors. Presumably, those still occupied had been evacuated. Police vehicles lined both kerbs, half a dozen uniforms with helmets and riot shields gathered behind a makeshift barricade of wheelie bins. 'What's the state of play, Dougie?'

Fraser lifted a finger, took a radio call, gave a few sage nods, right-ohs. Rocking on the balls of his feet, Harries scanned the street again, still couldn't locate Sarah. Neither should be here by rights, it was uniform's baby. 'Too many bloody chiefs, or what?' Fraser clipped the radio back on his belt. 'Anyway, old son. State of play. Some joker rang. Gave an address. Claimed all hell was breaking loose. Needed checking out. Patrol in the area, why not?' He shrugged. 'Lads couldn't get in, could they?' He turned, pointed to a derelict property fifty metres on the right, downstairs window boarded up, racist graffiti scrawled across the front door, upstairs window a gaping hole, tell-tale black stains pointed to a fire some time in the past. 'The little shits are up there. Barricaded in. Chucking gubbins every time anyone sets foot.'

Missiles littered the road: bricks, bottles, floorboards, slates, tiles, toilet seat, taps. Harries drew his collar tighter trying to keep out the rain that tipped down now. Oily puddles reflected the leaden sky. A scrawny black cat sat in a doorway licking its arse. Some of the crowd shuffled off, kids still enjoying the floor show.

'Puts a new spin on house clearance, don't it?' Fraser's sniff was sceptical. He tapped the radio. 'I hear they're out of ammo.' According to hastily set-up surveillance in the next house, there'd not been a peep for twenty minutes. Thinking was either the youths had stripped the place, or they'd drunk the contents before lobbing the bottles and were now paralytic.

'Either road, SWAT's going in, take away any toys left.' He dug a hankie out of his pocket, dried his face. 'Sooner the better in my book. Frigging brass monkeys out here and I could do with a slash.'

Surely he'd have said? 'I heard an officer . . .'

Harries spun round at a roar of mixed jeers and cheers from the crowd, turned back just in time to glimpse the battering ram take off the door, and riot officers stomp through shouting, 'Police!'

'It's not like they were expecting the Avon lady, is it?' Fraser batted his eyelids, dropped the simpering smile. 'Little gits; waste of space. Down to me, they'd get a good slapping, not a tap on the wrist from some lily-liv—'

'Fuck's sake, Doug.' Shouting over the crowd's din. 'Has a cop been injured?'

'Young lad. Probationer.' Apparently a rookie had been hit by a flying brick, patched up by paramedics then taken to hospital for further checks. 'He'll live.'

Harries expelled a deep breath. So much for gut instinct. 'Is DI Quinn around?'

'She is.' And standing at his shoulder. 'What's the problem?'

He rubbed a hand across his chin. 'Long story, boss.'

'Save it.' Unsmiling, she nodded down the road. 'It's our lucky day.' He turned to see two youths in cuffs being frog-marched to a police motor, doors open, engine running. 'Guess who, Dave?'

SEVENTEEN

S afe to say it was not the luckiest day of Zach Wilde and Leroy Brody's short and distinctly unsweet lives. Slumped on thin blue mattresses on low benches in adjoining police cells at Lloyd House each unwittingly mirrored the other's miserable-sod posture. Heads hung between hunched shoulders, scrawny arms hugged bony knees, each jigged a bare dirt-encrusted foot. Not so much dumb and dumber as glum and glummer. Mind, in the brain department, two cells between them was about right.

On arrival, they'd barely been able to stand, let alone string a coherent sentence together. After booking them in, the custody sergeant had had no choice but to let them sleep it off. *It* being a staggering amount of cider and dope. Slur and Lurch as Harries referred to them hadn't long come round. And given the overwhelming eye-witness evidence, pretty soon they'd be going down. For what and how long were the imponderables. Disorderly behaviour, assaulting a police officer, criminal damage, possession – went without saying. But would the rap sheet include robbery with violence and murder?

Sarah and Harries sat and pondered in an airless overheated observation room along the corridor. Wilde and Brody were showing on separate CC screens. Tom Cruise had nothing to worry about.

'Give us one, Dave.' Gaze fixed on Wilde's image, Sarah slid a hand along the table.

'Thought you didn't like 'em.' Salt and vinegar crisps. He'd just ripped open his third pack.

'Smell's making me hungry.' Make that ravenous. The beef pasty and Penguin lunch long gone. Coming up to five now, her scheduled day off was the latest in a long line to go by the board. She could've pulled out, but the prospect of interviewing the youths held appeal, a lot rested on it. He-who-must-be-informed Baker had been called at home, wanted a piece of the action, too, according to Hunt. Sarah had yet to set eyes on the chief. While Brody and Wilde had been out of it, she'd cracked on with the rest of the admin, now owned a clear desk for the first time in months. Harries had taken off for a couple of hours in the interim, returned clean-shaven and smelling of shampoo. The pull of the Brody Bunch Two had proved irresistible.

'I'd've brought in popcorn if I'd known,' he said. 'Choc ice. Hot dog.' She rolled tired eyes. 'Yeah, you're right.' He nodded at the monitor, opened a can of Red Bull. 'It's not exactly *Mission Impossible*, is it?'

Blues Brothers more like. She gave a fleeting smile, licked salty fingers. 'You're not here to enjoy yourself. And nor are they.' They were there to face a bunch of questions. 'What are the odds d'you reckon, Dave?'

The can paused halfway to his lips. 'That they're behind the muggings?'

'No. I'm thinking Shergar in the two thirty.'

He pulled a face. 'Get you.'

'Well don't be a plonker.'

'You're the one always banging on about evidence-based facts, analytical minds. Since when did idle speculation get the Quinn seal of approval?'

'Since I said so. Are you answering or not?'

'Not. I'd rather wait for proof.'

'Suit yourself.'

Wouldn't they all? FSI guys were currently picking a path through what was left of 14 Jubilee Way. In an ideal world, they'd unearth evidence before the interrogation got under way. Back in the real world, initial forensic feedback had revealed nothing to point to the youths' involvement in the street attacks. Nothing to set the world on fire either, only that fires had been lit in the house: grates upstairs and down contained ashes and embers. Several scuzzy sleeping bags had also been found lying round, plus a stash of canned food and grubby clothes in Asda carrier bags. It didn't take a PhD in the bleedin' obvious to conclude the place was being used as a squat. As much as anything, the findings confirmed statements taken during house-to-house inquiries and anecdotal stuff from some of the crowd. It had quickly emerged that number 14 was well known locally as a magnet for dossers and druggies. Whether Wilde and Brody had taken temporary refuge or lived there illegally was still up in the air.

As was Wilde's middle finger. His expression was pure loathing.

'Cheeky sod, look at that.' Harries pointed a crisp at the screen. 'If I was taking a punt – which I'm not – he's odds on favourite.'

Wilde had clocked the security cameras, clearly took exception to being filmed. Jumping up on the bench, he shoved his ugly mug as close as he could to the lens and was mouthing off big time. Hiring a lip reader wasn't necessary. Fuck off scum was hardly original. Sarah shook her head. The cocky little git was flashing V signs now. He sure wasn't camera shy, and certainly not blessed photogenically.

'Wouldn't want to wake up next to that of a morning, would you?' Harries sniffed.

She cut him a glance, said nothing, resumed watching Wilde's pathetic antics. Short and painfully thin in the flesh, his looks had changed since the Facebook pic to the extent there was more hair, fewer teeth. The layer of stubble resembled a dark skull cap, the black gap a poor substitute for a missing incisor as well as the absent molar. Could be down to decay, oral hygiene not being a priority, or Wilde got into a lot of fights. Looking at him now, she'd opt for the latter. It also struck her that in a less crude setting, the large pale green eyes would be beautiful.

'Seen enough, boss? Reckon they're up to a grilling?'

'Oh yes.' Eyes wide, she turned her back on the screen. Wilde had just dropped his trousers, his arse in close-up was too much, talk about dark side of the moon. Brody was still head down, rocking if not rolling. They'd need clearance from the custody sergeant first but as far as she was concerned the sooner the show hit the road the better.

It was nearer six before everyone got their act together. Fed and watered but refusing briefs, Brody and Wilde slouched in separate soundproofed interview rooms. Baker and Hunt were in with Wilde, the chief had waltzed in at the last moment demanding first dibs. Fine by Sarah, like she had a choice. Besides, she'd seen more than enough of Wilde.

She and Harries sat across the table from Leroy Brody in IR2. Décor of muted blues and grey was meant to be relaxing. She'd already snapped one pen in half. Twenty minutes since Harries had run through the spiel for the audio and video recordings and apart from her increasingly terse questions, the tapes were mostly redundant. A ticking clock, rustling papers and the occasional sniff wouldn't sway a jury. Brody hadn't uttered a word. Not even the catch-all 'no comment'. For

Christ's sake, he'd not even cracked a knuckle. Oblivious of her cold glare, the youth hunched forward, elbows on knees, head in hands, black curls still with blue tinge. The slight but constant rocking of his slender body was sending her up the wall. Now she knew why the bloody furniture was nailed to the floor. Frustration didn't begin to cover it.

She rolled the sleeves of a crisp white shirt. 'This is doing you no good, Mr Brody.' And it certainly didn't help the police. Worst interviewees in the world are those who won't open their mouth. Ziptits, Baker called them. With no version of events to go on, detectives had nothing to follow through, stand up, knock down. Semi-literate though Brody might be, he was canny enough to know the more he came out with greater the chance he'd give himself away. She could hardly catch him out in a lie, when the only sound he'd produced so far was a fart.

'For your own sake, I really think you should take the offer of legal advice, Mr Brody.' And a shower: the guy stank of stale flesh, unwashed hair, cheesy feet. Given the temperature in the room, the odours weren't getting any sweeter. She poured water into a glass. 'If not now, you'll need representation in court, because make no mistake you will stand trial and this time it'll be a custodial sentence.'

He must know the stand-off had attracted a bigger audience than Madonna's Super Bowl gig. OK, she ceded, that was police licence. But eye-witness evidence at Jubilee Way was overwhelming, conviction virtually a given. And they hadn't even touched on the muggings. She took a few sips, willed him to respond. Eyes creased she studied Brody's humped back. Perhaps a stay at Her Majesty's Pleasure was preferable to life on the street? As far as they'd established, the nineteen-year-old had no family, no fixed abode, no job, no deodorant. She sniffed. More to the point, she had no way of gauging his thoughts. Since the minimal eye contact when she'd made the introductions, Brody's entire focus had been on the tiles. Body language said bowed if not beaten. But what the hell was going on in that head?

'Well, Mr Brody?' Nothing. She exchanged the latest in a series of voluble glances with Harries. He raised an eyebrow, but she wasn't ready to pass the baton yet.

'I'll take that as a yes then.' She made to stand, wanted to force the issue, force something, anything. Brody shook his head a few times, gaze still on scuffed trainers. Progress of sorts, she supposed. She sank back in the chair, regarded the youth again. His arms were stick thin and grimy, one wrist bore a fraying friendship bracelet. A tiny cross hung quivering silver fish style from an ear lobe. For a second or two, she felt almost sorry for the youth. With a shit background like that, what chance had he stood of a bright future? Not her baby. As a cop, she reserved the lion's share of her sympathy for the victims.

'The police officer you attacked? Want to know how he's doing?' The slow rocking stilled momentarily. The emphasis on *you* getting through? She paused, gave him an opening. Mind he'd had more openings than Broadway. Still, nothing. As it happened, the mild concussion wouldn't keep the rookie in hospital overnight but Brody could stew. 'Course you wouldn't. Why would you care? Casual violence's your thing, isn't it?'

Chair grated tiles as she got to her feet. She paced slowly up and down for a fat minute while Harries lounged back, legs crossed, fingers drumming thigh. The silent treatment could work both ways. It often unsettled edgy suspects, eventually most filled the void. Eventually. Most. She rolled her eyes. The method wasn't foolproof. Maybe Brody wasn't a fool? How could they break his story when he hadn't offered one? Maybe the heat, maybe tiredness, it wasn't often she lost her cool, but she was pretty damn close.

Stifling a sigh, she resumed her seat, took up a file from the desk. 'Moving on, Mr Brody.' That was rich, they hadn't gone anywhere yet. She removed glossy prints of the mugging victims so familiar with them by now she could probably produce copies from memory. For Brody, she'd brought along the most graphic, the results of violence needed to hit home. She slid Duncan Agnew's picture across the desk.

'Not pretty is it? The man's still in hospital. What can you tell us about the attack?' Brody barely gave it a glance. 'We have several witnesses placing you and your buddies at the scene, Mr Brody.'

Nothing.

'Keeping shtum isn't going to save your sorry little neck.' She snapped, sensed Harries' gaze, the outburst rare. She took a deep breath, dropped her voice. 'Who put the boot in this time?' Brody recoiled slightly when Foster's pic hit the desk. 'Take a long hard look, Mr Brody. See the tread on his cheek? The impact broke the bone. He's lucky not to have lost an eye.' Again, the youth barely took his gaze off the floor. She walked round the desk, thrust the third victim's pic in Brody's line of vision. 'We don't know who this is yet, but he bled out at the scene. Your blade was it, Brody?' Assuming his eyes were open, they'd be meeting the victim's lifeless stare. Still, no response. 'Doesn't matter either way. Joint enterprise, Mr Brody: as the law stands, you'll go down for life.'

His so-what shrug did it. Throwing down the pic, she whacked the desk with a palm. 'Look at me when I'm talking, you little . . .' Harries laid an arm on hers. She shook it off, walked away, counting under her breath. Ten didn't do it, she hit twenty, still couldn't stand the sight of the youth. With her back turned, she softened her voice, even injected a little warmth 'It could go easier if you tell us who else is in on it, Leroy.' The elderly witnesses from the first crime scene had mentioned four or five youths. 'Think about it. Why do the time if you didn't do the crime? If I can, I'd like to help you, Leroy.'

'Boss.' Harries tilted his head. Frowning, she followed his gaze. The youth's narrow shoulders shook, wet tear trails were leaving white tracks down his grimy arms. Even Brody's crying was silent.

'Yes, but why the waterworks? Remorse . . . self-pity . . . his goldfish copped it?' Sarah provided her own answers, which was a damn sight more than Brody had.

Harries slid his metal tray on the table next to hers. 'Come on, boss. Give him a break.' Tired and hacked off, she'd wandered up to the canteen. Sunday evening fare was notoriously thin on the gourmet ground, but beat a still-empty fridge. Dave had tagged along, maybe at a loose end, too.

'Break?' She sniffed. Brody might as well be on bloody

leave. In no fit state to continue not answering questions, the youth's non-interview was on hold until morning. Time. Waste. Of.

''Sides, you've changed your tune.' She tore the wrapper off a straw with her teeth, not convinced strawberry milkshake was the wisest choice to wash down beans on toast. 'It's not that long since you were ready to throw away the key.' What was it he'd said when Brody and Wilde's names were left on the hotline? Cooking with gas.

'He's no angel, I'm not saying that.' Harries had boned up on Brody's back story and social reports: family break-up, children's homes, YOIs. 'Given the shit cards he was dealt, it would've been more of a shock if he'd not taken wrong turns, run with a bad crowd. A small part of me feels sorry for him, I guess.' Pensive, head down, he speared a chip, incipient lines round his eyes giving her a glimpse how his face would age. 'Must've been bloody tough growing up like that.'

Her smile was bitter-sweet. 'Yeah I know.' Knew emotional intelligence like that made Harries a decent bloke, that he'd develop into a good detective. The touchy-feely stuff wasn't just for show, learned in a lecture hall. He wasn't afraid to open up, admit emotions more macho cops wouldn't even acknowledge. She recalled her own flash of sympathy: fleeting, not heartfelt.

'But he's not the only one, Dave. And his welfare's not down to us. We lock away bad guys, not lick their wounds.' Glancing at her runny beans, she curled a lip, pushed the plate to one side. Blamed the appetite loss on thought association. And on the issue of blame, in her book, whether Brody was culpable of the muggings or not, he'd undoubtedly committed offences that day. Either way, he'd be held on the lesser charges while the squad bust a gut trying to gather incriminating evidence on the street attacks. If it existed. 'I'd still like to know why he broke down like that.' She slurped milkshake.

He gave a lopsided smile, pointed his fork at the glass. 'That come with a volume control?'

'Cheeky sod,' she snapped. 'Piss off.'

'Probably the way you spoke to him.'

'Bollocks.'

He lowered a calm-down hand. 'Not the shouty stuff – he'll have had verbal kickings, and worse, all his life. God, I'm stuffed.' He rubbed his stomach, pushed away the plate, only swirls of yolk, brown sauce, ketchup remained. Where did the guy put it? 'I mean towards the end, the soft voice, calling him by his first name, offering help.'

'Yeah right.' Brody was hardly a child. 'Remind me not to do my Mother Teresa next time.' She sat back, laced her fingers.

'Made a change from your Mike Tyson.' He turned his mouth down. 'Not sure what got into you back there, boss.'

'Long day. Short fuse.' Deep sigh. Christ, she was only human. Operation Steel was unwieldy, frustrating, a drain on resources and a drag on squad morale; she'd hoped for a break in the case not the interrogation.

He studied her over the rim of his tea mug. 'Not quite got the hang of the good cop bad cop routine have you, boss?'

She tried reading the glint in his eye. 'Enlighten me.'

'It takes two to work it . . . y'know, more double act than—' Both whipped their head round when the door whacked the wall.

'Fucking comedian.' Snarling, Baker stomped towards them suit jacket flapping like wings. Sarah turned away, watched his approach via the reflection in the picture window, the second hand view only delayed the inevitable. Baker pulled up at the table, hands thrust in trouser pockets, sounded like a heavy breather. 'Well, chaps, I've heard it all now.'

He wanted an audience, she turned reluctantly, met his gaze. Frowned. 'What's wrong with your eye, chief?' Swollen, bruised, classic shiner in the making.

'Wilde landed one on me.' He helped himself to a piece of cold soggy toast.

She cut Harries a glance, hoped she didn't look as gobsmacked. 'And you think that's funny because . . .?'

Still chewing. 'Little gobshite's only claiming self-defence.'

Oh, shit. She stiffened. 'So . . . he's injured too?'

'Yeah.' Wiping his mouth with the back of a hand. 'He fell off a chair.'

'You are joking?' She scanned his face for clues.

'Fuck's sake, Quinn. He lashed out when I helped him up. What d'you take me for?'

Hot head cop? She narrowed her eyes. But he wasn't stupid. She'd no doubt Baker was a loud-mouthed bully, but he'd not have laid into a suspect. Not with John-play-it-by-the-book-Hunt sitting in and certainly not with tapes recording blow-by-blow action. 'What's Huntie saying, chief?' Casual delivery.

Baker shrugged. 'Nipped out for a leak, hadn't he?'

Three, four second pause. 'So you'd terminated the interview?' And switched off the recordings. She swallowed.

He must've registered the look on her face. 'What is this, Quinn? The sodding Spanish Inquisition? I'm telling you Wilde attacked me.'

'And Wilde? What's his take?'

'What do you think?'

EIGHTEEN

Sarah reckoned Baker would be lucky not to be up on an assault charge. Wilde was throwing accusations as well as punches, swearing the chief had used Hunt's absence to launch an unprovoked attack. From what she'd heard, it was *just* conceivable the youth's injuries were self-inflicted: the split lip, bruised cheek, scratches near the eye were superficial. The medical examiner hadn't delivered a verdict yet. With no witnesses, nothing on tape, currently it was Wilde's word against the chief's. She pulled her camel coat closer. What a frigging mess.

'Never rains, eh, Dave?' She gave a thin smile as they dashed across the car park huddled under Harries' golf-sized Guinness umbrella. Not that she was talking weather. They'd just left a nick buzzing with rumour, gossip, bets on Baker's future, sweepstake on how long he had left.

'Reckon the old boy's on the level, boss? Shit!' He'd stepped in a puddle deeper than it looked.

For once, she let the 'old boy' go. 'Of course he is.'

Her instant unequivocal backing contrasted with the scepticism she'd clearly failed to hide earlier. She shuddered, recalling Baker's exit line. White-face, balled fists, low voice oozing contempt: *Thank you for your vote of confidence, DI Quinn.* The use of her rank was bad enough. But he walked away minus the strut, seemed somehow diminished. She'd neither seen nor heard him like that, ever, and the impact was greater for being suppressed.

'Without a shadow, Dave.' But there was doubt and she wished to God she *knew.* Christ, she was the so-called Snow Queen and she'd almost lost it with Brody. The chief had a hell of a lot more Mike Tyson than Mother Teresa in him. And he'd been acting erratic, of late.

'Bloody daft thing to do though, boss.'

Couldn't argue with that. If nothing else, the chief was guilty of gross stupidity. Staying alone with Wilde, laying himself open to wild allegations was dumb enough, on top of that the youth had retracted what amounted to a confession to the attack on Duncan Agnew, claimed now it had been given under duress. Maybe the fact Wilde had incriminated three so-called mates in Agnew's mugging factored in the volte face. Though names hadn't been named, if it emerged he'd opened his mouth to a cop, Wilde wouldn't be Mr Popular with his peers. The toe rag would be seeking police protection, not banging on about brutality. Course, if he'd been telling the truth, three attackers were still at large and needed rounding up pronto.

'Car's there, Dave.' She aimed the fob, heard rustling by a line of bins against the wall. The thunk must have startled a foraging cat or something. No, a mangy fox. Skulking away in the shadows, head down, wet ginger pelt matted to painfully thin body, brush lightly tracing the ground. When Baker's image flashed in her head, she told herself not to be ridiculous.

Alongside the Audi, they huddled closer under the umbrella. So close, for the first time she noticed darker flecks in Harries' chocolate irises, saw the tiny piercing in an ear where he could still wear a stud. Despite the shelter, one shoulder of his leather jacket ran with rain. Not that he seemed in a hurry to get away.

'I guess the brass'll examine the tapes first thing?'

'You bet.' *If not before.* An assistant chief constable most likely. Not so much for Wilde's contribution – that was still CID's baby – but scrutinizing Baker's every move, every word. She bit her lip. Whatever way it panned out, she had some massive bridge building to do with the chief. Think Forth. And double it.

'We'll need to view them, too.' She ran a hand over her hair. 'Preferably before the early brief.' She wanted at least a transcript to go through, particularly the part where Wilde confessed to Agnew's attack. Maybe read something between the lines. They needed to nail the youth down on Foster's mugging as well as the murder; Baker had barely had time to touch on those. They'd definitely need to question Agnew again. And Brody. And . . . the to-do list was a hell of a lot longer than her arm.

'Anyway, Dave,' she said with a smile, 'you know what they say . . .' A siren blared, ambulance it sounded like.

'Tomorrow is another day?' Smiling, he opened the door.

Turn up or what? She laughed out loud. 'How'd you possibly know that?'

''Cause I read you so well?' He held her gaze.

She raised an eyebrow, fully aware what he was – or wasn't – saying, knew it would take one word from her and they'd embark on a more than professional relationship. She could live without the frigging complication. Sod it. She could do with the company. How about a nightcap? No harm in that. Yes, right. 'Cause of course it would stop there. Thoughts still racing, she scanned his face. He looked so . . . serious . . . vulnerable . . . tasty? *Stop dithering woman.* One drink wouldn't hurt. 'Why don't we—?'

'Shit, boss. I forgot.' She almost smiled at the cartoon hand to mouth. 'I meant to pass on a message.'

'From?'

'Caroline King. Don't look like that, boss. She only rang me 'cause she couldn't get through to you. I swear I'm not . . .'

Seeing her? Screwing her? She tightened her mouth. Should've known. Caroline King made a bad penny look reclusive. Harries *knew* there was bad blood between them, more bad blood than in a septic wound. Hard to believe how close she'd come to inviting one of the fucking reporter's cast-offs back for . . . coffee. 'What's she want?'

'I'm only the messenger, boss.'

'I said, what does she want?'

'To speak to you. Something to do with Jas Ram. Says it's urgent.'

Always was with King. She nodded, got in the car, slung her briefcase on the passenger seat.

Still holding door and juggling brolly, Harries leaned in to speak to her. 'You said, "Why don't we?" Why don't we what?'

'Call it a day, DC Harries.' She slammed the door, would've burned rubber were it not so wet. Aquaplaning the puddle wasn't mature. The umbrella no protection. She saw Harries' drenched figure get smaller and smaller in the mirror as she put her foot down. *Honey I shrunk the cop.* Her lip curved. Childish? Yes. Did she give a damn?

Frankly not.

Four Years Earlier

T
he girl steeled herself, pretty sure everything was ready and in place. Candles shed sufficient soft light, cast flickering shadows across the walls and ceiling of the small room. Perched on the edge of the single bed, she tenderly stroked her naked body, tiny breasts. Though she didn't smile, it gave her pleasure. The flesh was firm; smooth and cool like ivory silk. Touching it felt good, how it was meant to be.

Peeping through curtains of fine blonde hair, she observed her actions in a full-length mirror, made believe she was watching a stranger, pretended the reflection was someone else, a character in a movie maybe. Though only fourteen, she'd long ago learned to distance herself from reality, disassociate from others. She'd heard social workers call it survival strategy.

It's how she got through the nights when the man came; stole in reeking of beer and fags. He was supposed to care for the kids in the home. She bit her lip, winced. He certainly cared for her all right. She'd learned other things, too. Like it hurt more when she writhed and screamed; he'd only bind her wrists with flex, stuff cotton wool in her mouth. Once she thought she'd choke, die. Back then, she almost welcomed death. Now when he raped her she didn't move or cry out. She lay motionless working out how to make it stop.

Asking for help was useless. No one in the place believed her. No one even listened. Only other kids who'd been there. If her mum knew, she'd kill him. She screwed her eyes tight. No, don't go there. Her mum was dead and the girl could barely recall her face. She'd remembered one of her favourite songs though. Maybe the song had given her the idea. That and the man starting to tell her it was her fault he had to fuck her. That she was a slut, teasing him with her tits, flaunting her body. Perfect, he called it. Perfect.

Trembling slightly, she held out her left arm, ran a fingertip from the tiny wrist to her elbow; the pale blue vein was barely perceptible under the skin. Lightly, she traced its course with a delicate pink nail. The razor lay on the duvet cover. Gingerly, she prised away the blade, careful not to nick herself then laughed softly at what an adult would describe as irony. Candlelight gleamed on steel as she cut a fine line, just parting the skin. Mesmerised, she barely felt the incision as blood beaded and oozed like a chain of tiny red glistening pearls.

The girl positioned the blade again. The lyric was wrong. The first cut wasn't always the deepest.

NINETEEN

'**M**onday, Monday. So good to me.' The tune had been playing on the radio as Caroline drove in to the city centre. It still spun in her head now as she sat in Starbucks sipping Kenyan. *So good to me.* Might as well take it as a promising sign. Her lazy smile bordered on smug. The booze-free early night showed in a glowing complexion, sparkling indigo eyes. She perched happily on a high stool, a window seat, the strategic positioning primarily so she could keep a lookout on New Street. Not that it excluded the occasional glance at her reflection in the glass. Dressed to kill crossed her mind. The scarlet jersey dress was supposed to soften the black trench coat and high leather boots. She pursed her lips. Thank God she'd ditched the beret. According to Nat, it made her look like a cross between Mata Hari and the Resistance woman from *'Allo 'Allo*. She raised an eyebrow. Come to think of it, her lodger had been very . . . perky . . . earlier, too.

She lifted her cuff, checked her Tissot: 10.05; tightened her perfect red lips, she loathed being kept waiting. Who did the blasted woman think she was? Craning forward, the reporter scanned the street. Considering the crap weather, shit economy, it looked business-as-nigh-on-usual. Women buying up the shops, a few pinstripes striding past looking stressed, kids who should clearly be at school dawdled along cramming fast food. She gave a thin smile when a grubby-looking dosser pitched on the opposite pavement waved at her. Even though the rain had dried up, the poor sod must be freezing. The ill-fitting crusty cast-offs and army blanket were no match for minus three. Mind, the beanie hat beggar bowl between his spindly legs would be better placed on top of the straw-coloured dreadlocks. Passers-by were giving the headgear a wide berth, and from what she could see donating very little else.

Sighing, she checked her watch again. *Where the frigging . . . ?*

'So sorry to keep you waiting. I got held up. Would you like a refill?' Wallet at the ready, Ruby Wells tilted her head at the almost empty mug. She had a stunning smile. For a second or two it stopped the reporter in her mental tracks.

'Cool. Thanks.' Aware of a rare sensation, Caroline smoothed a hand through her hair. It wasn't often she felt outshone by another woman's appearance. Ruby's unconventional features were striking. Pictures she'd seen of the lawyer didn't do her justice, not by a long shot. She'd clocked a snapshot in the open wallet, too. Mind, to Caroline all babies looked like Winston Churchill. Was the sprog daughter, niece, god child?

Caroline swivelled on the seat slightly to cast a glance at the queue. Ruby Wells stood out like a poppy in a weed patch. Porcelain skin, huge green eyes, wide mouth, body to die for. OK, the dark Armani suit helped, but she wore little, maybe no, make-up. When a dumpy middle-aged bloke alongside made some joke, she laughed aloud, head tossed back, lustrous red locks rippled like waves. Caroline sniffed, turned her back. If she wanted a shampoo ad, she'd have stayed at home watching telly.

'So you're a television reporter, Ms King?' Chanel Number Five wafted as Ruby deposited the drinks on the ledge then effortlessly hiked her no doubt pert buttocks on the neighbouring high-rise stool. Caroline, who virtually needed a stepladder, curled a lip as she raised her mug in thanks.

'That's right. Mostly BBC. Not exclusively. And please . . . it's Caroline.' Her warm smile was forced. She felt uncharacteristically wary. The woman was like a stealth bomber. Caroline hadn't heard her approach and even though she'd been keeping a casual watch through the window hadn't registered her late arrival. Could explain Caroline's slightly off-guard emotion, too. One of the reasons.

'TV journalism must be –' stirring sugar into coffee – 'fascinating.' It had been a struggle coming up with the word. Probably edited a few along the way, if the genteel sneer wrinkling her patrician nose was anything to go by. 'And you specialize in . . . crime?' Licking the spoon, she made more than token eye contact for the first time.

Caroline bristled mentally. Fighting the urge to fidget,

under the lawyer's barely disguised scrutiny-stroke-contempt, she forced another smile, cracked her usual come back. 'Hey –' hands high in mock surrender – 'I only cover it. Not—' *Commit it.*

'Quite.' The restrained moue suggested she'd heard the line a million times. 'Why am I here, Ms King? What is it you want?'

Friendly chat not. Wells had clearly run a few checks, must have an inkling what Caroline was after. Obviously, the reporter had done her homework, too; journalistic territory and all that. She knew Ruby's date and place of birth, that her parents were dead, that despite leaving home at sixteen, had graduated at twenty-five with a First in Law from King's College London. She also knew Ruby was a partner at Spedding & Rowe's over the road where she specialised in criminal law, that she lived alone, drove a Mazda MX-5 and must be on a damn good whack and/or have independent means. The history had holes, but Caroline hadn't been digging long. Besides, her research was force of habit more than the need for a full exposé.

'I'll be honest with you, Ruby.' Patently the woman was nobody's fool and she'd already checked her watch

'An honest journalist? Isn't that an oxymoron?' Seeing the reaction, she lost the smile, raised a palm. 'Sorry. Don't take it personally.'

There was another way? 'I could say the same about lawyers. Start again, shall we?' They locked glares for several seconds. Seemed to Caroline, the woman was weighing up the odds: talk or walk. Caroline held a mental breath, vaguely aware of hissing coffee machines, rattling crockery, low-level conversation. She needed the lawyer on board a damn sight more than the lawyer needed her.

Slowly, Wells crossed her legs. 'Go ahead, Ms King.'

Phew. She told Ruby about the book, how she wanted to expose the grooming trade, stop vulnerable girls from being fooled by false promises, flash cars, fake affection. She said she'd covered the recent crown court trial and was desperate to secure an in-depth interview with at least one of the girls involved. Ruby listened, sipped coffee, nodded once or twice. Caroline threw in the few stats available, mentioned a couple of cases in other parts of the UK. 'It's tip of the iceberg stuff, Ruby, Ms Wells.' Hot under the collar wasn't in it, Caroline knew her colour had risen. 'It shouldn't be happening at all.'

Ruby held the reporter's gaze. 'And this is to do with me because . . .?'

Caroline leaned forward, palms spread. 'The book has to be authentic, has to have real impact, has to move readers to get off their arses and actually do something. Sorry. I get worked up about it. It's just . . . if the major players tell their story . . . it'll have real punch. People need to know what's going on out there, how easy it is for girls to fall in the groomers' trap.' It was a wonder she hadn't fallen off the bloody stool.

Ruby traced a finger round her mug. 'That's all very laudable, Ms King. I wish you luck. I ask again: what's it—?'

'You have access to the girls.' It was a punt, she'd no real proof. Amy carrying the lawyer's card didn't necessarily mean the others had contact with Ruby. Caroline's news sense told her they did. And Ruby hadn't denied it. Besides, Amy Hemming was the girl Caroline most wanted to talk to. Her case highlighted how a solid middle-class background was no safeguard; made no difference in a groomer's twisted mind. 'I need to speak to them. They've been there, know what it's like, how it happens, how – dear God – to avoid it. They're the only ones who can tell the real story.'

The mug stopped halfway to her mouth. 'And why on earth would they want to?'

Keep up. 'As I say, to help others. And as a reporter, writer, whatever, I truly believe opening up makes it easier for people to move on. I've seen it. Lots of times. Once it's out there, victims put it behind them.'

'That's highly debatable to say the least.' She turned her mouth down. 'I still don't see why you need me. Why not approach them yourself?'

'You were on the money earlier. The oxymoron gag? You know as well as I do a lot of people don't trust journalists. Don't have a good word these days. How can I interview them if I can't get near them?'

'And you think I'll open doors? Give you credibility?'

'Got it in one.'

Ruby ran her tongue along her top teeth, clearly weighing sides again. Caroline masked her impatience but reckoned the bloody woman must have a set of scales in her head.

'What's in it for you, Ms King?'

She stifled a sigh, only surprised it took so long to ask. 'A piece of work to be proud of? A book that might actually save kids from the likes of Jas Ram. Might even make it impossible for the Jas Rams of this world to commit grooming crimes, let alone get away with them.'

'And the big fat advance? The royalties?'

Caroline shook her head. 'I'm not doing this for money, Ruby.'

'You'll be giving it to charity then?'

'Could do.'

'Tell me.' She sipped coffee, studied Caroline's face. 'Have you spoken to any of the girls yet?'

'Amy Hemming. Briefly. I think she'd be perfect.' Please don't let that have blown it.

Ruby nodded. Like Caroline had passed a test or something. 'If you'd lied, I'd have told you to get lost.'

She narrowed her eyes, gave a tentative smile. 'That mean you'll help?' *Monday Monday.*

'I'll think about it.' Uncrossing her legs, she slid off the stool. 'I'll be in touch later. Maybe.' Several heads turned to watch her saunter to the door.

Caroline glanced at her phone. Whoop-dee-woo. Quinn had finally got back, left a voice mail. *So good to me . . .*

'Just a thought.' The stealth bomber. Ruby Wells had done it again. 'When you pushed your card through my door Saturday night, you didn't see anything strange, anyone hanging round?'

Standing now, Caroline made a mental note to get the Louboutins out next time. 'No. Why?' Frowning, she nodded towards the exit. 'I'll walk out with you.'

In the street, Ruby told her about the dead bird on the windscreen. Made light of it. 'Probably kids messing around. No worries. It was a long shot. Just thought I'd ask. You were in the neighbourhood around the time it must have happened.'

They were headed in the same direction, walked in step. 'Have you reported it?'

'The police have got enough on their plate.' As they walked past the beggar, she tossed a few coins in the hat.

He flashed a toothless grin. 'Bless ya, Tuesday.'

She laughed when she saw Caroline's face. 'As in Ruby?' she explained. 'We got chatting one day. His name's Art. Always calls me Tuesday.'

'Reckon he was in a Stones' tribute band?'

She laughed again. 'This is me.' She pulled up outside the Victorian monstrosity that housed Spedding & Rowe. Pigeons cooed on high window ledges, pooped too going by the state of the pavement. Caroline glanced up ready to dodge droppings.

'One more thing . . .' Ruby paused. 'You say you want to talk to the major players? Does that include Jas Ram?'

'I think it has to.' Bets hedged.

'Have you approached him?'

Ruby was on the side of the angels. Caroline lied instinctively. 'Not yet. Why?'

'Be careful, that's all.' She tapped the side of her nose. 'I wouldn't believe a word he says.'

Caroline narrowed her eyes. 'You've had dealings with him?'

'Trust me.' Smiling, she gave what could have been an ironic wink. 'I'm a lawyer.'

TWENTY

'I ain't opening me mouth till you get me a lawyer, Pig Man.' In the margin, someone had written the 'oink oink' sound on tape.

'Make your mind up, sonny. Five minutes ago you didn't want a brief in spitting distance.'

'Yeah, that was before you started twisting my words.'

'I won't tell you again . . . get your effing feet off the table.'

'Gonna make me?'

'Don't tempt me, sonny.'

Elbow on desk, Sarah dropped her head in a hand and shuddered. Jesus. It made depressing reading. The exchanges between Baker and Zach Wilde were more like a shit script from *Life on Mars* than an interview under police caution. She'd found the transcript propped on her keyboard first thing, a note from Harries attached: 'You wanted to see this before the brief?' He'd been in even earlier than her. Currying favour? She'd been surprised the little toady hadn't left an apple as well.

She'd skimmed through the transcript then. Was rereading it now, post brief. What a bundle of laughs that had been. A squad split down the middle over Baker's quandary. Comments ranged from 'best copper that ever walked' to 'time the bastard got his comeuppance'. The inquiry could do without a distracting division. Sooner the issue was sorted the better. After soothing gripes, wiping metaphorical brows, Sarah had assigned tasks, and troops were now mostly out in the field. It felt like she'd already put in eight hours and it wasn't even ten o'clock.

She circled a temple with her finger. Three paracetamol hadn't touched the headache. The overheated stale air in the office wasn't helping. She'd opened a window briefly, but the incoming chill threatened hypothermia. Wrapping a hand round a mug of tepid tea, she returned to the passage earmarked earlier.

'How should I know the guy's name? You're the one saying it's this Agnew geezer. Whoever it was hit me mate first.'

'Which mate?'

|Wilde shrugs|

'For the tape, Mr Wilde.'

'Dunno his name.'

'Close mate, then.'

'Go fuck.'

'Let's go back. You're claiming Duncan Agnew started a fight in the street in which you became involved?'

Another annotation: slow handclap on tape.

'Quick for a cop, ain't ya?'

'Talk me through it.'

'I dunno. He was pissed or something. Mouthing off. Started kicking out.'

Here, Sarah had jotted: epileptic fit? Drawn a circle round the words.

'What was I supposed to do? Stand there and let me mate take a hammering?'

'How noble. So what did you do?'

'Told you: give him a smack. Him against me, wannit?'

'You said you were with four mates. So it was him against five of you. Very Queensberry.'

'Yer what?'

'Odds don't sound fair to me.'

'What you banging on about, old man? He started it. I slapped him back. Self-defence. End of. 'Sides, when we left he was fine.'

'Beaten within an inch? All his valuables nicked? Duncan Agnew is still in hospital, Mr Wilde. Lucky to be this side of the pearly gates.'

'Nah. That wa'nt down to me. We ain't talking the same geezer. And if you think I'm saying anything else – you're as thick as pig shit. Make that thicker.'

The youth had talked more – only to refute allegations. He denied robbing and beating Agnew, hadn't a clue about the Foster mugging and was nowhere near Chambers Row last Friday night.

Sarah raced through the rest of the transcript, winced at increasingly hostile exchanges. She could well imagine it winding Baker up, almost hear his exaggerated sighs, drumming fingers, the heel of a fist pounding the table.

Was that all he pounded after John Hunt left the room? Surely, there'd be news from the bosses soon?

She pinched the bridge of her nose. What had Baker said? *Don't tempt me, sonny.* 'Oh, shit.'

Shot out a hand when the phone rang. 'DI Quinn.'

'Good morning, inspector.' Bright breezy. 'Your favourite friendly neighbourhood hack here.'

'I don't have a favourite hack, Mr Hardy. And I'm up against it. So get to the point.' She wondered vaguely why Caroline King hadn't got back. Couldn't be that bloody urgent.

'Up against it?' he paused. She sensed something suspect. 'Is that cause they've got you acting up already?'

'Sorry?' Genuinely clueless.

'The powers that be.' That telling silence again. 'Now you're a man down.'

Man down. She stiffened, senses on full alert. 'Not with you, Mr Hardy.' She so was. Man down meant one thing. She blamed her throbbing head, or she'd have seen it coming sooner. The newsman had picked up a sniff on Baker and was on the scent. Blood probably.

'Stands to reason. With a senior detective short – they need someone filling in.'

Sounded to her like Hardy did, too. He'd left the silences, hoping she'd inadvertently oblige. But how much did he actually know as oppose to guess? How long was the fishing rod? She saw a verbal minefield, needed to tread very softly. 'Short? How's that?'

'As in suspended.'

'Nope. Definitely not.' Hardy was off-beam there, his source dodgy. No decision had been made. Last she'd heard Baker was skulking in his office waiting to hear his fate.

'Punched some youth during questioning.'

Who was feeding him this stuff? Her laugh sounded hollow even to her ears. 'Is there a stand-up convention or something in town, Mr Hardy?'

'You think it's funny? A senior detective clouting a defence-less kid? You think it's some kind of joke?'

A lecture from a sodding reporter? She took a calming breath, chipped each word out of ice. 'I think . . . if you publish one word of unsubstantiated rumour . . . you're in serious danger of ending up in court.'

'I agree, DI Quinn.' No he didn't, the lie was in his voice. 'So why not confirm it? Is Detective Superintendent Fred Baker on gardening leave or not?'

'Absolutely. Utterly. Categorically. Not.' She scored unwit-ting holes in the transcript with the nib of her pen. 'Write one word different and you're fucked.' Detective *Chief* Superintendent Baker might be in the market for a new spade soon – that was a bridge she'd cross later. Assuming it wasn't broken. 'Is that clear, Mr Hardy?'

'Your position is, inspector. Perfectly.'

*   *   *

Harries had assumed he'd be in on the Brody bunch interviews, but the boss had tasked him with squad room duty: taking calls, making calls, checking backgrounds, cross-checking witness statements, rereading police reports. All the really exciting stuff. Yawn. He scowled, knew he'd been put in his place. Bottom of the pecking order. Talk about insult to injury, she'd actually taken Jed Holmes in with her to grill Zach Wilde. Known as No Shit, DC Holmes was a decent enough bloke but thinking on his feet – never mind analytically – wasn't his forte. Most of his peers reckoned he had the brain power of a comatose snail.

Harries gazed through the window, saw Shona Bruce step in to a police motor, presumably off to the QE again. Christ, she spent so much time there the hospital ought to name a bloody wing after her. Glancing round the open plan office, he told himself it might not be so bad if the place didn't make the Marie Celeste look like an overbooked cruise liner; virtually the whole inquiry team was out following leads. Actually, scrub that. It was bloody bad, he did feel miffed. Not being landed with plod work, it went with the territory. He resented what he saw as a kick in the balls for his reluctant go-between act, struck him as mean-minded unprofessionalism. Wouldn't be beyond Baker's management style maybe, but he'd thought better of Sarah Quinn.

'What you do to piss her off then, Dave?' Paul Wood glanced up from his monitor, reached for a can of Diet Coke.

'Who? DI Quinn?' *So* glad it wasn't obvious.

'Nah, the Queen Mother.' The DS rolled his eyes. 'Who else?'

Christ, if Twig had picked up on the froideur, it'd be all round the nick. 'Nothing, mate. We're cool. She reckons No Shit needs the experience. Anyway, there's loads—'

'No Shit needs a lobotomy.' He crushed the can in his fist. 'And Quinn should get over herself.'

Harries picked up an apple from the desk, glad now he'd not left it on the DI's. 'Not with you, sarge.' And didn't want to be. He took a large bite. It was one thing Harries bleating on about Sarah, an entirely different ball game when someone else took a pop. Hypocritical? Sure. Besides, before the Wilde debacle, Twig would never have bad-mouthed the boss.

'Baker's a frickin' good cop. OK he's been going through it . . . but innocent till proved guilty, right?' Wood leaned back, tucked thumbs under belt. 'It wouldn't hurt to show a bit of support, solidarity. Quinn could've put in a word at the brief.'

Harries shrugged, office politics he could live without. 'She's got an inquiry to run, sarge. Pressure to get a result.' He bit off another chunk.

'Yeah?' Derisive sniff. 'Well she needs to man up.'

Momentarily, his chewing stopped. So when push comes to shove, the boys stick together? Women bosses are fine when they don't rock the proverbial? Blokes like Twig just pay lip service to equality? Were attitudes surfacing because Baker's crisis was polarising opinion? Harries chucked the rest of the apple in the bin, reached for the ringing phone.

Talk about fallout. Vesuvius wasn't in it.

TWENTY-ONE

Zach Wilde appeared every bit as obnoxious in the pasty flesh as on paper. And small screen come to that. Spread legs stretching tight black denims, he sprawled in a chair in IR1 cupping his crotch. Sarah, who'd seen it all before, kept her gaze on his face. For one she wanted to examine the injuries, for the other she'd not give him the satisfaction. Tugging up the sleeves of her white shirt, she decided the damage was superficial: minor scratches near the eye, barely perceptible bruise on left cheek. Someone had mentioned a split lip – couldn't see it herself. If Baker had been riled enough to lash out, would he really have had the restraint to pull the punch? She couldn't see that either.

'Hey, bitch.' Wilde's leer was almost laughable. 'What you staring at?'

'What do you think knob end?' Jed Holmes, who was supposed to be sitting in, observing, lunged across the desk, thrust himself into Wilde's personal space. 'And to scum, it's

DI Quinn. Got that? Scum?' The voice was a Brummie Vincent Price on nasty pills. The youth straightened slowly, gaze darting as he hugged both arms round skinny torso, definitely rattled. Scared of lightning – make that cops – striking twice? Or like most bullies did Wilde have a yellow streak a mile wide when someone bit back. Sarah reckoned No Shit had hidden depths. Fact he looked like a middle-aged anorak – he'd have to.

'All set, ma'am?' He resettled the horn-rims, smoothed a hand down the mustard coloured knitted tie.

She raised a 'hold on' finger, confirmed with Wilde he definitely didn't want a lawyer. The youth had changed his mind yet again that morning, just wanted to get on with it, he said. It had suited her. She gave a brisk nod. 'When you're ready, DC Holmes.'

No Shit might be slow, but he knew when the tapes were running. Starting them now, he reeled off time, date, people present.

'Let's go back to the fourth of January, Mr Wilde.' Sarah played a pen between her fingers. 'Kings Road, Selly Oak. Around eleven o'clock at night. Yesterday, you told Detective Chief Superintendent Baker you got into an altercation?'

His curled lip revealed the orthodontic black hole, his vocabulary had a gap, too. 'Alter what?'

'Fight?' She raised an eyebrow, he didn't take the cue. No Shit interpreted her subtle nod and slid a colour print across the desk. 'With him.' She tilted her head at the pic. 'A man we know to be Duncan Agnew.'

'You might, sister. Never seen the geezer before. And now I've had chance to think – without a pig breathing down me neck – I ain't even sure I was there.' He folded his arms, stuck his bottom lip out. 'Nah. Deffo. I remember now. I wa'nt there.' Like that was it.

'Fine.' She flipped the lid off a paper cup. 'So you'll be able to tell us where you were.'

'Fuck's sake. How'm I supposed to know?' No Shit cleared his throat. Wilde flinched, almost slipped off the chair.

Was that what happened last night? Baker said he'd helped Wilde off the floor? What was the cliché: did he fall or was he pushed? 'Let's get this right, Mr Wilde.' She took a sip of coffee. 'You remember where you weren't but not where you were? Are you playing games with me?' She'd love to know what was going on behind those shifty bloodshot eyes, she could almost hear the cogs turn in what passed for a brain.

'I made a mistake, got it arse about tit. Even you lot cock up.' For the first time, he stared directly at her, fingering the scratches under his eye. 'What's happening to the fat cop by the way? 'Bout time me and him kissed an' made up. No harm done. Move on, eh?'

She narrowed her eyes. Was the little shit really saying what she thought? Did he imagine for one second he could fashion some sort of deal? Let me walk and he's off the hook? Was it conceivable Wilde had lied from the start? Fabricated the whole scenario about Baker beating him up to secure a bargaining chip? A Get Out Of Jail Free card? God, you almost had to admire the brass neck.

She gave an incredulous snort. 'Play a lot of Monopoly, do you, Mr Wilde?'

'Yer what?'

It wasn't until No Shit started softly whistling 'Please Release Me' that she had to stifle a laugh. The next forty minutes held nothing remotely funny. Apart from Wilde's continuing chorus of 'I know nothin' which put her in mind of Andrew Sachs's Manuel. They went through the same non-comedy routine with intense questioning on Foster's mugging and the Chambers Row murder victim. No matter which way she probed, the youth didn't move a gnat's. She was on the point of calling it a wrap. 'Tell me, Mr Wilde—'

'Read my lips, sister.' Maybe he hadn't heard the knock on the door. Either way he didn't bat an eyelid. 'I wa'nt there. I know nothin' and I've never set eyes on the dudes in my life.'

Standing in the doorway, Harries cocked an eyebrow. Sarah nodded, told him to go ahead.

'Maybe in another life, Mr Wilde? Because one of those dudes knows you. Swears you and your merry men beat seven shades of the proverbial out of him.'

'The wot?'

*   *   *

Duncan Agnew had positively identified Zach Wilde's ugly mush from a police mugshot. Not exactly a handsome pay-off for DC Shona Bruce's patient bedside manner, but a big evidential return. The sooth-talking DC had also flashed Leroy Brody's pic at Agnew. Scored another hit. Kerching. Shona would happily have treated Foster to the same visual delights but the second victim was unconscious most of the time.

'What a turnaround, guys.' Sarah perched on a desk in the squad room, circling an ankle. She'd stood a round of tea and doughnuts. Only half a dozen detectives were dotted round, so either way the celebration wasn't massive. It was a start. When confronted with Agnew's statement, Wilde and Brody had fallen like a pack of cards, stacked on jelly, on a spin cycle. No Shit said he'd never seen anyone put up his hand so fast. Both youths admitted the attack. Came clean on the robbery. Violently denied involvement in the other crimes.

'Shame they didn't go the full house,' John Hunt said. 'Bang-to-rights-bingo.' The detective sergeant leaned against his favourite wall, brawny arms folded. He'd conducted Brody's second interview alongside Beth Lally, a DC back that day from maternity leave whose butt was currently parked on a corner of Harries' desk.

'Talking of houses, Twig.' Sarah shielded her eyes from a welcome if not warm ray of sunlight. 'Anything back from the squat?' A forensics team was still out at the Sparkbrook crime scene. Brody and Wilde had eventually admitted living there off and on for five months.

He tapped the side of his head. 'Soon as I hear, ma'am.'

'Big diff, isn't there, Huntie?' Harries, who had a dab of jam in the corner of his mouth, had clearly been musing on John Hunt's earlier comment. 'Owning up to a relatively minor street robbery's one thing. But, near as damn it, *two* murders?'

'Hanged for a lamb? Stuff the sheep bit?' Twig's take.

'Nearly two murders, Dave? How's that work?' Beth tucked a lock of blonde hair behind a petite ear.

He shrugged. 'You know what I mean.'

Everyone in the office knew. Foster's condition didn't look good. If he pegged it, Brody and Wilde could face two life sentences. Assuming they were guilty. Surprise surprise, the youths had suddenly produced alibis for the times of both Foster's attack and the murder. Hanging with chicks, as Wilde put it. In English: staying with girlfriends. The girls were being traced, would be questioned, soon as.

'But why cough at all?' Twig again. 'Surely they'd be best off keeping their mouths shut?'

'Unless they know they're on a loser,' Hunt said. 'Know there's evidence out there. Just a question of us finding it.'

'To Agnew's attack? Or all three?'

Hunt held out empty palms.

'I sure as hell think they know more than they're letting on.' Sarah drained her cup, slung it in the nearest bin. 'The numbers game, for instance.' Wilde and Brody had clammed up on the aspect completely. Agnew had told Shona he believed the gang was five-strong, even provided sketchy descriptions of the other assailants. Brody and Wilde wouldn't be drawn, point blank refused.

'Keeping it up their sleeve for later?' Holmes breathed on a lens of his specs. 'Maybe see it as leverage?' Polished it with his tie.

More bloody bargaining chips? 'Maybe, Jed.' Strolling to the window, she tapped the side of her mouth as she passed Harries. He blushed, cottoned on instantly. 'Either way –' Sarah perched on the sill – 'if Agnew's feeling up to it, we'll get someone over there this afternoon, pull together an e-fit.' She'd already asked Ted White to knock out a news release, issue it to the press pronto. She frowned. That reminded her. She needed to check the local rag's lunch edition, see if Nat Hardy had gone into print with the Baker line.

'Reckon Brody and Wilde are in the frame for the lot, DI Quinn?' Beth was probably just trying to make her presence felt after six months' leave. As a psychology graduate, she'd know it was a stupid question to ask. Her charcoal skirt suit and crisp white blouse suggested she'd dressed to impress, too. Maybe a touch too hard?

'Honest answer?' Sarah laced her fingers. 'Damned if I know.' Early on in the inquiry, she'd certainly favoured the attacks being down to the same perps, similarities spoke for themselves. But now? Wilde had gone into meltdown denying numbers two and three, virtually begged her to believe him. But then he would, wouldn't he? He'd even said he might have been mistaken about Baker, might be willing to withdraw the allegations.

'What I do know is we need hard evidence.' Her phone beeped a message alert. She glanced at the sender's name, curled a lip. King could 'king wait.

'Brody pissed himself, you know,' Hunt said.

'What, laughing?' Holmes asked.

He shook his head slowly. 'Scared shitless, wasn't he?' Whether it was Hunt's hangdog expression, deadpan delivery, or doughnut sugar rush, after the briefest pause, someone's snigger set everyone off. Probably why no one heard the late arrival.

'Fuck is this?' Hands jammed in pockets, Baker raked a glare over every officer. His left eye looked like a bruised damson. 'Happy hour on the friggin' funny farm?'

'Chief . . .' Sarah started.

He flapped a hand. 'Party's over, Quinn. Everyone. Get back to work. I want to see Wilde's balls nailed to the wall. Lying little bastard.' He cupped an ear. 'You lot gone deaf all of a sudden? Come on, chaps. Chop chop.'

TWENTY-TWO

'You following me, Quinn?'

Baker did have eyes in the back of his bloody head. Sarah had exited the squad room in his wake, now followed the Paco Rabanne trail down the corridor at what she'd judged a discreet distance. First she wanted to ask the DCS's state of play, make that work. Second she didn't want an audience for the inevitable exchange between them, behind closed doors would do nicely. 'Yeah. I wouldn't mind a word, chief.'

'Nor me,' he called, still walking, still showing his back. Pulling up outside his office, he turned to face her. *God, that eye looks sore.* 'Sorry'll do for a start.'

'Sorry?' Frowning. 'Not with you, chief.' As if. But she wouldn't just roll over, not for anyone.

'Got that right, Quinn.' He opened the door, flicked his head. 'Inside. Sit.'

Yes sir. No sir. Woof-dee-woof. She glanced at the executive desk covered in files, printouts, reports, half a dozen cups with coffee dregs scattered round, accompanying plastic spoons reminded her of the 'measured out my life' line from Prufrock. Best not mention it. She couldn't see Baker as a member of the T.S. Eliot appreciation society.

'This word then, Quinn?' Leaning back in his matching executive chair, he stared at her across the cluttered surface, stubby index fingers steepled.

She glanced down, brushed a few grains of sugar from her skirt. 'Welcome back?' Her smile was tentative. His position not exactly clear.

'That's two.' He scowled, illustrated the point digitally. 'Shit at maths as well?'

She gave a heavy sigh. 'I'm not looking for an argument, chief.'

'Nor me. I were you I'd take loyalty lessons, though.'

She cocked her head. 'As in teach them?' He was not amused. She knew she'd have to bend some time soon. His watch sounded like Big Ben in the uneasy silence. He could wait a while. 'I take it Wilde's dropped the allegations?'

'No. But he will.' Dead cert. Still staring at her, he outlined why. The forensic and medical evidence overwhelmingly backed the chief. None of his DNA had been lifted from Wilde's skin which indicated he'd not laid a finger – never mind fist – where it mattered. Blood under Wilde's nails turned out to be the youth's which meant he'd scratched his own face. And the clincher? A faint circle in the bruise on the chief's cheek was an exact match for the tiny raised skull on Wilde's cheap signet ring. An expensive mistake.

Baker leaned back, rested crossed hands on budding paunch. 'So whatever the lying little git comes up with next I'm Mr Clean. Absolved. Acquitted. Exonerated. Exculpated. Vindicated. Get the picture?' She nodded. More than. 'See, Quinn, like I told you . . . I never touched the scrote.'

He'd been sorely tempted though. Said it himself. It looked increasingly as if Wilde had engineered the whole incident. She'd not have given the oik that much credit. 'I'm glad to hear it, chief. It's great to have you back in the saddle.' Doh. Shouldn't have mentioned saddles. He probably thought she was taking the piss. The Wild West was Baker's big thing. He took regular riding holidays in Montana, wore all the gear, boasted encyclopaedic knowledge of American Indian culture. Baker on horseback was a concept she'd never been able to get her head round. His mind was one-track at the moment.

'You owe me an apology, Quinn. You thought I'd whacked him one.' He jabbed a thumb at the door. 'Out there, you said you weren't with me.'

She gazed at the ceiling. 'I meant—'

'I know what you meant, woman. I'm not thick. But we work as a team. If you're not with me – where exactly are you, inspector?'

'If you're saying, against – you're wrong.'

'*I'm* wrong?'

He was right: they had to work together. She had kind of jumped the guilt gun and, metaphorically, she was bigger than him, always known there'd be bridge building to do. 'OK, chief. I was out of order. I shouldn't have doubted you. I'm sorry.'

'Good girl.' He rubbed his hands together, leaned forward. 'Right, where we at?'

She shook her head. *Incorrigible old bugger.* As she brought him up to speed, it became clear he'd mostly kept pace anyway. She filled him in on who was doing what, the results they were waiting on, told him she was keen to check the youths' alibis, tackle the girlfriends soon as they were traced. Cut the risk of them being coached or nobbled. Winding it up, she mentioned Nat Hardy's fishing expedition, primarily to make Baker aware the nick had a leak rather than fears the story would appear. 'I told him one word in print and he'd be fucked.'

'Royally fucked now I'm in the clear.' Baker turned his mouth down. 'So you fought my corner with this Hardy bloke, then?'

'Course I did.' Smiling, she reached down for her bag. 'So what's the little word, chief?'

'Words, Quinn.' He held up four sausage fingers and gave a stage wink. 'Never apologise, never explain. Now shift your ass, lass.'

She rolled her eyes; PC was a lost concept on Baker. Her campaign to drag his thinking into the 1970s had a long way to go. 'I'll keep you posted, chief.' She was almost out the office when he called her name. She turned in the doorway, keen to get on.

'I meant what I said about nailing Wilde. Vicious little shit nearly cost me my pension.' *Nothing personal then.* 'Spit the lemon out, Quinn. There's nothing personal going on here. I'm not into vendettas. Way I see it, he's guilty as sin. They both are. The evidence is out there. All we need do is find—'

'Great. Two birds with one . . .' Paul Wood stood just behind her. 'Gov.' He nodded at Baker. 'Ma'am.' She manoeuvred out of his way. Twig was evidently eager to take pole position. 'Forensics. Said I'd let you know?' He gave a lopsided smile, flashed a piece of paper with a few scrawled lines. 'You're gonna like it.'

She *so* did. Twig's list detailed a cache of stolen property unearthed by the squat team. Sarah had motored straight to Jubilee Way for a bird's-eye viewing, parked the Audi just beyond two white transits. Togged now in a white all-in-one, she strode to the semi-derelict dive, down a narrow litter-strewn pavement. A brace of Vicki Pollards surgically attached to fags and mobiles parted in either deference or dumbstruck bemusement. No voyeuristic audience this time round, the drab back street was deader than a dodos' reunion. Mind, without Harries sitting shotgun, she'd have thought twice about leaving the car unattended. The DC was back in her good books, leaving him out in the metaphorical cold would've been pointless, petty, beneath her. No point them both trampling the scene though, he was better placed phoning round a few people trying to track down Wilde's alleged squeeze.

Not that Sarah had to be there, the site visit wasn't compulsory, the compulsion all hers. She always had the need to get the feel of a place, a mental hands-on. The visualizing, imagining, sensing had to be done in person, in situ. A DVD, even with Spielberg directing, was no substitute. Besides, the forensics team had done a bloody good job, made a face-to-face thanks only fair. She told herself it had nothing to do with a certain Ben Cooper being here. Almost believed it.

The cheap replacement front door was slightly ajar. She pushed it open, called her name, a voice from above directed her to a downstairs back room. It was the first time she'd set foot in the place, wouldn't lose sleep were it the last. Stenches stuck in her nose, caught in her throat: cat piss, stale smoke, cheesy vomit. Talk about olfactory overload. Maybe stinky crime scenes were behind Baker's heavy aftershave habit, a vat of Paco would have its work cut out here.

The room was small, gloomy, sparse, décor minimalist with bare floorboards and – apart from lurid semi-literate graffiti – naked walls. Presumably the furniture had been flogged or burned. Empty cans and booze bottles were piled high in the hearth, used candles lined the mantelpiece, fast food cartons screwed into balls lay in corners.

Stepping further in, she switched focus to the plastic sheeting covering part of the floor, primarily the evidence bags that lay on top. Most contained hairs, fibres, fag ends; useful if they could get a DNA match. She hunkered down, handled the bags that looked more interesting. Two cheap as chips watches, not a lot to go on there. The flashy ring was more promising – the initials WF engraved in the gold. A Saint Christopher on a silver chain. Duncan Agnew's? He'd told Shona his was missing. Though the credit card had expired, potentially it was the most valuable find. Frank Gibbs. The name didn't ring a bell, no reason it should. Maybe the theft hadn't even been reported. Maybe reporting it wasn't an option for the owner? She narrowed her eyes: was it possible Frank Gibbs was the Chambers Row murder victim? Or maybe there were victims out there the cops didn't even know about? Either way, the squad now had solid lines worth pursuing.

'Enough to be going on with, Sarah?' Forensic lead manager Ben Cooper stood framed in the doorway wiping gloved hand across glistening brow.

Glancing over her shoulder, she mirrored his smile. 'More than.' The findings certainly gave the inquiry impetus. She'd need to get the press on board, publicise details, soon as. The ring was a good bet, someone should recognise the initials. And a DC could contact the bank for pointers to the identity of Frank Gibbs.

Cooper entered the room, helped her rise, hung on to her hand a smidgeon longer than necessary. 'Always happy to help.'

It struck her again how attractive he was. Tall, blond, great build, the guy even managed to look hunky in a bunny suit. She knew he used to box, had won a couple of police titles a few years back. Harries knew she and Ben had shared the odd date which probably explained why he still referred to the guy scathingly as Henry.

'Where'd you find the personal stuff, Ben?' She assumed it had been squirrelled away or she would have expected it to surface sooner. Today was the team's second bite at the search cherry.

'Why? You think we took our time?' No aggression. Nor did he sound defensive. He was just quick on the uptake, even the tacit uptake.

She snapped off a glove. 'That's not what I said.'

His cocked head said she hadn't needed to. 'You're right though. It was behind the bath. One of the guys removed the panelling yesterday. We didn't spot it first time round.'

'We?'

He shrugged. She assumed he was protecting a less experienced colleague. 'Anyway I took another look. Being on the safe side and all that. Found the items in a Jiffy bag gaffer-taped to the far side. Either way it couldn't have been there long. The adhesive was still tacky. Packaging not damp.'

'Good thinking, great work.' She smiled, nodded towards the door. Seen enough. Smelt enough. Cooper followed her out to the pavement, probably needed a breath of fresh air even more than her.

'You about done here now?' She started loosening the suit. Felt clammy despite the cold.

'More or less. Rest of the team's finishing up out back then we'll call it a wrap.' He pulled down the hood, finger-combed a shock of expensively tousled dirty blond hair. 'Something bothering you?'

Was it so obvious? She shook her head. 'It's probably nothing.'

'But . . .?'

'Is there a chance the stuff actually wasn't there yesterday?'

'Hidden after we left, you mean?' He arched an almost amused eyebrow.

'I said it was nothing.'

'I guess in theory it's possible.' He turned his mouth down. 'But why?'

'I don't know. Just a vague notion.' Difficult even for her to pin down. She frowned trying to think it through. 'Thing is we suspect three gang members are still at large. If that's a regular cache maybe they came back to use it.'

'With police tape round the door? All the hoo-ha in the papers? You really think they're that stupid?'

'Yeah. You're probably right.' Except perps would have no way of knowing the search would resume today. Maybe imagined it was a dead clever move, going back to a place the police had already turned over.

'Boss?'

Sarah turned, forgot Ben was a boss, too. She didn't recognise the forensics officer, focused more on the evidence bag the young woman clutched in a blue gloved hand. The grey hoodie in it was torn and grubby. 'I found it under a pile of logs out back. Whoever put it there probably planned on burning it.' Smoothing the plastic, she pointed out a large liver-shaded patch that looked like a map of Africa. 'I reckon this is blood.' She cut Sarah a glance. 'And there's another one where this came from.'

TWENTY-THREE

'How long before we get the results?' No intro, no social niceties, oleaginous voice instantly recognizable.

'*We?* Mr Ram?' Ruby Wells glared at the mouthpiece, puckered her lips. If she'd talked the guy through drink-drive procedures once, she'd talked him through a thousand times.

OK. Five. It seemed a lot more, seemed like he was always calling and, even at the end of a phone, she found Jas Ram's manner insidious. Swivelling forward in her office chair, she reached for a bottle of water. 'You should still have a note of the date you need to attend.'

He'd been bailed to appear at the station towards the end of February. He'd hear then if the urine sample was positive. If clear, the cops would cancel bail beforehand. End of. Ram knew all this. Knew, too, the police had no reason to contact her either way. So what was his game?

'How's about we make another date, Ruby?' Ah, she thought, silly me. 'Discuss tactics or . . . something?'

How's about we don't? 'I really can't see there's anything to discuss, Mr Ram.' Unscrewing the cap.

'Really? I thought women like a good natter. Lot of birds *I* know have trouble keeping their trap shut.'

The bottle stilled halfway to her mouth. Was that an allusion to the unwanted gift on the windscreen? A subtle warning? A veiled threat? She kept her voice neutral. 'Could be you deal with the wrong sort of birds, Mr Ram.' Crows. Canaries. Under-age chicks. She heard traffic noise in the background. Wondered if he was driving, phone in hand. How great would that be? If the cops pulled him over? No doubt the law kept tabs on him. God, she was almost tempted to keep him on the line.

'We could chat about that when we meet. You could put me right, Ruby.'

'I very much doubt it.' Personality transplant and total gene therapy would be the better bet. She took a swig of water, swilled her mouth, still had a nasty taste. A soft thud outside the window startled her. A pigeon had swooped onto the ledge. Should be used to birds landing there by now, but talk about ironic timing. She gave a wry smile, watched it waddle along, head bobbing. If it was pecking for crumbs, it'd go hungry.

'OK. I admit it. I like you, Ruby. You're my kinda girl.' Face screwed, she mimed a finger down throat. 'I'd like to get to know you better. Not a crime, is it?'

'Tell you what . . . let's meet for a drink.' Get a few things straight. Ram didn't scare her but if she didn't nip the pestering

in the bud it would only get worse. Last thing she needed was
a stalker. Besides, she was curious. Wanted to find out – among
other things – if and/or why he'd decorated her car with a
dead crow. And what was the saying? Keep your friends close,
enemies closer. But it would be on her terms. 'Let me check
my diary. I'll get back.'

He was still whingeing when she hung up.

Friends? Ruby reached for a framed photograph on her
desk: Michelle, Charlie, Lily, Shannon on a day trip to
Blackpool. They'd commandeered some stranger on the beach
to take the shot. It was all sunny smiles, Kiss Me Quick hats,
ice cream and candy floss. Ruby found her lip curving too.
Empowered and emancipated now, the four genuinely seemed
to have put appalling pasts behind them.

Sighing, she replaced the pic. Images of four younger girls
in the forefront of her mind: Ram's victims. Dawn, Amy,
Laura, Natasha had gone through a different kind of trauma,
abuse. Weren't out of the dark emotional woods yet. Could
they be helped to move on, too? Would opening up to someone
like Caroline King really be cathartic? They had the reporter's
number now, the ball was in their court. Amy was the only
girl who hadn't turned the offer down flat. Whatever course
they chose, she'd back them. But in Ruby's book, ultimate
closure for all four would be seeing Ram sent down, knowing
he'd be behind bars for years.

She flicked through her diary, settled on time and place,
picked up the phone. Who knows? She might elicit more from
Ram than he bargained for.

'Let's get this straight. You want a meet, and you'll make it
worth my while?' Striding back to the Audi, phone clamped
to her ear, Sarah seriously regretted taking the bloody call.
She had bigger things to do than play word games with Caroline
King. The reporter was trying not-so-clearly to cut some sort
of deal. Seemed to Sarah like everyone – from Zach Wilde
up – had a pack of cards these days. Not concentrating, she
stepped in a stream of dog pee. 'Yuk.'

'Sorry?'

'Make it snappy,' she snarled, simultaneously working on a

mental get-people-to-do list: chase press office, hassle pathologist, contact the credit card company, check Agnew.

'Not now. Why don't we do dinner, Sarah? Talk it through
properly. On me, natch.'

On expenses, more like. As for the *Sarah* – King was clearly
in full sycophant mode. Approaching the motor, she hand-
signalled Harries to unlock the boot. 'Give me a steer here,
eh? Why'd I put myself out to talk to you?' She struggled,
extricating herself from the white suit was difficult enough
with both hands free. No rush: King still hadn't responded.

Eventually: 'Jas Ram. I'm meeting him.' Like it opened
doors.

'And?' Sarah drawled. King didn't call the shots, whatever
she thought.

'You make it look so easy, boss.' A whisper from Harries
who'd left the car to help Sarah slough off the suit. Soon as
she was shot of it, she gave a cartoon simper, held a palm flat
for the keys.

'I can't say too much . . . not . . . over the phone.'

What was this? A spy movie? Sarah shook her head. Who
did King think she was playing – Modesty Blaise? 'Look, I'm
sorry – I don't have time for this.'

'Then make time, inspector.' Snappy. No more Mrs Nice
Spy. 'You owe me a big favour.'

Sarah stiffened, the hand with the key paused on the way
to the ignition. 'I beg your pardon.' Like hell she did. Harries
cut her a glance, clearly earwigging.

'Your boss man. Baker. I'm told he stepped so far out of
line, he hit the equator.' King's volume dipped when she
delivered the ostensibly casual punchline. 'Hit something
anyway.'

Sarah tightened already taut lips. So her favourite friendly
neighbourhood hack had spilled what he thought were truth
beans to his best mate. King waited for a response. And waited.
Seemingly undaunted, she took up the fairy story.

'Yeah, I reckon Baker's a lucky boy.' The tone suggested a
lot of nail admiring was going on at her end. 'I can't tell you
how close he was – still is as a matter of fact – to finding
himself splashed all over the front page. You could say I saved

his bacon. Whoops.' King gave a deliberately hollow laugh. 'Pun not intended. So when I say *favour . . .*'

Sarah sat back, fingers tapping thigh, cut the reporter more verbal rope. She knew exactly where King was going with this. Shame the stupid woman had the wrong map.

'Thing is, Sarah . . . I'm not sure how much longer I can hold him off? Goes way against the grain – a reporter sitting on an exclusive. Nat and I are close, but . . .' Cards on the table then. Scratch my back and I'll make sure the piece is spiked. King's bargaining chip was more blackmail than bribery. Except of course . . .

'Thing is, Caroline . . .' She aped King's tone and delivery. '*As a matter of fact*, Nat Hardy's sitting on an exclusive pile of shite.'

'Nice try. And looking out for the boss does you great cred—'

'Don't patronise me, Caroline. Your source is dodgy, the story past its sell-by. As a *favour*, I'll tell you this: Baker's in the clear, the evidence backs him, the suspect admits fabricating the allegation. But do urge Hardy to go ahead with his fiction.' Her turn for a telling pause. 'Make my day.'

Harries gave a thumbs up from the passenger seat. Sarah returned his smile. *Royal flush or what?*

'OK you win.' King's capitulation came surprisingly quickly. 'But what about Ram? I think I can get him to talk, Sarah.'

She read King's verbal shorthand. Whatever Sarah thought of the woman personally, the reporter was a sharp operator, skilled interviewer. She couldn't see King delivering Ram's head on a plate, but she might elicit material the cops could take a look at. Against that, Ram was no easy target, it would be a bloody miracle if he dropped his guard. Take into account the fact he was a sleazy depraved thug, King could be on a hiding to nothing. A dangerous hiding to nothing.

'He's toxic, Caroline. Are you sure you know what you're getting into?'

'No. That's why I'm asking for help. I need to pick your brain.' Ram would be getting back, she told Sarah, but the meeting with him could be any time.

The DI chewed a pensive lip; King had been angling for

this since the get-go. Doubtless the reporter had something else up her sleeve. Still, it could be worth playing along. Plus she'd need to eat later. 'OK. I should be free around eight. I'll meet you in the Queen's Head.' Cops' local, Sarah's work turf, the hack wouldn't like it.

'How about the—?'

'That's where I'll be.' She turned the ignition. 'Take it or leave it.'

She'd take it.

TWENTY-FOUR

'**D**on't push it, Dave.' Sarah pulled up outside an unprepossessing terrace in Balsall Heath; Harries' phone bashing outside the squat had come up with the not-a-million-miles-away-address. She cast the place a quick once-over, no obvious signs of life. But, then, the visit was on spec. There'd be zilch mileage in giving Wilde's lady friend advance warning. Sarah had brought Harries up to speed on the squat scenario during the drive over. He'd fed the findings back to Paul Wood who'd make sure forensic irons were in the fire. Then Harries had started clearing professional air.

'I'm not pushing, boss, just saying, is all.'

Despite the fact she'd grudgingly apologised for drenching him in the car park and reluctantly agreed assigning him squad room duty had been a gnat's out of order, he'd just accused her of showing Jed Holmes preferential treatment that morning. She suspected Dave's tongue was embedded in both cheeks. Either that or he was fishing for compliments.

'It's horses for courses, Dave. Nothing to do with favouritism.'

'Oh, I see. So No Shit's got a winning way with yobs, has he?' His hand was on the door.

'You'd be surprised.' She recalled Jed's lightning lunge across the desk. 'What he can't do is charm the birds from the trees.' Masking a smile she made a sharp exit.

Harries was alongside fast. 'Is that my area of expertise then, boss?'

She simply raised an eyebrow but his beam bordered on smug as he rapped the letterbox. Music was playing inside, maybe they hadn't heard. 'Once more with feeling, Dave.'

Music got louder, footsteps approached, door opened. Sarah almost asked the girl if her mother was in. But appearances can be deceptive, closer study suggested the small, slight blonde was late teens, certainly a few years older than a first glance suggested. Mind, she still looked to Sarah like a cross between Tinkerbell and Tenniel's Alice. Her hair fell almost to her waist except for the stab at a mini beehive pinned more or less in place with knitting needles. The wardrobe was Helena Bonham Carter on benefits: scuffed pink pixie boots, humbug striped tights and a diaphanous lilac dress. Sarah cocked a cordial head, warrant card raised. 'Michelle Keating?'

'Who wants her?' Staccato. Her eyes were the palest blue Sarah had ever seen. Almost like discs of ice. Her wary glance darted from Sarah to Dave, hadn't even skimmed the ID.

'I'm Detective Inspector Sarah Quinn. My colleague here's DC David Harries.'

'Phew.' Her heart-shaped face broke into a broad grin. 'That's all right then. For a minute there you had me worried.'

Relieved to find cops at the door? That was novel. Most householders ran a metaphorical marathon. Sarah slipped the card back in her pocket. 'Worried?'

'Yeah. Had you down as Mormons.' Still smiling, she twisted a strand of hair through her fingers.

Sarah smiled back, waited for the invite.

Sudden narrowing of the eyes. 'You're not flogging anything are you?'

Dead horse by the sound of it. Was she dense or disingenuous? 'I said we're detectives. We'd like to come in.'

'You can but I'm not Michelle.'

Go ahead. Waste my time. She stifled a sigh. 'Is Michelle your sister?'

The seemingly artless grin again. 'Don't you think *all* women are sisters? Under the skin? What's your name again, I didn't catch it?'

You're certainly getting under mine, love. 'Quinn.' *And, no. I don't.* She'd come across women she wouldn't want as long distance pen-pals let alone close relatives. But was the girl really into gender politics, the sisterhood and all that jazz? Or was she taking the Michael? Doing a clinging ivy on the door, she certainly didn't look the part. Those pale eyes held the hint of a tease and the glance she cast over Harries wasn't exactly withering.

'Who're *you* then, love?' He tried his lopsided smile. It usually went down a treat.

'Lily.' She offered Dave a tiny hand. 'Lily Maitland.'

Ding dong. Sarah's eyes lit up. Harries clearly hadn't dug far enough; his inquiries should've revealed Brody's girl lived here, too. Still. One stone, two birds . . .

'Stroke of luck, Lily.' Dave nodded at the door. 'Go in, shall we?'

Three of the room's four walls were papered in magazine articles, glossy picture spreads. The bright budget chic tickled Sarah's fancy, made her smile – until she registered the man mountain in front of the window. *Stone me.* Lost in thought or ignorant bugger? Staring out, presumably onto a back garden, his bulk blocked a good deal of daylight. The sludge-coloured trackie bottoms did Michelin Man no favours. The shapeless hoodie – in similar shade of shit – had Chicago Bulls emblazoned across the back. Sarah swallowed. Reckoned it was a safe bet lard arse didn't play. He wasn't big on people skills either.

She nudged Dave's elbow, mouthed, 'Here's your big chance.'

Harries cleared his throat. Glanced at Sarah. 'Hey, mate.' Cleared it again. Bar the tapping of scruffy trainer on thread-bare carpet the greeting had no effect. Sarah was part-way through counting the guy's neck rolls when Lily breezed in fresh from euphemistically washing her hands. Had she gone to the loo or was it – as the DI suspected – hogwash?

Lily picked up the vibe soon as she entered. Standing close to Sarah, she placed loose fists on her boyish hips. 'Hey, Charlie? Manners!' Apart from the tapping toe, nothing. 'Doh.'

Lily's frown morphed into another grin, she sauntered to the window, tapped a shoulder you could ski down.

He executed a pretty nifty turn considering, simultaneously tugged on the white wires of telltale earphones. Even from the other side of the room, Sarah could hear the tinny leak from the iPod. His eyes lit up when he saw Lily. Sarah's narrowed as she did a double take.

Even the ugly shaven head didn't detract from the fact Charlie was female and not even the suet flesh could completely disguise her striking features.

'Visitors, Charlie.' Lily jabbed a thumb over her shoulder.

The glance was cursory and spot on. 'The fuzz. What they doing here?' Not hostile. Seemingly indifferent. She was certainly sharper than Miss Twinkle-toes. Maybe watched a lot of cop shows, or she'd had first-hand dealings with the law?

'Is it so obvious?' Sarah asked.

'Yep. What do you want?'

'Cuppa tea'd be good.' Harries rubbed his hands, gave a boyish ice-breaking smile.

She sniffed. It certainly wasn't *his* charm school offensive she bowed to. 'Lil?'

'Sure go ahead. They don't want to speak to you anyway, hun. Just me and Mitch.'

Charlie stared at the girl for a few seconds, nodded. 'Cool. Shout if you need me.' She shuffled past plugging in the earphones. They'd need a megaphone then.

'Have a seat.' That grin again. 'Or should I say *the* seat.'

The settee had seen better days. Avoiding the lumps, Sarah and Harries sat side by side. Lily bagged a rug, made the lotus position look like a doddle. Sarah, who could never manoeuvre both legs into place, reckoned the girl must be double jointed. God knows what Harries thought, he clearly needed more time assessing. If it was Lily's idea of a distraction tactic, it wouldn't work.

'Leroy Brody.' Sarah nudged Dave's elbow, mimed writing. 'How long have you known him?'

'Depends what you mean by "known"?' She selected another strand of hair to play with.

Playing silly buggers, too. And for time. Sarah stifled a sigh. Answering a question with another was a classic delaying tactic. She could almost see the girl coming up with a good wheeze. She opened her mouth to clarify but . . .

'Known as in met – couple a years.' She let the hair fall, made – and kept – eye contact with Sarah. 'Known as in go out with – six months. Seven, maybe. Why?'

Pass a slice of humble pie. Talk about misread signals. She smiled. 'We can get on to that. Let's start from the beginning, shall we?' Harries made notes while Lily talked them through the relationship. She'd met Brody in a pub, the Fighting Cocks in Moseley if she remembered right, they were both with friends and though they'd swapped numbers, apart from bumping into him a couple of times in the street, they'd not taken it further until last July, maybe August. He rang inviting her to some party, they'd talked, had enough in common to get on, started seeing a bit more of each other. He wasn't 'the one' or anything, they didn't hang out that often and she certainly hadn't slept with him, but she liked him, he made her laugh, he was sound. 'Why do you need to know?'

'What about his mates? Zach Wilde and the others. Do you see them, too?'

'Zach now and again. Him and Mitch used to go round quite a bit.'

'Used to?'

'Not my baby.' She raised a palm then quickly tugged a sleeve that had fallen down her stick-thin arm; the milky skin was a network of tiny silver scars. 'Ask Mitch.'

I will. 'I'm useless with names.' Sarah flashed a thin smile. 'Remind me who the others are.'

'Trying to think who you mean.' She chewed her lip, shook her head. 'Nah. Can't really say I've noticed anyone.'

'You're sure?'

'Can't you tell me what this is about?' She appealed to Harries as if he might be a softer touch. 'Is he in some kind of trouble? It's not like I owe him and if he is . . . surely I need to know?'

'Bear with us a minute, Lily,' Sarah said. 'You say you don't hang out that often?' She glanced at Harries who was already rifling his notebook. 'There's a few dates.' She dropped her gaze to the page. Brody had supplied six nights he'd spent with the girl, not just those of the attacks. Sarah reeled them off including last Wednesday and Friday. 'Leroy says you and he were together. Is that how you remember it?'

'I don't need to remember.' She rose in one fluid movement, dashed out, calling, 'Back in a min.'

Sarah and Harries synchronised shrugs. Another comfort break? Couldn't be, the door opened within seconds.

'Where's Lil?' Charlie's piggy eyes scanned the room as she shuffled in, clutching two thick white mugs. It was almost comical, like they'd sold Lily into slavery or something.

'It's OK,' Harries said. 'We've not . . . Ow!' Sarah removed her foot from his.

'She nipped to the loo, I think, Charlie.' Standing, she relieved the girl of the drinks. 'Is this your home, too?' Warm smile.

'Nah. I broke in. Course it is.' Fuck's it to do with you was written over her face.

'Nice place.' Bit of a dive, as it happened, but hey . . . 'Lived here long?' She sat back on the settee, handed Harries tea that looked like wood seal.

'Look, lady. I don't do small talk.' She ran a hand over her scalp. 'If you've got something worth ask—'

'Leroy Brody. Do you know him?'

She rolled saliva round her tongue, like she was ready to spit.

'Told you I didn't have to remember, didn't I?' Lily pranced back, brandishing a diary. The fluffy pink leopard print cover said a lot. She glanced up, clocked Charlie, glanced at Sarah. 'Did I miss something?'

'She was asking about Leroy Brody.'

'And?'

She shrugged. 'Don't know the dude, do I? I'm off. Later, Lil.' The girl didn't just know Brody, she loathed him. And if she'd misread that, Sarah reckoned she'd best look for another job. She let it go for now, Charlie was almost at the door anyway.

'Don't mind, her. She's not keen on . . . strangers.' Lily resumed the lotus position, diary on lap. 'Right, those dates.'

TWENTY-FIVE

'Liar, liar. Pants on fire then?' Harries was driving like an octogenarian, on slow juice. Sarah had asked him to take the wheel of her Audi. The offer didn't come along that often, he'd grabbed it with both hands. Boy racer wasn't living up to his billing. Visualising the work piling up back at the nick, she almost wished he'd step on the gas. 'You on the same page as me, boss?'

Mouth twisted, she averted her glance from the speedo, reached in a coat pocket for a tissue. 'More like Lily's pages plural but I get the drift. And, yes, it sure looks that way.' Lily's cross-checking of the dates had resulted in four big yeses confirming she and Brody had been getting it together. But whatever Leroy Brody had been up to late on January 11 and 13 it hadn't been with Lily Maitland. Adrian Mole had nothing on Lily. Lily Maitland aged eighteen and three-quarters seemed compelled to record every detail of her not so hectic highlife. She'd let Sarah read some of the entries and according to the gushing pronunciations, she'd spent both nights at home drinking plonk, scarfing pizza and watching chick-flick DVDs. With Michelle, Charlie and a fourth housemate.

Which meant Zach Wilde's putative alibi had gone down the deep-pan pizza pan. They'd need to confirm everything with Michelle of course and check the girls' stories far as they could. But why would Lily make it up? Sarah could see why she might lie to get Brody out of the shit but not to dump him in it up to the ear lobes.

Harries slowed to let a 2CV join the traffic. Not that the line was moving much. 'She was dead helpful, I thought.'

'You would.' She sniffed, glanced through her window. The mutual ogling had got up her nose from the start.

'Meaning?' He knew damn well what she meant.

She shook her head, hit Baker's speed dial number – again. She'd already called for an update; Huntie didn't know where the chief was hiding either. He'd set her mind at rest about the news release though. Details on the squat findings had already gone out and a couple of local reporters had put in interview requests.

'And that's another thing – why stamp on my foot?'

'It was about to go in your mouth.' Sarah suspected any smart arse remarks about Lily would have gone down like a concrete dinghy, effectively zipping Charlie's lips. Not that she'd let anything slip, but when asked about Brody the body language had been big. Sarah grimaced at the mental pun then glared at the phone. *Where the heck was he?* She drummed fingers on thigh, had a bunch to do before the brief. Rush hour traffic was a pain, and rain had just started spitting. 'Surely you picked up how protective she is, Dave? She followed Lily round with her eyes? Hung on her every word? Mother Bear wasn't in it.'

He turned his mouth down. 'Dunno about bears. Lily was more Goldi—'

'Enough already.' She flapped a hand. Charlie's hero worship could explain her aversion to Brody though. There was no love lost there.

'Maybe she fancies Lily?' Sarah's withering look didn't stop Harries warming to the theme. 'Women get crushes, don't they?'

She rolled her eyes. 'In your wet dreams, detective.'

'Yeah you're right. If Momma Bear had a crush, it'd be curtains all round.'

'Bee-itch.' She bridled a touch on Charlie's behalf. Dave didn't normally go in for personal remarks and certainly not sexist. 'What's her size got to do with anything?' *Let alone the case.* If he didn't stop blathering, she'd never get her head round it.

'Sorry, boss. But what a state to get in, carrying all that weight can't be healthy.'

'Lily's scars weren't either.' They were old, long since healed, but the girl had obviously had problems.

'Can't say I noticed, boss.'

'Wasn't her arms you were looking at, Dave.' As for Charlotte, God knows why, but Sarah felt a sliver of sympathy for the young woman. 'There could be good reason why Charlie's so big, Dave.'

'Eating all the pies'd do it. And the cakes. And the . . .'

'I get the picture.' She closed her eyes, laced her fingers, leaned her head on the rest. Hoped Harries would get the message.

CU DNBL8 Caroline grimaced as she deleted the text. What was so tough about typing: See you. Don't be late. She slipped the phone on the bottom stair, slung her coat on the banister, marched to the kitchen, mouth like a desert. Maybe textese was a generational thing. Kid-speak. Lazysod-speak more like. The reporter couldn't be doing with it, her every message a grammatically correct, properly punctuated, cleverly crafted missive-ette. Bottom line, top line, every line had to be about communication. And Amy's first string of initials had been virtually indecipherable. Caroline had read it – tried anyway – in the car twenty minutes ago, put through a call instead. The girl wanted a meet to test the waters before deciding whether to commit to an in-depth interview.

Caroline grabbed Evian from the fridge, raised it in silent toast. *Thanks Ruby. I owe you.* She'd maybe celebrate with a proper drink this evening. If Quinn was in expansive mood as well, she'd even make it a double. But that was counting chickens territory. Amy came first in the pecking order. And getting her to talk openly was by no means a done deal.

God, she was thirsty. She drank half the contents, ran the back of her hand over her lips. She had a sneaking suspicion she'd end up paying the girl, too. Amy hadn't come right out and asked for moolah, but the hints couldn't have been heavier. *How much is it worth?* was pretty unambivalent. Caroline sniffed. Max Clifford had a lot to answer for. The world and its aunt was media savvy nowadays.

Snatching the phone, she took the stairs two at a time. Tape recorder and transcript still lay on the desk where she'd abandoned them the other night. Sitting down, she ran through her notes, refreshed her memory, prepared to tackle the rest of the tape. She'd need to keep Amy on track this evening, couldn't afford to keep 'She Who Must Be Obeyed' Quinn twiddling her thumbs. Shouldn't be a problem. The girl's proposed venue was a playground a stone's throw from the Hemming pad in Harborne. With the best will in the world it'd be a damn sight too parky to hang around. With a bit of luck she'd make it to the Queen's Head before Quinn. Give herself a head start, as it were. Mind, she needed to finish her homework first.

Pen in mouth, she cued the tape, hit play . . .

'Of course I didn't judge her. I still don't. How could I? Amy's my baby, my little girl. She always will be. If I blamed anyone it was myself. Why hadn't I protected her? Why hadn't I questioned her more about where she was going, who she was seeing, what she was up to. I'd ask myself how could I possibly not have known what was happening? More realistically, how could I possibly have known? Not for one second did the truth occur to me. Why would it? Something so far removed from our lives? From normal existence? How could I even suspect that virtually every time she went out, my child was being repeatedly raped by men old enough to be her father, her grandfather?

'It was worse for Ian, my . . . husband. Being the only girl, Amy was the apple of her daddy's eye. Is the apple of his eye. I'm sorry, it's so easy to slip into the past tense talking about what happened. In a way, you see, so much of our lives is . . . over.

'To go back, when Ian found out what those . . . animals . . . had done to her, a part of him died. And another part of him wanted to kill. I saw it. You know how they say when someone hears bad news they crumple? I'd never seen it before but that's what Ian did. He fell to his knees, clutching his chest. I thought . . .

'I swear he aged ten years in two minutes. In Ian's eyes he'd failed, you see. It was his job to look after his precious princess.

'I know what Ian thinks, but . . . I don't blame him. And you know what? I don't blame myself any more. I know exactly who's to blame for violating my daughter, ruining her childhood, potentially wrecking the rest of her life. And I hate every cell of . . .'

*   *   *

Shit. Caroline stopped the tape, answered the phone.

'I can give you an hour tonight, Caroline.'

Give? She very much doubted Jas Ram was into the free economy. 'What time?'

'Grab a pen. And listen up.'

TWENTY-SIX

S arah wrote the word again, added a question mark, underscored it, stared at her efforts, willed enlightenment. 'Bod? What's it mean?' Tapping her lip, she spoke quietly, almost to herself. Richard Patten leaned back in the chair opposite, desert boot resting on denim-clad knee.

'Devil if I know, Sarah. Bod*ies* are my territory.' The pathologist's appearance in her office was rare. Good though it was to see him, he'd brought more questions than answers. And the pack of chocolate Hobnobs they'd almost polished off between them. She suspected the personal touch was to compensate for what he saw as a professional, if not error, then oversight. He'd already apologised for not spotting it sooner. Bod had been written in blue ink on the upper arm of the Chambers Row murder victim.

'The lettering's small and if it registered earlier at all I just assumed it was part of the design.' He took a sip or two of coffee, kept his gaze on her over the rim of his Styrofoam cup.

Nodding, she laid down the pen, recalled the body on the slab, virtually covered in lurid tattoos. If it was Richard's failing, it was hers too. 'But you took a closer look this afternoon?'

'I'll not lie to you, it was more luck than judgement, Sarah. We needed to move the body.' He flicked a dog hair off the hem of his jeans. For the first time she clocked he wasn't wearing his wedding ring. '*Then* I took a closer look. Even then, I read it first as dad. Probably 'cause there's an ever so tasteful "Mum 4 ever" lower down the arm. "For" written as a number, can you believe?' He shook his head. 'Anyway . . . dad seemed odd given the nature of the tattoo.'

'A bird, you said?' Frowning, she crossed her legs. Needed to keep an eye on the time. Brief o'clock was fast approaching.

'Ye-es. A bird, Jim, but not as we know it.' He waggled an eyebrow. 'Apologies to Spock.'

'Spock never said that line anyway.' She smiled. 'He's always misquoted.'

'Like, "Beam me up, Scotty." No one said that either.' He hunched forward, elbows on knees. 'You're not a closet Trekkie too, are you?'

Patten was a Trekkie? She masked a cross between disappointment and amusement, not difficult. 'This bird . . .' Reached for a can of Red Bull.

'Right, sorry, yes. It's grotesque. Think Edvard Munch's take on a Quentin Blake phoenix. You know, mythical creature, long tail . . .'

Rises from the ashes. Yeah, yeah. She raised a palm. 'Can you get me pics? I need to see the word blown up.'

'Already in hand. I just popped by so you'd be the *second* to know what I'd found.' The skin crinkled at the corner of his eyes. 'I wish I'd come through with it sooner.'

Whatever 'it' is. 'Don't beat yourself up, Rich. It may not figure either way. 'Til we find out what it means, we won't know.' She wondered vaguely why he hadn't just put in a call.

'Until *you* find out, detective.' He drained the cup, tossed it in the bin, sprang to his feet. 'Thanks for the tea.'

She curved a lip. 'It was coffee.'

'God, my day's just packed with insight, isn't it?' Rueful mouth turned down, he tapped a salute. 'See you round.'

She smiled. Patten was the only man she knew with a legible wardrobe. Tiny white writing on the back of today's black T-shirt read: I see dead pixels.

'Rich?' Struck by a totally unrelated thought.

He turned at the door, bowed his head, mock servile. 'Ma'am?'

'Could he have written it on himself?'

His brown eyes narrowed fractionally as he gave it some

thought. 'In theory, I guess. It's on his left arm. Most people are right handed. I need to have another look at the angle of the writing. I'll get back to you. Is it important? I mean, Sarah, even if he could, why the hell would he want to?'

Aye therein lies the rub. She couldn't put it better herself.

'Why the hell would who not want to do what? See you, general.' Baker breezed in, helped himself to a couple of biscuits. Glancing over his shoulder, Sarah realised General Patten – nickname long bestowed by Baker – had beat a hasty retreat. 'I'm putting a biccie behind me ear. Man has to keep up his strength, you know.'

Stifling a sigh, she walked round the desk, closed the door after him. 'Where've you been, chief?'

'I had an appointment.' The tone brooked no argument. When she looked round, he'd helped himself to her seat, too. 'Go on then –' licking chocolate from a finger – 'what was the general pontificating about?'

Arms folded, she walked to the window, perched on the sill, related what Patten had found. 'He was answering a hypothetical question. I'd asked if the guy could have written it on himself. Rich came back with why the hell would he want to.'

'Misses the point big time.' Baker sniffed. 'Question that needs asking's – why would *anyone* want to?'

'Silly me,' she simpered. 'If only I'd thought of that.'

He pursed pensive lips, reached for a third Hobnob. Not that she was counting. 'Bod. Body. Boddington's. Bodleian. Stiff sups bitter in toff library.' She gazed at the ceiling. 'It's called thinking outside the stationery-box, Quinn.'

'Beer-drinking stiff? That's thinking outside the sodding coffin, chief.'

'OK, OK.' An airy wave of the hand sent crumbs flying over the desk. 'Not the posthumous imbibing bit, too surreal, but anything that gets a cop's thought processes going.' He held out empty palms. 'I rest my case.' And reached for the pack.

'Glad to hear it.' She rescued what was left, tipped them into her drawer. 'Case isn't resting though, chief.'

'Not far off.' He ran through his take on the findings at the squat, the alibis that had been blown out of the water. She realised that wherever Baker had sloped off to – as per – he'd kept on top of developments.

Standing, he slipped a hand in his pocket. 'Strikes me, Quinn, we're damn near throwing the book at Wilde and Brody.' Winking, he pulled out another biscuit. 'If not the Bodleian.'

TWENTY-SEVEN

The frisson in the air at the brief was almost tangible. It vied with the metaphoric scent of blood: Brody and Wilde's. For the first time in several days, Sarah saw the squad energised, enthused. Saw being the operative word. While she perched on the corner of a desk swinging a leg, chief cheerleader Baker basked centre stage. The chief's offer to run the late brief was similar to Don Corleone's in *The Godfather*. Refusal wasn't an option. She was inured to Baker adopting a more hands-on approach the nearer the squad got to a result. Right now, he put her in mind of a hyperactive octopus.

'As you know –' slinging his jacket on her desk – 'we can charge the little scrotes any time with the public order stuff, possession, assaulting a police offer – the lad's out of hospital by the way – the attack on Agnew, criminal damage, Uncle Tom Cobbly etcetera. But right now . . . we're only a gnat's pisspot away from nailing the buggers for the biggies.'

Sarah traced her lip with a finger. The biggies. It was one way of describing the assault on Foster and murder of Tattoo Man. She glanced at the dead guy's photo pinned slightly askew on one of the whiteboards. Why had no one come forward with a name? She'd make damn sure the next news release majored on the distinctive as well as extensive body art. Made a mental note to get a DC to chase the ink parlours, extend inquiries beyond the Midlands.

Wilde and Brody certainly weren't going anywhere. The bog standard twenty-four-hour detention period had been extended by a further twelve. Baker made it clear to every officer in the room, he wanted every second to count before questioning resumed again first thing.

'Right then –' rubbing gleeful hands – 'let's see what we've got, chaps. And chapettes, natch.' He cast Sarah a knowing beam. Christ he'd be talking chapattis next. 'I'll run through what's cooking.' He addressed the squad. 'Feel free to throw in the odd two penn'orth.'

How big of you, chief. Sarah folded her arms, listened and observed. Had to admit as ingredients went they were pretty tasty.

Late afternoon, Duncan Agnew had positively identified the Saint Christopher. Apparently he recognised a nick in the silver where an old girlfriend had bitten into it. Let's not go there, Sarah thought. Agnew had also been asked about helping draw up an e-fit of the three supposedly extant – and absent – gang members. Beth Lally, who'd given Shona a break from out-of-hours hospital visiting, said he'd been iffy, wanted a while longer to think about what he'd seen. Sarah reckoned it was about time she had another word with Agnew. Made another mental note: see DA.

Media coverage had led to a trickle of calls on the stolen items: the engraved signet ring, watches, credit card. Baker predicted an increased flow if the regional TV programmes went with the story this evening. Sarah glanced at the clock on the wall. Any time now then given it was gone half six.

The bank was dragging its heels on supplying Frank Gibbs' credit card details. The data protection form had gone in and Jed said he'd followed through with a couple of fruitless phone calls. Baker told No Shit to give him the number. God help the lucky sod who picked up when the chief rang.

Michelle Keating and Lily Maitland had agreed to drop by the station early tomorrow, to make statements. Harries had arranged it on the phone with Michelle – mobile number courtesy of Twinkle-toes. Sarah wanted the girls to take a look at the hoodies forensics had uncovered at the squat. She entered that in the mental log too. Wilde and Brody could deny owner-ship until the cows came home and swanned off out again, but if the girlfriends – probably exes by now – had seen them wearing the gear, they wouldn't have a leg to stand on. Lab results on blood-stroke-DNA samples might not be back for days but knowing a possible match was imminent should – if not scare them witless – at least focus the youths' minds. Sarah's drifted slightly when the chief embarked on some anecdote from his glory days. She gave her shirt a surreptitious sniff, wondered if there'd be time to nip home, freshen up before meeting King. Wouldn't normally consider it except the reporter always looked so frigging immaculate. Mind, the way Baker was droning on, they'd be lucky to get out of the place this side of Easter.

The squad appeared to be soaking it up though: rapt attention, lots of eye contact with the old boy. Truth told, she envied his easy rapport; the light touch didn't come naturally to her. Dave had it, too. When he noticed her gaze on him, he winked. Maybe she ought to let him teach her a few tricks.

Baker wound up the state of play in typical bonhomie and back-slap style, then straddled a chair. *Gee thanks, chief.* Sarah looked away sharpish, caught Dave's lip twitching.

'Way I see it, chaps,' Baker rolled his sleeves. 'Tomorrow we go in flat out, full throttle, guns blazing. Take no prisoner shit from anyone. Everyone agree? Quinn?' Like that would be a miracle.

She humoured him with a brief hesitation, then: 'I'm on board, chief.'

'Hallelujah. First time for—'

'More or less.'

He cut her a glance. 'And the caveat would be?'

She pursed pensive lips. How to explain? Brody's tears in an interview room? The look in Wilde's eyes when she talked murder charges? The willingness – eagerness almost – in admitting the attack on Agnew. But the stonewall denial of more serious offences? And what if Agnew and the anonymous calls to the hotline were on the money? It meant the involvement of three more youths who might even have initiated the attacks. Brody and Wilde were no angels, but they could be led astray fall guys. Jesus wept. The blend of sentimental mush and hunch sounded lame. Baker would tear it to shreds. And her. But then she had no personal axe to grind. Of course she wanted to nail the perps' balls to

the wall as Baker so eloquently put it. But they had to
be the right perps' balls.

No. Sod it. She'd hold fire. 'Forget it, chief.' She raised a
placatory palm. 'I'm with you.' She'd just feel happier if they
had extra bullets for those blazing guns of his. The squad knew
next to nothing about Foster and Tattoo Man. With more ammo,
questioning could be better directed, they'd know where to go
with it for a start.

'Got that right, Quinn. I want you sitting in. Both interviews.
Crack of sparrow's fart.'

Charmed, I'm sure. 'No worries. Before we split, I just want
to throw Rich Patten's find into the pot, chief.' If two heads
were better than one, establishing why 'Bod' had been written
on a body should be a breezy walk in the park. Except for the
wall of blank faces that ensued the telling. 'Anything?' She
ran her gaze over the troops. 'Help me out here, please.'

'It can't really be that important, can it, inspector?' This
from Beth Lally who'd bagged the same front seat and now
sucked a biro.

Sarah hid the bristle beneath a neutral smile. 'You tell me.'

'From what you say, Patten only came across it by chance?'

She gave a get-on-with-it nod.

'Well, surely if it was meant to be some big wheelie dealie
message it would have been a lot more in-your-face. I mean
if Patten hadn't stumbled across it, as it were, nobody would
be any the wiser.'

'Good thinking, Lilly.' Baker all but patted the blonde's
pretty little head.

'It's Lally, sir. Thanks.'

'I know that, detective. Problem, Quinn?'

She shook her head. Not one she could pin down.
'You're right though, Beth. The guy could have gone to the
grave without anyone knowing.' Sarah narrowed her eyes. *And
you're wrong, too. The person who wrote the word knew it was
there.* What if he or she never intended it to be found? Or it
didn't matter whether anyone else saw it or not? That it being
there on the man's body was enough? If Sarah was on the right
lines, Beth was wrong again in assuming its unimportance.
It had to be devilishly important to whoever wrote it.

'. . . on the phone, yeah, just now, gov.'

Young voice, Welsh accent. Sarah hadn't even heard the guy come in. She glanced up, frowning, knew his face from the incident room, wondered why he was clutching a scrap of paper. 'Sorry, detective, say again.'

'Keep up, Quinn. Go on, lad.'

'This woman rang the hotline. Says she knows the guy who was attacked in Stirchley. Saw his photo in the local rag.'

'Foster.' Sarah nodded encouragement.

'No, ma'am.' His colour rose. 'Not according to the caller.'

'Go on.'

He glanced at the paper. 'She says it's Walter Fielding. Wally Fielding.' Tiny hairs rose on the back of Sarah's neck. 'Reckons she'd know him anywhere.'

'How come?' She kept her voice level.

'Wouldn't say, ma'am.'

She crossed both sets of fingers, very near crossed her legs. 'Did you get her number?' And please let it be pukka.

'Number, name, address, the lot. Thought it might be important, like.'

'I think you might be right, detective.' Smiling, she took the paper from him.

The name Walter Fielding meant absolutely nothing to the DI. But the initials did.

TWENTY-EIGHT

'It could be a coincidence, boss.' Harries tapped a Winson Green postcode into the satnav.

'That's right, Dave. And the Pope might not be a Catholic.' Sarah glanced in the mirror, cursed the glare from some idiot's full beam headlights. She was slightly more miffed that Harries didn't appear to share her sense of urgency. Heading down the Hagley Road, they were en route to the address taken by, would you believe, DC Tom Jones. God knows how she'd forgotten that name. Not exactly unusual. *Ouch.*

'Besides, you've no way of knowing Sean Foster uses his second name. And even then, there must be loads of blokes with the initials W.F.' Harries concentrated on opening a KitKat.

Zillions, at least. Even Sarah was hard pushed to explain her conviction. 'Humour me, just this once, eh?' It wasn't often she acted on instinct but if Sean William Foster and Walter Fielding weren't one and the same, she'd eat Baker's Stetson. And chaps. Shee-oot. She'd best be spot on.

'You could've left a message, boss.' Harries shrugged. 'She's probably not even in.' Sarah heard the KitKat snap, glanced across to check the size of the bar.

'I could but, hey I didn't. Get over it.' No one had picked up when she phoned but even while keying the number, Sarah knew a home visit made more sense, see the woman in the flesh, gauge the body language, clock what the face was doing. She'd asked Jones if he'd read anything into the caller's voice. Middle-aged, quite posh, didn't strike him as a time waster, he'd said.

Harries broke off another piece. Smell of chocolate made her mouth water. 'Could be a wasted journey, is all.'

'Look, Dave, if you'd rather not be here, just say.' He was off shift by rights. She'd asked him along for the ride, it wasn't compulsory. Baker thought she could've tasked it, but she wanted the job for herself. If Patricia Malone could supply a few bullets ahead of tomorrow's interrogation: bring it on.

Harries sniffed. 'It's not that, boss. I just can't see why I can't join you for a bite in the pub.' She gave a thin smile. Suspected what he really wanted was for *her* to see something, see sod all going on between him and King. She'd already told Harries it was a private party. King would only play to an audience; Sarah could live without the distraction. She cut a glance at the dashboard clock: 18.55. As it was, she'd be pressed to get back on time to meet the journo.

That KitKat was fast disappearing. 'Don't I get a bit?'

'Wouldn't have thought you'd want any. Seeing as how you'll be eating later. Enjoying a drink or two. Girls' night out and all that.'

'Grow up, sweetie.'

'One finger or two, boss?'

Not bad. She masked a smile. Hadn't she more or less fed him the line?

The Edwardian villa stood a few streets from the Victorian prison where Fred West topped himself. Not that Sarah read anything into it. In Winson Green, a lot of property did.

'Don't say it, Dave.' Sighing, Sarah unlocked the motor after her fruitless mission at the front door.

'What's that, boss?' Rocking on his heels, hands behind his back – all Mr Innocence.

I told you so. 'I still think dropping by was better.'

'Shoving a note through the door beats leaving a message any time, boss.'

Sarky git. At least she'd seen where Patricia Malone lived. The house was neat, tidy, windows clean, door intact, more than a cut above its boarded-up neighbours. Casting the place a final glance, she got back in the car. She'd left a stack of numbers asking the woman to call. All she could do was cross fingers and wait.

'Not been stood up *again* have you, Quinn?' Baker took a slurp of beer, yanked out a chair, flopped down uninvited. Sarah, drumming the table with three fingers, didn't miss a beat. Mind, she could've banged out Ringo Starr's entire play-list by now. Nearly an hour she'd hung round waiting for King to show, checked the phone every five minutes. The dark mood she was in, Baker was going the right way to get another bloody black eye.

'How'd you guess, chief? Tom Cruise cried off at the last moment.'

'Got a better offer, did he?' He winked at her over his glass. 'Short-arse like that'd be no good to you anyway, Quinn.'

Sipping on her third bitter lemon, she raised a wry eyebrow. 'Like I'd know?'

'How'd it go at Winson Green?' He turned his mouth down as she told him it hadn't. 'Likely she'll get back, lass.' If it was important being the subtext. 'I reckon the case is coming together, either way. I feel it in my water.' He tilted his glass before sinking another mouthful. 'Any road, no shop, not tonight, if that's OK. You eaten?'

She frowned. *Something not right there.* 'A finger of KitKat. Does that count?' She casually scanned his face for clues.

'Only to one.' His smile was almost tentative. She took another sip, watched as he leaned across the next table, grabbed a couple of menus. 'Here y'go. The world's your oyster baguette. My shout.' He struggled to hold her gaze.

If that's OK. She stiffened mentally. *That's* what had jarred a few seconds ago. Since when had the chief given a flying fuck about consensual anything? It was his way or the super highway; made no bones about it. She thought she'd detected a hint of uncertainty lurking in his eyes, too. Not about shelling out for a meal – certainly couldn't accuse him of being a tightwad – more a case of nervy how the offer would go down.

'Well, lass?'

She weighed it up a couple seconds more. 'Why not?' Intrigued as much as anything, she gave him a warm smile. 'Best offer I've had all week, chief.'

'Better than Cruise?'

'Close.' Skimming the menu, she reckoned she'd plump for the salad again. 'Must've had a run on oysters, chief. I'll go for the caesar—'

'Look, Quinn, there's *nothing* your bum'd look big in. Why not get some proper grub down your neck?'

Had he just paid a compliment? 'Go on then, twist my arm. Steak and ale pie.'

'Chips?'

'You spoil me, chief. Talk about showing a girl a good time.'

He stood, gave her shoulder a paternal pat. 'Mebbe you should get out more, dear.'

A smile still played on her lips as she watched him amble to the bar, hand delving in trouser pocket for wallet. Maybe she'd imagined the old boy's more engaging, even slightly apprehensive manner. Having said that, his banter with Laughing Len came across as a little subdued, forced even?

Brushing away the thought, she pulled her phone closer, checked the screen again. King could at least have texted.

Forget Cruise. In the better offer department, she reckoned the reporter must've struck oil.

'Get that down you, lass.' Baker handed over a glass. 'It'll take away the taste of the bitter lemon.'

Sauvignon Blanc. Her usual poison. She'd eschewed it earlier, dealing with King even with a clear head was sobering enough. 'Cheers, chief.'

'Please, lass.' He stilled halfway to his seat. 'We're not on the job here. Y'know the name.'

Easy for you to say. He'd told her to use it before, but she found Fred impossible to spit out. Clowns at the nick had no trouble calling him The Shred. Behind his back. She raised the glass to her lips, took a tactical sip. The chat was light, amiable, the occasional silence not uneasy. The pie was heaven on a plate. She relished it while Baker waxed lyrical about his times out West. Told her she'd love it there, ought to learn to ride. She'd laughed, said there was more chance of her piloting Richard Branson's *Galactic*.

Her mood mellowed. In his current state, Baker was decent company, good talker, entertaining tales, surprisingly interesting – and equally happy to listen. He wasn't exactly a different man, but certainly showing a different side. Or she was prepared to see it.

Suddenly he shoved his plate to one side then: 'I was at the solicitor.' Blue Out Of.

She certainly wasn't prepared for the verbal curveball. 'Sorry?'

'This afternoon. You couldn't reach me.' His gaze didn't reach *her*.

'Ri . . . ght.' She stretched it to two syllables. *And you're telling me why?*

'It'll get out soon enough, but . . . her indoors – the missus – isn't. She's left me. Pushing hard for divorce. I needed to sort a few details.' Dipping an index finger in a little spilled beer, he kept his gaze on the table. Poor bloke. She wondered if she ought to tell him his exclusive was the worst-kept secret since news broke on Jeremy Clarkson's gagging order.

'I'm sorry to hear that.' True, but she was still hazy why he'd chosen her as confidante.

'I didn't see it coming, reckoned we were hitched for good.

Till death do us and all that. Fact is, I'm finding it . . . difficult. I'm a grumpy old bugger at the best of times. Know that. But these last few months have been . . . shite. I've prob'ly not been the easiest person in the world to work with.'

Probably? No point rubbing it in. That was as close to an apology he'd ever come. 'No worries, chief.'

He sighed. 'Not sure how much longer I can hide it from the lads.'

Bit late in the day if what he was really saying was, have a quiet word with the squad. As in: cut the chief some slack cause he's going through the wringer.

'I think one or two might have picked up on it, chief. Look, if there's anything I can do . . .?'

'Thanks, lass. Guess I just needed someone to tell.' *For tell – read, talk to?* What was the saying? It's tough at the top. Must be pretty lonely up there, too.

'Any time. I mean it.'

He finally lifted his gaze. 'I miss her.' The simple statement had more impact than if he'd wrapped it in some glib so-called wit. *And was that a tear in his eye?*

'Hey, it'd be a wonder if you didn't.' She felt a rush of sympathy, almost reached to comfort him. 'It's only natural . . . Fred.'

'I mean, Quinn, I can't boil toast and as for the sodding washing machine.' He threw his hands in the air. 'Don't fancy shacking up, do you?'

The line didn't fool her for a second. For whatever reason, he'd shown vulnerability, an emotional Achilles heel. Now it was business as normal. Smiling she shook her head. 'You'd get a shock if I said yes.'

'Shock? I'd have a bloody stroke.'

Her ring tone – at last. She was still smiling when she grabbed the phone. King could bloody well sod off. Except it wasn't her number on display.

'Boss?' Harries. *What was he playing at?* 'Sorry if I'm breaking anything up . . . thought you'd want to know.' She waited a few seconds while he got his breath back. 'Patricia Malone's place . . . looks like it's been torched.'

TWENTY-NINE

'Where are you?' Sarah glanced at her watch, calculated the wine intake: 21.35 and pushing it. Baker who'd wandered off to take a leak would definitely be over the limit. If need be, she'd call a police driver.

'Across the street from the house. Crews are still in there.' Harries said he'd driven back to Winson Green on the off-chance, knew she placed importance on what the woman might have to say, wanted to try and get something out of her before the interviews tomorrow. *Chasing Brownie points.* Christ, woman, don't take a pop at him for showing initiative. 'I couldn't believe it when I saw the engines, boss.' Must be a generator she could hear in the background. 'I feel a right numpty now for taking the piss.'

'And Malone? Where's she?' Eyes closed, she mouthed a prayer. *Dear God – don't do this.*

'Hold on a tick.' She heard engine noise, shouts too muffled to make out the gist. *Come on, come on . . .* 'Sorry 'bout that. One of the guys just came out, says they're pretty sure the place is empty. I'll feel happier when I've had a word with the lead fire officer. He's up against it at the mo.'

Pretty sure? Proof positive'd be better. 'What's the damage like?'

'Could be hell of a lot worse. Neighbour putting rubbish in his bin out back spotted it. From what I hear, the crews managed to stop it spreading upstairs. I can't see the place being habitable for a while though.'

'And you reckon it was torched?' She shook her head at Baker who stood at the bar waggling an imaginary glass.

'I'm told there's been a spate round here in the last couple of weeks. Burning rags shoved through letterboxes. They suspect it's kids, copping a buzz. Mind, this fire started at the back of the house and it's the only property that had someone living in it.'

'Had' was about right. When Patricia Malone eventually turned up, she'd find herself at least temporarily homeless. Whether she'd be too afraid to move back was anyone's guess. Maybe scaring her off was the point: scaring her off from talking to the police.

Given the circs, she saw no mileage going out there, asked Harries to knock on a few doors, find out if neighbours had any idea where the woman had gone and more important when she'd be back. 'Either way, Dave, have a word with uniform. Tell them I want an officer posted there till they hear otherwise.' They'd need to nab Malone the minute she showed.

'Looks like your instinct was sound, boss.'

She chewed her lip. 'If there's been a spate, I s'pose this could just be coincidence?' In the clutching straw department, she suspected she'd grabbed onto a burning hayrick.

He gave a sceptical sniff. 'Bless. What was it you said about the Pope?'

Yeah right. 'Look Dave, I'm still in the pub but I'll be heading off any time soon. If there's anything I need to know—'

'Gotcha.'

'And thanks, Dave. Good work.'

'No worries. How's the girls' night going then, boss?'

She glanced at Baker hunched over the table, tongue stuck out in concentration as he gingerly added a beer mat to a perilously leaning tower. *Like a house on fire.* 'Like a dream. You just wouldn't believe it, Dave.'

Four Years Earlier

Moonlight glinted off stainless steel sinks and work surfaces, cast silver grey shades over the rest of the room. Silhouetted against a tiled wall, the girl sat on cold lino, bare legs spread wide. Fridges hummed, a tap dripped. Oblivious, she stared ahead, tears trickled down her face. She crammed the last doughnut in her mouth. The sauce that glistened round her lips was all that remained of a twelve inch pizza. The red stain looked like lipstick – applied by a ham-fisted clown. Or as if someone had smacked her in the mouth.

Stifling a sob, the girl tried working out when it all went pear-shaped. Not ending up in care. Christ, she was used to that by now. No. This shit situation with the man. Six months back she'd been well in. He'd singled her out, shown her preferential treatment, a touch of favouritism. She wasn't going to say no. She'd have a bit of that. In all her fifteen years, she couldn't remember anyone showing interest, and she'd liked helping him in the kitchen. It was all unofficial, he gave her a few bob pocket money on the sly and she got first dibs on food, any seconds going spare. She wasn't fussy. It'd be a shame to see it go to waste. She didn't see it as stealing. Not until the man threatened to dob her in.

She couldn't get her head round it. He'd been the one who'd taken her under his wing, looked out for her. He'd said she was all skin and bone, needed fattening up a bit. He used to push the extras her way. Then a few weeks ago, he started making her look for them, told her it was a game. He'd hide plates of food in store cupboards or in the room where they kept the cleaning things. It was all right – until he started following her in, locking the door, touching her. Even that was OK at first. He was still nice to her then and she was pathetically grateful. Then he started bringing friends in, other men, men who treated her like meat.

She'd begged him not to, threatened to tell the woman in charge but he told her he'd kill her if she breathed a word. The woman didn't believe her anyway. Called her a fat lying tart.

Shivering, the girl felt round on the floor for her knickers. She didn't think they'd be back tonight. And there was an almost full tub of chocolate ice cream in the fridge. She couldn't be arsed with a spoon, scooped it out with her fingers then licked the tub clean.

Comfort food they called it. Yeah right.

When he eventually came back to unlock the door, she'd head for the bathroom and shove the same fingers down her throat.

Dead comforting, that.

THIRTY

Baker decked out in Rhinestone Cowboy costume cavorted on stage astride a palomino stallion clad in a pink satin tutu. The National Indoor Arena was packed, the concert in aid of the Police Benevolent Fund, the whip-cracking crowd going wild during the chief's raucous rendition of *Rawhide*. Tammy Wynette joined him for a duet – *D-I-V-O-R-C-E*, natch – there wasn't a dry eye in the house. Crowning moment came when the pink limo glided on stage and Dolly Parton popped out in a low-cut pink cowgirl mini dress. Her fuchsia Stetson had fetching puce feathers and flashing red hearts. Dolly and Fred's interpretation of *Hillbilly Willy* had to be seen to be believed. Sarah watched in toe-curling embarrassment from the front row then broke into a broad smile. Of course, all the pink made sense now – no one wanted the horse to stand out looking like an ass.

Dripping with sweat, palms clammy, Sarah threw off the duvet, lay back trying to work out if she was about to throw up. Not so much at the vomit inducing visions but the indigestion-stroke-heartburn that had broken the dream. She put both down to last night's flaky pastry and thanked God she'd not eaten cheese, any more rich food might have prompted a nightmare: she could've found herself starring in the stage show. Shuddering at the thought, she swung her legs over the side of the bed, sat with her head in her hands till her heartbeat slowed.

Clock read a minute to six, almost rise and shine time anyway. She took a deep breath, slowly exhaled. The nausea seemed to have passed. Rising shouldn't be beyond her. She wandered to the window, pressed her forehead against the cool glass. Icing sugar frost tipped the reeds and grasses along the canal bank, patchy ice floated on the surface of the water. Forget the sun cream then.

Like she'd slipped King's mind? The reporter failing to turn up was one thing but no text apologising was slack. Sarah tightened her lips. Her sleep couldn't have been that deep, surely? Strolling to the bathroom, she checked the phone again. Nada.

Last call was Dave's around eleven just before he pulled out of Winson Green. He'd told her Patricia Malone's neighbours had mostly been a waste of space, but one old girl reckoned Mrs Malone did a fair bit for the homeless: soup runs, volunteer stuff at night shelters, that kind of thing. Pretty ironic given what had happened. Uniform had obviously failed to track her down or Sarah would've heard.

Stepping into the shower, she reckoned Malone would have to go on to the mental back burner for a while anyway. She rolled her eyes; there were better ways to put it. Whatever. Wilde and Brody's interviews would take precedence. She'd skimmed through some of the files before bed, jotted down a few thoughts. For the youths, it didn't look good.

Ten minutes later she glanced at her reflection in the cheval mirror, reasonably happy with her own image. She'd opted for black. Tailored linen trouser suit, crisp white shirt. Even applied a hint of slap. The gear was more severe than her normal soft taupes. A sartorial message. She gathered the paperwork, slipped it into her briefcase. An earlier peep into the fridge had confirmed it was running on empty. No matter. She'd already decided to hit the canteen.

The call came when she was in the car. It explained why Caroline King had been a no-show. And handy, it meant Sarah could drive straight to the hospital.

'Christ, Caroline. What happened?' The reporter lay in bed in a private room at the QE. Sarah hoped the shock didn't show in her face: Caroline's resembled marbled beef. Outside in the corridor, the DI had learned that the reporter had been found in a side road in Edgbaston. Beaten, robbed, not sexually assaulted, she'd been treated for shock as much as the injuries, kept under observation for several hours, as well as sedation. Sarah's knee-jerk reaction? One way to keep the bloody woman's trap shut. That was before witnessing the damage. Even the whites of King's eyes were red. Soon as she'd come round apparently, she'd badgered a nurse to call Sarah.

'That bad, huh?' Caroline turned her head to the wall.

'How did it happen, Caroline?'

'Sod knows. You tell me.' It sounded as if teeth were missing or damaged. Though the lisp could be down to swelling. The lips looked bee-stung. By a swarm.

Sarah stepped further into the room, dragged a chair closer to the bed. 'You were found around half-eleven last night unconscious near the cricket ground.' By a bloke taken short, on the way home from the pub; if he'd not waded into the bushes it would've been hours before medical treatment arrived. If hypothermia had set in . . . The DI had picked this up just now over the phone, a control room inspector had read her the attending officers' report. They'd not had a name to go on back then, the assailant or assailants had left nothing that identified King.

A clearly still woozy Caroline picked listlessly at the sheet with her fingers. 'Last thing I remember is being in Harborne.' Less lisp more slur. Made sense though, her BMW had been found in Harborne, Park Road.

'Where in Harborne?'

'Leaving the park, around half-seven. Heading to meet you.' Pitch black, freezing cold. 'What were you doing in the park?'

Hesitation, prevarication or medication slowing reaction time? 'Meeting . . . someone.'

Probably all three. 'This someone have a name?' *Beginning with J ending in M.* Last time they'd spoken, Caroline said the meeting with Jas Ram was imminent. Did he have anything to do with this? He mightn't like getting his hands dirty but he had henchmen who'd be willing.

'Yes, but . . . hold on . . . I . . .' She narrowed her eyes. Something else had struck.

Sarah leaned forward, placed a hand on the covers. 'What?'

'I'm not sure. No, it's gone.' Impatient shake of her head. 'I thought I remembered . . .'

Past tense bad. 'Remembered?'

'Shadows, dark figures. Over my shoulder.'

Figures plural. 'How many?' Three perhaps? Wilde and

Brody's absent buddies? No. Sarah dismissed the thought. The leap was way too large. Besides, the gang hadn't attacked a woman before. *As far as the cops knew.* Was it possible, then? Just? Or was the DI only giving the notion mental house room because the youths occupied much of her mind most of the time recently?

'I just don't know. It was dark, there's a bunch of trees out there. It was a hazy glimpse. Corner of my eye. I might have imagined the whole thing anyway.' Tearful, nervy, touch of am dram, too? No. That was churlish. She'd never seen King look so lost, so fragile. Tread lightly.

'No worries.' Sarah smiled. 'It's more likely to come back when you're not thinking about it anyway.' She'd ask Dave or Jed to take a look after sun rise. Couldn't do any harm. Burning questions were how she'd got from Harborne to Edgbaston? And what had happened in the hours in between? 'Any idea what—?'

'I wish. Doesn't the brain blank what it can't handle?'

She nodded. 'It's been known.' *Amnesia could be selective too.* Was she holding back information, pursuing her own agenda? Sarah wouldn't put it past King but the ordeal was real enough. For the moment she'd give her the benefit of the doubt. And have another word with the medic – they must have done blood tests.

The earlier notion still bugged Sarah. Had the reporter been in the wrong place at the wrong time? A random mugging for rich pickings? Or had the gang targeted her? But why? More likely something to do with her work: journos, like cops, made more enemies than friends. Given King's recent dealings, surely if anyone had singled her out . . .

'This meet you had in the park?' She paused, waiting on eye contact. 'Wouldn't have anything to do with Jas Ram, would it?'

'Nothing.' Rapid response. Too rapid? 'Pass my water, would you?'

Keeping her gaze on King, she handed her the glass. 'And you'd say if it was?'

'Thanks.' Was slaking her thirst more important than answering the question?

'Well?'

'Of course I would.' She lifted a hand let it drop. 'Sarah, can we do this later? I'm really beat.'

That she was. Sarah's fist clenched. Had Ram got a hold on her? Was she protecting him? 'I warned you he was toxic, Caroline.' She recalled her take on Caroline getting involved with the bastard: a hiding to nothing.

King pointed both index fingers at her face. 'This isn't to do with him.'

'Weird that.' She raised an eyebrow. 'If you can't remember anything – how do you know?'

'Look . . . please—'

'Look please nothing. I'm not here for the good of my health. You asked to see me.'

Caroline lowered her head, and voice: 'I want you to pick up a few things for me from home. Nat's away.'

What? 'For fuck's sake . . . isn't there someone else?' A solitary tear trickled down the reporter's battered face, dripped off her chin, dampened the sheet. The sight staunched the flow of Sarah's tirade. She was pretty sure King had no family, certainly none in Birmingham, colleagues were mostly London-based. Christ, if her only option was to call a cop that made her Milly-no-mates big time. Maybe they had more in common than she'd assumed. 'OK.' She reached out tentatively, patted Caroline's hand. 'I'll see what I can do. What do you need?'

'I've written a little list. It's here somewhere.' She gave a weak smile as she scrabbled under the pillow. 'Bastards took everything: phone, watch, jewellery, bag.'

'Keys?'

'Coat pocket. There's a spare BlackBerry on the kitchen dresser. I'll need my laptop, too. But mostly it's toiletries, decent nightie, make-up bag.'

Sarah glanced at the ceiling. Saw a leopard with spots. 'Thought they were only keeping you in one more night?'

'Long enough, isn't it?' She gave a one-shouldered shrug. 'Look I'm still a bit shaky but I know I've got to try and come up with more detail. I'll do my best, honest.'

Nodding, she took the paper and keys from Caroline. 'Yeah,

well when I get back I'll have a list, too, and it won't be short. So think on, eh?' She rose, slipped the things into her bag.

'Sarah?' The DI turned her head at the door. 'Straight up? If I want to look half decent, how much slap am I gonna need?' Her laugh was brittle and too loud, the fear in her eyes telling, as she searched Sarah's face for the truth. She'd not have looked in a mirror then.

'I won't lie to you, Caroline. Probably more than you've got.'

A full English would be pushing it but still just shy of half-seven, Sarah had time enough to grab toast, banana and coffee. Huntie had already been roped in to hold the early brief. Waiting in line, she glanced round the canteen, spotted Dave, Jed and Beth Lally in cahoots over by the window. She'd have to break up the party. Wanted Jed and Beth to take a gander round the park in Harborne; Dave, she'd almost forgotten, would have his hands full with Michelle and Lily first thing. Picturing the image, she smiled. Her nose wrinkled: a waft of Paco Rabanne had cut through the bacon odours. Talk about olfactory early warning.

'Call this crack of sparrow's fart?' Baker's tray appeared alongside hers.

'Give it a rest, chief. I had to drop by the hospital on the way in.'

'Nothing serious, I hope.' Mouth tight, she cast a glance, caught him eyeing the suit.

'Where's the hearse, Quinn? You look like a funeral director touting for business.'

Hearse sounded far too close to horse. She had a sudden and certainly unwitting vision of Baker belting out *Rawhide*. If she'd been on stage, she'd have corpsed, as it was she had to press a hand to her mouth to stifle a giggle.

'Sodding hell, woman. It's not that funny.'

'Oh, I don't know.' She could barely get the words out. 'Horses for courses and all that, chief.'

'Yeah, well, get it out your system while you can, Quinn.' He was not amused. 'I can't see today being a barrel of laughs.'

*   *   *

'Rohypnol?' Sarah had left Baker to it, carried the tray to her office, opted for a working breakfast. She'd skimmed the overnight reports, responded to emails and was now on the phone picking the pathologist's brain. Richard Patten was more at home talking stiffs, but made the odd exception for Sarah's live specimens. He was up to speed on Caroline King's symptoms, particularly the memory loss. 'Rohypnol as in roofies?' Sarah asked. 'What people think of as the date rape drug?' Not that any cases had been confirmed in the UK. 'There's no indication of sexual assault, Rich.' Pensive, she popped in the last piece of toast.

'Yeah, but it's a recreational thing these days, rave parties and the like. Kids use it for the buzz, the euphoria. It gets them intoxicated quicker, combined with other drugs – cannabis, coke, heroin – it intensifies the effect.'

Wilde and Brody? They both smoked cannabis. Presumably their missing mates would too. She jotted a note, already considering a further possibility. Pimps, sexual predators, groomers had been known to subdue their victims with Rohypnol. Groomers like Jas Ram.

'From what you say about the woman's condition – the drowsiness, confusion, memory loss – Rohypnol is a definite possibility.' Nothing like committing yourself. 'Not that I'm saying she took it herself. She's not a raver is she, Sarah?' *As if.*

'How would it have been administered though?' She grimaced, reckoned the lingo was infectious.

'It comes in tablet form, usually slipped in a drink. It dissolves easily and it's colourless, odourless, tasteless and ten times more powerful than Valium. Even more potent when mixed with booze. It'll act faster, effects'll last longer. Victims can pass out within a few minutes, stay out for up to eight hours.' She heard a bark and Patten's slightly muffled voice saying, 'Shush, Scottie, old boy.' She smiled: the dog wasn't stuffed after all. 'Sorry where was I? Yeah. Rohypnol. In theory it's only available here on private prescription. The manufacturers changed the formula a while back, added a blue dye to make it easier to detect, but there are street versions out there that don't have the dye – as I'm sure you know.'

Easy to get hold of, dirt cheap, too. 'She says the last thing she remembers is walking across a park?'

'Yeah but what happened immediately before? Has she no memory of that?' As if she should.

Good question. 'Let's just say she's not sharing.' *Yet.* Medical tests would detect if the drug was in her system, only King would know how it got there. If it was. Sarah blew out her cheeks on a sigh.

'You sound as if you need a lift.'

'In need of something, Rich.' A fan and air freshener would do for a start. The prospect of spending x number of hours confined in stuffy interview rooms in the hygienically challenged company of Zach Wilde and Leroy Brody didn't have a lot going for it.

'Actually, I was gonna give you a bell later anyway.' Touch hesitant? 'Couple things. The pics you asked for? The writing on the body? I'll email them soon as I get in.'

'Great.' Brushing crumbs off her lap.

'Yeah and the other . . .' Definitely hesitant. 'Don't know whether you're up for it, but I've got tickets . . . let me just check the date.' She ran a wish list: Coldplay, Radiohead, Stones, RSC, Comedy Store. 'They're for a convention.'

Legal? Medical? Professional? Oh no. She gave a mental grimace, knew what he was about to say.

'At the NEC early April. Patrick Stewart's a cert. Shatner a maybe. 'Course Len doesn't do appearances any more. Real shame that but—'

'Rich?' Rapping the desk with her knuckles. 'Can I get back to you? I've got someone at the door.' A real McCoy knock startled her. She glanced up, frowning; Dave entered as per without summons. Cutting Patten off in his prime, she drawled, 'Do come in, detective.'

'Cheers.'

She twisted her mouth. *Should've laid the sarcasm on with a trowel.* 'To what do I owe . . .?'

'No pleasure, boss.' His clenched jaw, curt tone underlined the point. 'Hospital's just been on. Sean-William-Foster-Walter-Fielding, whoever he was?'

Was? She felt the colour drain from her face.

'Had a heart attack this morning, boss. He didn't make it.'

THIRTY-ONE

'God. That's awful. I'm really sorry to hear it. And you've no idea what happened?'

'That's right. I get the occasional hazy flashback. Like a dream you know is in your head, but can't grasp?' The reporter hadn't phoned Ruby Wells to burden her with news of the attack. Apart from needing something – anything – to help fill the interminable hours, the call was primarily to thank the lawyer for pointing Amy Hemming in the right direction. Caroline's chat with the girl last night had gone better than she could have expected. Doubtless, the carton of Silk Cut and Diet Cokes helped strike the deal. That and the promise of a few bob once the interviews were in the can, as it were.

'How long are they keeping you in, Caroline? I could come visit if you like?'

She wouldn't. Even looking her best, Caroline struggled next to Ruby. By now she'd seen her face. She'd cajoled the nurse who wheeled in the phone to fetch a mirror. Caroline could still picture the damage. She bit her lip, winced at the pain. Not all of it physical. OK. Nothing was broken, bruises faded, swelling went down, but violence had always been something she reported on, not taken the brunt of. She'd have to live with the experience now, but what if the psychological legacy hit again and again? She brushed away the fear, now not the time . . .

'That's kind, Ruby but, hey, don't put yourself out.'

'It's no hassle or I wouldn't have offered.'

Not for you maybe. Caroline rubbed a hand across her forehead. Her concerns went a lot further than the prospect of a visit by the stunning lawyer and the attack's potential future impact.

Just what the fuck had happened after she'd left Amy?

To say the least, her recall of events was patchy. And, God, she'd tried. She'd caught the odd tantalising glimpse in her mind's eye, shadowy shapes, muffled sound track, all just beyond reach, on a sort of mental tip of the tongue. Frustrating wasn't in it. The not knowing was driving her doolally. La Quinn probably thought she was prevaricating but it was like trying to pin down fog jelly. God knows when Sarah would deign to get back, but when she did she'd want answers. Irony was if the reporter had them, she'd almost certainly give.

'So what do you say, Caroline?'

Her concentration was shot to shit as well. 'Sorry?'

'About my dropping by.' She heard a smile in the lawyer's voice. 'Do you like grapes?'

'I do if they're in a bottle.'

Her laughter sounded good. 'That settles it then. See you later.'

Resigned, Caroline hung up, flopped back on the pillow. A bit of company might be just as well. Christ. It wasn't even ten o'clock yet. If she didn't get out of the place pdq, she'd die of TB anyway: terminal boredom.

'The guy's dead? When?' Baker was standing gathering papers from his desk when Sarah popped her head round the door. He tapped his watch. 'And where the bloody hell have you been?'

'He died about an hour ago. Some of the fallout needed sorting.' Christ she was only five minutes late. She lingered in the doorway, no point entering the den when they were supposed to be in IR1 by now. 'The hospital put a call through just now, let us know the score.'

'Know? That's rich.' He grabbed his jacket off the back of the chair, slung it over a shoulder. 'He's been there – how long? – a week – and we still know jackshit about him. Christ, according to you, even the name we're going on could be wrong.'

She reversed into the corridor as he careered out. 'Yeah, that's why it's even more imperative to track down Patricia Malone.' She had two DCs working on it plus the uniform presence outside the Winson Green house.

'Nothing doing yet?'

She shook her head, upped the pace to match his. 'I had

another word with the guy who took her call. DC Jones? He's adamant there was no indication she'd be going AWOL.'

'Like she'd tell him anyway?' he snapped. 'Don't be so bloody daft.'

He was right: as bright remarks go – it didn't. Nonetheless: '*So* glad you're in such a good mood, chief.' She didn't care if that overstepped the mark; Baker's arsey brake needed pressing, the interrogations called for cool heads, subtle handling. Strategy they'd worked out was to start slow, open with the easy ones, move on to the big guns. Good cop: not-so-bad-cop.

Pulling up sharp, he turned, glared, clenched the jaw. Psyched up for a full frontal attack, she was taken aback when his face relaxed into a sort of smile. 'You're right, Quinn. I'm wrong and I'm real sorry.' She *was right and* he *was sorry?* That had to be a first. Was a new Baker finally struggling out?

'Hey, no worries, chief.'

'And if you believe that . . .'

THIRTY-TWO

'I'm not the liar here, mister.' Wilde struggled to retain his laid-back sprawl in an unyielding upright chair, the bolshie front seemed less pronounced since the previous interview and in the last five minutes had backed off more. Sarah reckoned it was a show – a show that wouldn't make the ratings.

'*You're* not the liar?' Baker's exaggerated gaze swept the room, he glanced over his shoulder, bopped his head down to check under the table. 'Nope. Definitely not. No one's sneaked in while I wasn't looking. How about you, DI Quinn? Catch anyone lurking around?'

Staring, impassive, at the youth, she shook her head.

'Unless?' The chief lifted a podgy finger, like it was all a big mistake and he'd got the wrong end of the stick. 'You're suggesting me and the inspector are spinning porky pies?'

He sniffed. 'You said it, mate.'

'DI Quinn?' Baker all faux shock. 'You're absolutely sure you're not fibbing?'

She nodded. Wished he'd get on with it, drop the act, his amateur dramatics were nearly as lame as Wilde's. They all knew the youth was making oblique reference to his girlfriend in response to Sarah's initial line of questioning. She'd suggested Wilde might like to think again about his movements on January the eleventh and thirteenth. No, he wouldn't, check with the chick, he'd drawled, like it was a done deal. She'd watched his face fall as she assured him she already had, that his dates didn't add up, that Michelle Keating and Lily Maitland had blown both his and Brody's alibis so far out of the water, they were orbiting Venus. Baker said last time he looked it was Uranus. It was then the youth's attitude shift really took off.

Looking at him now, the body language screamed 'get me out of here', the panic had to be more than skin deep going by the rank odour coming off him.

'So you're saying your lady friend's a lying tramp?' Baker made to lean across the table, decided against. 'Is that it? Just so's we know.'

He shook his head, gnawed hard on a thumbnail.

'For the tape, Mr Wilde.'

'En. Oh.' He spat a sliver of nail, skin whatever on the floor. 'Either you shoved words in her mouth or she's got it arse over tit.'

'Let's see if I've got this right.' Baker sat back, legs crossed, fingers steepled. 'Miss Keating's not a liar, she's a div. But a div as honest as the day's long?' She'd bloody better be, Sarah thought. Both girlfriends were in the nick now, hopefully by this stage casting an eye over exhibits. Frowning slightly, she felt a draught, realised Wilde's leg was pumping like a piston.

'Total bollocks. You think you're so smart, don't you, cop? But that's exactly what I'm saying – you lot twist everything.'

'If that's what you think,' Sarah intervened, 'that's *exactly* why you should have a lawyer.' She reckoned Wilde eschewed a brief assuming he'd be in for an easy ride, that the girlfriends would gold-plate the alibis: end of. He knew he'd go down for the Agnew attack, had no idea how far, but now the ride was going a different route.

'Ask her again.' He cracked a bad boy knuckle. 'I bet you scared her shitless. Knowing Mitch, she'd come out with the first word—'

'Lots of words, Mr Wilde, all written down.' Sarah showed him a pen, in case he'd forgotten what they look like. 'A record of where you and Brody *weren't*. All *not* there in black and white.'

'Nah. Can't be right.' He cracked another knuckle. 'Let me have a word with her.'

Baker guffawed. 'Funny boy.'

'Look, I don't know why she's saying this stuff, but I ain't lying, mister.'

Baker put a hand to his ear. 'Is there an echo in here, DI Quinn?'

'Fuck's sake, stop dicking round.'

'Dicking around?' Baker snapped. Sharpened the act in a heartbeat. 'I don't think so, sonny. I'm *dead* serious. Foster snuffed it this morning.' He let the breaking news sink in. Wilde's leg stilled, his glance darted rapidly between the detectives. 'Way I see it,' Baker said, 'you're now looking at two murder charges. Is that serious enough for you?'

'No way.' He shrank back in the chair. 'I don't know the guy, never been near him in my life.'

'Does the name Walter Fielding mean anything to you?' Sarah's constant watch on Wilde paid off, she was pretty sure she'd detected a fractional narrowing of his eyes.

'Nothin'. Why?'

'You tell me.'

'Frank Gibbs. Heard of him?' Baker barked.

'No I soddin' haven't. What is this?'

Sarah and Baker took turns to reveal the findings at the squat, the baton passing between them aimed at keeping the youth on his toes. He came back every time with flat denials, increasingly desperate. So desperate, she was almost inclined to believe he didn't have all the answers.

'Take my advice, Mr Wilde. If you're shielding anyone, protecting accomplices – now's the time to say. As it stands, you and Brody are on your own. Are you really prepared to take the entire rap?'

'No I'm sodding not. But I haven't got the first idea what you're banging on about. All I know is I'm innocent. I ain't killed no one. Please . . . you've gotta believe me.'

'Because of course . . .' Baker leaned across the table this time, pointedly fingering the fading bruise round his eye. 'You never tell lies, do you?'

'I want a break.' He dropped his head to his chest. 'I need a piss.'

'Makes a change from taking it, sonny.'

Wilde couldn't have timed the stoppage better if he'd tried. His problem? It was in the cops' favour. Half-an-hour later when the interview resumed, Sarah and Baker were already installed. She'd grabbed a coffee, not had a chance to drink it yet. The lidded cup stood on the table, out of harm's way from another recent addition – a plastic evidence bag. Wilde flicked it a glance as he shuffled to his seat.

Baker did the honours with the tapes this time, ran through the spiel, dived straight in: 'That your hoodie, Wilde?'

'No.'

'Take a closer look if I were you.

'You're not.'

'That's right, son. And I'm not facing the rest of my mean miserable little life behind bars. Now take a look. Is that your hoodie?'

'Can't see it proper.'

Baker signalled Sarah. Forensics had lifted multiple DNA and blood samples from the material, the latex gloves she snapped on were superfluous, wouldn't hurt though if the touch of drama unnerved Wilde. Holding it by the shoulders, she glanced at Wilde then at the hoodie. 'What do you reckon, chief? Good fit or what?'

'Perfect, DI Quinn. Cinder-sodding-rella.'

'Never seen it before in me life.' Why was he trembling then?

'Another echo.' Baker shook his head. 'Need to get the acoustics sorted. Or you're gonna have to change the record, Wilde.'

'Read my lips, cop: it ain't my gear.'

'Read mine: Michelle Keating's given a sworn statement identifying it as your property.'

'Bullshit.'

'Even has a happy snap. You wearing it sitting outside some pub, having a fag. Might even have been that same fag that burned the sleeve? DI Quinn?' Sarah helpfully pointed her pen at a small hole near the cuff. 'Michelle recalls you being right racked off about that.'

'OK. Lay off. It's mine.' He dropped his head in his hands. *Result.*

Every interview has a pivotal moment: were they seconds away from a full confession?

Sarah cut the chief a glance, saw the film of sweat across his top lip.

'And the blood?' Baker went for the metaphorical jugular. Wilde's tapping foot overrode the sounds of the tapes. Five seconds. Ten. Scared of losing it, or playing for time? The chief gave a gentle nudge. 'Well?'

He looked up, ran both hands across his shaved head. 'I dunno. Look, mister, it's my hoodie but I ain't set eyes on it in weeks. I left it somewhere, thought I lost it.'

'*Evidently* not, Mr Wilde. I'll tell you what you've lost.' Baker's cold civility sent a shiver down Sarah's spine. 'You've just waved goodbye to every shred of credibility.'

THIRTY-THREE

'**A**re we charging them then, chief?' Sarah winced; a sip of coffee had scalded her tongue. Baker's plate was barely visible under a mixed grill. She averted a hungry gaze. Have to grab a bite on the hoof. She needed to nip out, hoped the chief's debrief wouldn't take long. No reason it should. Leroy Brody's interview had followed similar lines to Wilde's. If anything Brody had capitulated quicker even though the hoodie Lily identified had no telltale burn, handy name tag, as if. He'd claimed ownership anyway, had no explanation for its recent whereabouts. But, like Wilde, flatly denied any knowledge of the murder.

'We've got a few hours yet. I'm tempted to let them sweat. See what comes out.'

Perspiration? She didn't share. 'Think they'll cough? Ouch.' She reached for more milk. Even with pretty solid forensics on the table, cops always favoured full taped confessions. A recorded mea culpa often eased cases past the crown prosecution people, could make a trial easier on victims and/or their families, sway juries and factor in the sentence meted out by the court. Confessions weren't bulletproof, they were easy enough to withdraw. But PACE worked both ways. Defendants found it a damn sight harder to claim police threats, let alone fists, forced their hands. Wilde and Brody had yet to oblige with a full admission – so it was academic anyway – and as it stood, Sarah reckoned the evidence including forensic could be harder.

'Don't rightly care.' He was having trouble squirting the ketchup. 'Case against is solid enough.' *Bit more dirty linen packed in wouldn't hurt.* She kept shtum, stirred the coffee. 'I can see you've got a poker up your ass, Quinn. Come on, spit it out.'

She swallowed, so didn't want that image in her head. 'I'm not really sure, chief, it's just—'

'Feminine intuition? Don't say it, Quinn. They're going down. Bang to bloody rights.' Like the ketchup, she watched as he dabbed a blob off his shirt.

'I know that.' Blowing on the coffee. 'I guess I'd be happier if we could flush the others out, put a bit of flesh on the thing.' It seemed more and more to her that Wilde and Brody were only part of the story. She could, just, get her head round the honour-among-thieves concept. But with murder in the equation? That surely upped the stakes? As cops, they obviously couldn't offer the youths a deal, but hints dropped by Baker had been heavier than a lead coffin. 'Wouldn't you think they'd want to spread the blame, chief?'

'Are you back on the naïve pills, Quinn?' He took a slurp of tea. 'Besides, we only have it on hearsay there's anyone else involved. And if there are more bad boys skulking round out there, d'you really think Wilde and Brody are gonna drop mates in the shit? Get real, woman.'

She shrugged. He was entitled to an opinion, didn't mean he was right. Didn't stop him trying to convince her otherwise either. At knifepoint, given the way he was jabbing his eating iron. 'There's an old saying, Quinn, about birds and bushes. Well, seems to me we're holding two cocks by the short and curlies. So what's your grouse?'

God he was milking the avian line. She tried hard not to roll her eyes. What they could really do with were results from the labs, a blood match with the murder victim and/or Foster-Fielding would mean a case so tight David Blaine would have trouble wriggling out.

'OK, OK, Quinn, I get it.' She raised an eyebrow, hadn't said a word. 'Call the labs. Get 'em to fast-track the results. Break the sodding budgets.'

She masked a smile. Telepathic, eyes in the back of his head, Rhinestone Cowboy, was there no end to the man's talents? 'Cheers, chief. You know it makes —'

'Say sense, Quinn, and I change my mind.'

She so hoped not. It was more than twenty-four hours since she'd put a rocket up the lab's backside.

'The stupid woman can't just change her mind.' Sarah held open the driver's door as she stared up at Harries who was gazing down from the squad room window. He'd spotted her crossing the car park and caught her on the phone.

'Well she has, and she won't.' Harries shrugged. Talk about good news, bad news, no news. Patricia Malone had finally surfaced but no longer wanted to talk to the police. She'd arrived at the fire-damaged house a short time ago, refused to cooperate with the uniformed officer posted outside. Ideally, he'd have driven her to the nick so she could help police inquiries. As for no news: Beth Lally and Jed Holmes had so far drawn a blank at Harborne. A few house-to-house inquiries needed mopping up, but that would have to wait until owners got back from work. 'She just won't budge, boss. And another thing – report just in says the fire wasn't arson, a chip pan had been left on a low burner.'

Another theory bites the dust? 'Where is she now?' Sarah tapped a foot. *If she's disappeared again . . .*

'Gone back to the friend she was visiting before the fire. It's why she wasn't around last night.' *DC Einstein.* Sarah's foot was doing a Wilde. 'See, this friend took ill and—'

'Not what I asked.' Curt. Even from where she stood she saw him bristle.

'Bartley Green. Reservoir Road.'

'I take it the house has a number?' The civil tone belied the snide intent. What was wrong with the bloody guy?

'I don't think it'll do any good, boss.'

'What's the frigging number?' He'd have heard that without the phone. The holler had sent a magpie flying off the wall, yacking nineteen to the dozen. One for sorrow? Would it count double if she crossed her eyes?

'Sixty-seven.'

'Thanks. Sorry, Dave.' She took a deep breath. Hardly his fault Malone was pissing them round. Sarah couldn't explain even to herself why she'd invested so much in what one woman might have to say, it was a hell of a lot riding on someone who could turn out to be a flake. 'Fancy meeting me there?' She checked her watch: half-two. 'Say around four?'

'Sure thing boss.' He gave a thumb's up from the window. She was forgiven then. 'Where you heading now?'

'Visiting the sick.' On a mercy make-up mission. 'Seeing your ex.'

'Below the belt and then some, boss.' He raised a wry eyebrow. He ought to know it was a wind-up. If anything convinced her Dave no longer held a torch for the reporter, it was his muted reaction when she'd told him about the attack. Sure he'd shown interest, but not the impassioned concern of someone who wanted to get into King's pants.

'Later.' She threw him a smile. 'Actually, Dave, hold on a min. Did Patricia Malone say why she wouldn't talk?'

'Yeah. Apparently it was about the only thing she did come out with. She said it was wrong to talk ill of the dead.'

*   *   *

The hinges on King's front door had the loudest creak Sarah had ever heard. Though the nervous tingle she felt entering the modest semi had nothing to do with the Hammer Horror sound track, more the weird sensation she shouldn't really be there. Like she was a cat burglar or something. The concept was absurd given the list of items in her hand and King's specific instructions in her head where to locate them. Maybe the temptation to carry out a little extra-curricular snooping had brought on the fanciful notion about breaking and entering. Even though they'd known each other getting on for twelve years, she'd never set foot in any of the reporter's homes. No great surprise, she supposed. They'd socialised occasionally early on but were hardly bosom buddies. But there was a saying about gift horses – make that hacks – and mouths. Cops learned a lot about people, seeing the way they live, what books they read, music they like. Any insight she might pick up here would be trespassing into King's personal space not private property. A thought crime then? Sarah curved a lip. No way, given that at King's request, she'd be rifling her knicker drawer in a minute.

Gasping for a drink, she headed for the kitchen first. The spare BlackBerry should be on top of the dresser and if there was a microwave, her pasty could be zapping while she rummaged round finding the rest of the bits and bobs. Bingo times two. Phone located and ping-cuisine. Timer on the microwave set, she ran the cold tap, eyed the mess as she slaked her thirst. A plate in the sink held a solitary bean, a sliced white loaf lay open on top of the bread bin, surfaces were cluttered, cupboards ajar. King was no closet Delia harbouring desires to clean up on the domestic front. Sarah could live with that, she'd eat out every night and rather take collars than iron them any day.

The sitting room was off piste but she popped her head round the door. It was lava lamps meets Laura Ashley with an ailing orchid in the far corner. She seemed to recall Caroline had inherited the house when her mother died some months back. Either the reporter had gone for the retro look or Momma King had been stuck in a time warp. A couple of Dulux brochures splayed on a corduroy bean bag more or less answered the point. Would Sarah's place resemble as much of a tip if she didn't have a cleaner? Oh yes? One question she couldn't answer: was Caroline intending to tart up the house prior to putting it on the market, or wanted it looking good because she planned on using it more. Surely she wasn't thinking of moving back to Birmingham? As if. She shook her head, dismissed the thought.

Standing in the bathroom, she gave a low whistle; she'd seen beauty counters with fewer products. Shelf after glass shelf was lined with bottles, canisters, tubes; porcelain containers held blusher brushes, cotton wool, tweezers, scissors, shavers, hair brushes, combs; refills and overspill crammed a three-drawer trolley. Looking like King must cost a small fortune. She could certainly check if she was worth it: *Mirror, mirror on the wall? Every sodding wall.* Sarah sniffed. The make-up wasn't even in here. She shook her head, bagged toiletries and electric toothbrush, took off for the bedroom muttering, 'Who's the fairest . . .'

She half expected animal prints and scarlet satin sheets so wasn't surprised, a little disappointed at the predictability perhaps. The slap had its own vanity case, she grabbed it then padded across the room, vaguely musing whether Dave had savoured the delights of the king-size? Probably best not to go there. She opened the top drawer of the oak tallboy, found the ivory lace knickers, had a nose at the label: size eight. Damn. The silk nightie was under the pillow along with a Kindle. So far so . . . She raised an eyebrow, bet Caroline had forgotten she'd left the vibrator there. *Moving on . . .*

The office down the landing looked as if a bomb had hit it, freezing, too. If the tidy-desk-tidy-mind maxim held true, King's head must be a right shambles. Sarah picked her way across a carpet littered with newspapers and magazines to a desk covered in files and loose papers. She lifted some of the clutter, still couldn't see the laptop. King had been spot-on up to now. Frowning, she shuffled more paperwork – nada, no voice recorder either. A bit of daylight might help. She turned, snapped the blind. Oh shit. The circular hole in the window was the neatest thing in the room, the glass expertly cut and removed. No wonder the room was like a fridge. Shivering she looked out, somehow doubting the burglar would have left footprints. Looked like a professional job to her. Was King's attack part and parcel of the break-in, or mere coincidence? Startled, she jumped when the microwave pinged. Nowhere near as much as when she felt an arm lock round her throat.

THIRTY-FOUR

'**S**tay exactly where you are.' Boozy breath on her cheek, menacing hiss in her ear. Voice faintly familiar? No time to pursue the suspicion. In the fight or flight stakes, fleeing was out. Adrenalin flooded her body, zinged in her veins, the rush more tsunami than tidal. Heart pounded ribs, blood whooshed in both ears. She *so* should have realised the potential danger. Almost instantly, her training kicked-in; she jerked a knee forward, kicked back, rammed her heel hard against the bastard's shin.

He screamed, buckled, lost the grip. 'Fuck you do that for?'

Spinning round, fist raised, breath coming fast and shallow, Sarah registered who it was even before seeing Hardy crouched over, gingerly fingering already reddening skin. 'If you ever try a trick like that again—'

'You'll what?' He cut her a pained glance, bloodshot eyes watering. 'Smash my head in. Beat me senseless? Passed the police brutality course with flying colours, did you, DI Quinn?' *Verbal attack best form of defence? Or was he hacked off at being brought to his knees?*

'Police brute . . .' Her mouth gaped. Un-sodding-believable. 'You know me for fuck's sake. What the hell did you think you were doing?' He was lucky she'd not aimed higher.

'As far as I was concerned, you were a burglar about to leg it through that.' He tilted his head at the window, presumably so she wouldn't catch the fleeting sly grin. She had. And the stubble, and sheen of sweat. Suit looked as if he'd slept in it.

Eyes narrowed, she crossed her arms. 'Total bollocks. You knew it was me. And you knew exactly what you were doing. I want to know why?' Frigging joker. Did he see it as some sort of puerile payback for their past crossed swords? A role reversal where he came out on top for a change? Or had he fancied a sleazy game of cop and robber? Bloody weirdo.

'Fair dos. I got it wrong.' Standing, staggering slightly, he brushed the fringe out of his eyes, ran his gaze up and down her body. 'I see now I caught you in the middle of a police raid.'

'Police raid?' She took a deep breath, cautioned herself not to get wound up. Patently, he was pissed as a fart factory. She told him why she was there. Caroline's attack was apparently news to the reporter. Toeing the carpet, head down, he put her in mind of a sulky schoolboy. And she still didn't know what game he'd been playing. He *must* have known it was her. She'd probably called it right a minute ago: it was a lame trick.

'I hear what you say, inspector. But it wouldn't be the first time your lot raided a journalist's house, took away files and computers, would it? That's when you get the right address, of course.'

'Hardy.' She took a step towards him, held finger and thumb tight inches from his face. 'You are this close to me running you in for assault.'

'Yeah and that's another thing.' Like she hadn't spoken. '*You* say I knew it was you. But you had your back to me. And it all happened so fast. I get home, see a man in black by the window, assume he's Burglar Bill – and boom. Mistaken identity, your honour. I rest my case.' Hardy's fairy stories were all over the place, he clearly liked his latest spin. But his lopsided smile fell flat when he saw her face.

'When?'

'When what?' He drew his brows together.

'When exactly did you get home?'

'Just now.' Jabbing a thumb over his shoulder towards the hall.

'You're a liar.' Even if the front door didn't sound like something out of Dracula's castle, Sarah's hearing was acuter than a colony of bats. 'You were here all the time.' More than that, she'd bet he'd deliberately crept into the office to scare the pants off her. He was torn, she could see that. Chewing his bottom lip, he couldn't maintain eye contact. Either he'd come clean or keep up the façade. If he lied again, he was a gnat's eyelash from being taken in for questioning.

'You're right.' He raised both hands in surrender. 'I saw you . . . I thought it'd be a bit of a lark. It was stupid and I'm sorry.'

'You're nicked, Hardy.' Not. She couldn't be arsed but she'd never seen anyone sober up so fast in her life.

Panic-stricken eyes searched her face, trembling hands reached out in appeal. 'Honest to God, I was only playing the fool, I'd never have hurt you, wouldn't hurt anyone. *Please* believe me. I could lose my job over this.'

'I should care why?' She slipped a hand in her pocket.

'Look, I know you don't owe me any favours.'

'Got that right.'

'I was supposed to be in London. I called in sick.'

'Sick? Got that right, too.'

'Please, inspector. I'd been on a bender. I was out of it. Sometimes, the pressure . . .'

Superman? How wrong can you be? Lip curled, she raised a palm then pointed to the stairs.

'Please, Sarah, I'll do anything.'

'Kitchen. Pronto. And it's DI Quinn to you.' Sodding pasty was probably cold by now. She ate it leaning against the sink listening to Hardy's whines. It took five minutes to elicit that he'd crawled back to the house around eight a.m., stumbled into bed in a drunken stupor. He told her the place could have been raided by the SAS and he wouldn't have heard a thing. Sarah's arrival seven hours later had finally penetrated his alcoholic fog.

As lies go it was piss poor; ironically she was inclined to believe it. She'd no doubt a reporter was capable of making up better porkies. Hardy's sob story wasn't one he'd share unless he had to.

She turned her back, brushed crumbs into the sink, told him he'd be let off with a warning this time. 'Clean up your act, Hardy.'

'Thanks. I owe you.'

Big time. And it could be useful having a tame reporter on side. She nipped back upstairs, made a quick call, picked up the bag and case of goodies. When she popped her head in the kitchen, Hardy still sat on a stool staring at his hands. 'Forensics are on the way. They'll need pointing in the right direction. Make yourself useful: scout round, see if anything obvious is missing, or something's here that shouldn't be. Don't touch anything. When you're in a fit state, go see Caroline. She needs a friend. I'll catch you later.'

Might well do at that. For the moment, he'd get the benefit of the doubt. Boozed up or not, Hardy had sneaked in, grabbed her by the throat, proceeded to spin a string of increasingly risible lies. Pathetic piss-head or man prepared to use force? At the very least, he needed keeping an eye on.

THIRTY-FIVE

Harries sat in an unmarked police motor a few doors down from the Bartley Green council house. Keeping an eye on the mirrors, he saw the Audi's lights flash and was stamping cold feet on the pavement as Sarah drew up behind. The showdown with Hardy plus the school-run traffic had both had a knock-on effect. Gone four already, the DI had yet to drop by the hospital, King's belongings lay on the back seat. Grabbing her bag, Sarah opened the door, scanned the road in both directions. Amber street lighting washed the near identical red-brick semis a sickly shade of orange, some downstairs rooms had curtains drawn against the dark and thin off-white lines where the material didn't quite meet.

'Thought you'd got lost, boss.' Harries jangled keys in his pocket. His dig was tongue-in-cheek, she knew her way round the city better than his satnav.

'I did, Dave. In a saddo's fantasies.' Walking in step to the house, she gave him edited lowlights of the not so brief encounter at King's place.

'Sounds hairy. Are you OK?' She heard concern in his voice, saw it in his face when she cut him a glance.

'The idiot took me by surprise, that's all.' Even sober, Hardy wouldn't measure up in the self defence stakes. After the initial shock, one of her biggest fears was that if she'd not clicked who it was so fast, she'd have inflicted real damage. The other was that both she and Hardy had inadvertently trampled a crime scene and potentially compromised evidence.

'He's lucky I wasn't there.' Manly sniff. 'I'd have punched his lights out.'

Testosterone central. 'Fancy directing traffic again, do you, Dave?' she drawled.

'Come on, you could've been hurt.'

'I can take care of myself, thanks.' Looking ahead, she narrowed her eyes. 'Tell me it's not the house with the gnomes.'

'It's not the house with the gnomes. He lied.'

'Shit.'

'Not scared, are you?' he joshed. 'Not the woman who can take care of herself?'

Gnomes gave her the creeps. In her head, they were on a puke-par with ventriloquist dummies and porcelain dolls. She could probably trace the revulsion back to childhood, but it wasn't something she'd go out of her way to pin down. Mostly, they didn't impinge. Right now the little freaks were unavoidable. The small lawn outside number sixty-seven was Gnome Village: garish figures with inane beams dangled fishing rods, others held pipes to their mouths, a few clung on to wheelbarrows. There were wishing wells, bridges spanning plastic ponds, miniature bird baths, spotted toadstools strung with fairy lights.

'Not a big fan then, boss?'

'How can I put it? No.' She shuddered as they walked past the colony on the way to the door. 'I'm surprised they don't get nicked.'

'They do. Are you after me?' Turning in sync, Sarah and Harries saw a small dumpy woman wearing a cloche hat and clutching a Co-op shopping bag to her chest. Her dark deep-set eyes shrank further. 'Are you cops?'

Their nod was synchronized, too. 'Yes, I'm—'

'Took your time didn't you? I phoned Friday.' The woman barged past, key in hand. 'You'd best come in. First on the right. I won't be a tick.'

Trailing in they watched her disappear through a door at the end of the narrow hall. The bloody things had invaded the sitting room, too. Open-mouthed, Sarah looked round, realised gnomes were the least of her worries, just the tip of the little people iceberg. There were dozens – make that scores – of dwarves, leprechauns, pixies, fairies, trolls. Just about every available space had been taken over; even the walls were cluttered with calendars, clocks, paintings, posters. Sarah sighed. 'Now I know how Gulliver felt.'

'Who?' Harries asked.

Finger to lips, she shook her head. The little woman bustled in carrying a stack of photo albums in her arms. 'Right then. Sit yourselves down.' She scurried across the room, flopped on a wing chair by the fire, slipped off her shoes. Her stockinged feet didn't quite reach the red carpet. 'I'm Mrs French. Dora. But you'll know that any road up.'

'Actually, Mrs French—'

'Take the weight off your feet, love.' She waved a tiny liver-spotted hand towards a gold velveteen settee. Sarah clocked lilac streaks in Mrs French's tight white perm and reckoned a brickie had laid her foundation. 'I don't mind you taking a few photos away. Long as I get 'em back. Think they'll put 'em on *Crimewatch* with that nice Kirsty Wark?'

'Young,' Harries muttered.

'Whatever.' She was leafing through an album with a beatific smile on her face. 'Yeah, here you go. This lot was nicked Thursday night. John, Paul, Mattie, Mark, Dai, Freddo—'

'Mrs French,' Sarah said. 'I'm sorry for your loss. But we're not . . .'

An incredulous Harries nudged Sarah, mouthing her words back at her, 'Sorry for your loss?'

'Thieving bastards. Think they're having a laugh.' Her head shot up. 'What did you say?'

'We're not here about the gnomes. We need a word with Patricia Malone.'

She rubbed the heel of her hand against a damp cheek. 'That's all well and good but what about my—'

'I'll get a patrol out, but right now can you tell your friend we're here?'

'She knows.' A tall, thin woman leaned in the doorway. 'Knew the minute I saw you get out the cars.' She pointed up. 'I was in the window.'

Watching? Why? 'Mrs Malone.' Sarah stood, bridged the gap, hand outstretched. 'I'm Detective Inspector Sarah Quinn.'

'You can be Sarah Palin for all I care.' Brushing away the hand. 'I thought I'd made it abundantly clear. I've got nothing to say to the police.' Almost Sarah's height, Malone still managed to give the impression she was looking down her nose. Her large washed-out grey eyes were rimmed red and virtually lash free. She dragged a hand down her beige face, leaving faint trail marks in the dry skin.

Sarah held the woman's gaze. 'But you did care, Mrs Malone. Enough to make the first move.'

'A mistake's what I made.'

Liar. Sarah bit her tongue. It struck her Malone was scared. 'Please, Mrs Malone, just tell me why you rang.' Apart from ascribing Foster a different name.

'There's no point.'

'Please, Mrs Malone.' Gentle voice, no pressure. 'Let me be the judge of that.'

'God's sake, Patsy, tell her. I'm making a brew.' Dora French jumped out of the chair, patted her friend's arm on the way out. 'Go and sit down, love. Remember, you don't owe the bastard waste-of-space nothing.'

Sarah watched Mrs Malone trudge across the room and sink into an armchair. The woman stared into the middle distance, wringing her hands. The DI waited thirty seconds or so then walked across and knelt beside her. 'Remember what, Mrs Malone?'

'He's dead now so it doesn't matter, does it?'

'What doesn't matter, Mrs Malone?'

'He can't hurt no more kids, can he?'

Once Malone started, the story seeped like sewage. Page after page of Harries' notebook was full: names, dates, dirt, sleaze. Twenty years ago, she'd been in a relationship with Wally Fielding a.k.a. Sean William Foster. Loved him, she'd said. Worshipped the ground he walked on. They'd not married, hadn't lived together. Maybe if they had it wouldn't have happened, social services' checks would've been more stringent. Malone might've picked up on signs. Fact was they'd been lovers, partners, call it what you will, on and off for a decade and she'd not suspected a thing.

That over a period of six years, he'd systematically abused every foster child in her care. Boys. Girls. Seven in all. Mostly teenagers.

Malone related how she used to take in troubled youngsters, kids no one else wanted, kids with no self-esteem, kids who already felt like rubbish. And who after falling into Fielding's paws ultimately felt like shit. Not at first. He was like a father-figure, invested his time, doled out pocket money, played games, helped with homework, built their trust, made them feel good – then demanded favours in return. For favours, read sex.

'How could she not have known, boss?' Harries sat alongside Sarah in the Audi, playing a bottle of water between his hands. She'd just put in a call to the squad, tasked a team of DCs with verifying Malone's statement, liaising with social workers, tracing victims. She and Harries needed a little time out now, mull over the sordid story before going their separate ways. What they really needed was a long hot shower.

'They say love's blind, Dave.' She pictured Malone sitting there, wringing her hands, tears streaming down her crepe face. 'Unless she knew all along, and cast a blind eye. Her reasons for not turning the bastard in sound dodgy to me.'

The last victim had finally plucked up courage to tell Malone what was going on. She claimed the minute she knew, she'd taken a knife to Fielding, threatened him with the police. He'd begged, pleaded, promised he'd never touch another child. He told her he'd leave the country, change his name, never show his face again. She eventually relented after he swore literally on the Bible he'd seek treatment. Malone maintained it was only after contacting the other kids that she realised the scale of the abuse. By then, she'd no idea where he was and decided, as she put it, to let sleeping dogs lie.

'Ask me she let a lying dog sleep with under-age kids,' Harries said. 'And why do the decent thing now?' Seeing the so-called Foster's picture on the TV news was the catalyst.

Malone said the thought he was back in circulation possibly harming more young people was one she couldn't live with. 'Did you buy that line, boss?'

'More I think about it, more I think she's a self-serving bitch.' Sarah tapped the wheel with her fingers. 'My feeling's she failed to come forward before because she was intent on saving her own sorry ass. I've no idea whether she was complicit in what went on but I reckon she was shit scared no one would believe her and she'd be implicated.'

'That's a bit harsh, isn't it?' He frowned.

She turned to face him. 'What's harsh is Fielding/Foster, whatever his fucking name is, getting away with molesting vulnerable youngsters for way too long. So pardon me if my heart's not bleeding for Patricia-mealy-mouthed-Malone.'

He turned a cold shoulder. 'I suppose you think she left the chip pan on deliberately so she could fiddle the insurance.'

'Don't be a twat, Dave. That line's even beneath Baker.' The bloody woman had seemed genuinely gutted about the fire and losing the house, more so than about kids losing their innocence under its roof. She sniffed. Mind, she'd be distraught, too, if it meant staying in Gnome Towers.

He faced her again. 'Yeah well, pardon me if I don't hang on your every word, DI Quinn. Your not liking Malone doesn't make her guilty of anything let alone helping someone molest kids.'

'That's the whole bloody point.' She clenched a fist. 'No one's guilty. She's dumped it all on him. He's in no position to answer back. Who takes the blame now? Crime and punishment, Dave. Crime and pun . . .' She narrowed her eyes.

Harries saw it too. 'It was payback time, wasn't it, boss? The mugging.'

Almost certain, she nodded. Perhaps if they'd not been wading through a sewer, they'd have spotted the connection sooner. Big question now, were the other attacks linked to sex offenders, paedophiles, perverts? The names Zach Wilde and Leroy Brody had meant nothing to Malone. So where, if anywhere, did the youths fit in? The potential development opened a new network of inquiry lines. They tossed round a few ideas: did either of the other mugging victims have a

murky past? Duncan Agnew was a captive audience, so to
speak. As for the Chambers Row murder victim, surely they'd
get an ID any time soon. Baker had elicited Frank Gibbs' data
from the credit card company; Beth Lally and Jed were working
on firming up any possible link with Tattoo Man. A news
release bigging up the body work had also gone out.

'Grab anyone you like to help with the digging, Dave. And
keep Baker sweet, tell him what's going on. Come on, shift
your butt.' She smiled, turned the engine. 'I'll see you back
at the ranch.'

'Betcha.' She watched him clamber out, waited for the door
to close but he popped his head back, pitiful look on his face.
'I'm sorry for your loss.' The head slowly shook. 'I can't
believe you said that, boss.'

She patted her chest. 'Under this hard exterior beats a heart
of reinforced granite, Dave.' Revved the engine. 'And watch
the lip. One more pop, and you're on gnome patrol.'

THIRTY-SIX

'Tell me you're joking.' Propped up on pillows, Caroline
King pressed a distraught hand to her face, winced,
then carelessly let the hand drop. Hearing about
the break-in had caused enough emotional damage for her
momentarily to forget the physical. Eyes glistening, she said,
'Tell me the laptop's still there.'

'I'm sorry, Caroline. The recorder's gone, too.' Hands clasped
in front, Sarah stood at the foot of the bed in the private room.
Ruby Wells, resembling someone on a Vogue shoot, lounged
back in an armchair with legs crossed. Half-a-dozen empty cups
and an almost empty box of Black Magic suggested the tea party
had been going on some time. When Sarah first walked in and
spotted the two women's heads together, she'd assumed Caroline
was after legal advice, hadn't realised the reporter and lawyer
were friends. Christ, why hadn't not-so-Millie-no-mates
recruited Ruby as errand girl? Mind, it looked as if the lawyer

had been too busy bearing gifts: a beribboned bottle of Chablis and a stack of glossy mags stood on the bedside table. Apart from depositing Caroline's bags, Sarah had brought only bad news.

'The forensic guys are still in there,' she said. 'But don't hold your breath. Thanks to CSI, even the densest crim knows about DNA these days.' Sarah reckoned the job had a professional cast to it anyway, the average opportunist thief didn't carry glass cutters and an apparent shopping list in his back pocket. 'On the bright side—'

'What fucking bright side,' Caroline snapped, grabbed a tissue. 'Sorry.'

She let it go, could see King was genuinely cut up. 'As I say, on the bright side, the rest of the house was untouched.' Nat Hardy had phoned Sarah with the info, his voice a cross between grovel and ingratiating. 'So either the burglar panicked for some reason before having a chance to move on—'

'Or the office was targeted.' Caroline nodded, licked a dry cracked lip. Clearly nothing wrong with the speed of her reactions now and she was patently thinking it through. Sarah wondered if their conclusions would tally, assuming King shared. She asked the reporter if she'd been working on anything sensitive. *Like, doh.* King's book on girl grooming had sod all to do with hygiene products. And they both knew she'd been sniffing round Jas Ram.

She blew her nose. 'Everything I work on's sensitive.' *Since when had King joined MI6?* The DI bit her tongue; King's self-pitying rant wasn't over yet. 'It's a nightmare. My whole fucking life's on that laptop.'

'Tell me about it.' Ruby handed King another tissue. 'I'd be in the same boat if I didn't back everything up.'

Sarah played a mental violin. Fact was King had told no one anything. It was an old trick: hyperbole a great way to dodge questions. Sarah gave a disarmingly warm smile and threw another. 'The most sensitive and recent assignment being?'

Jas Ram's finishing school for girls? As in finishing off any chance of a bright future. Now Sarah came to think of it, the last time she'd seen Ruby Wells had been the night of Ram's drink-drive incident when they'd been exiting the nick together. She cut the lawyer a covert glance. Was there more to her visiting the sick than met the eye? Were the women cooking up something tasty to go with the wine? Something that said Ram on the tin?

'Seriously, Caroline, maybe I ought to . . .' The lawyer placed both hands on the chair arms, made to stand, she'd already offered to leave when Sarah arrived. So maybe the DI's suspicions were wrong. Either way, the gesture had let King wriggle off the hook. Again.

'Don't go, Ruby.' The reporter waved her down. 'I'll need cheering up even more when she's gone.'

She? Thanks, pet. 'No worries. I've got to get back.' Missing the brief wasn't an option. Heavy traffic had already added to the journey time here and she had to battle through more to make it to the nick before six. She fully intended questioning King further, certainly needed more than a few snatched minutes. Besides, even if the reporter was happy to have a third partner in on the session, Sarah wasn't. She'd try and fit in a visit on the way home, King had lots to digest mentally in the interim. No harm throwing in an extra morsel before she left.

Slipping car keys out of her coat pocket, she kept her gaze on Caroline. 'Seems to me, whoever broke in to your place almost certainly knew it was empty. Maybe someone watched you leave, or knew where you were going?' *Because her absence had been rigged?* 'Think on, eh?'

The sighs of relief were audible as Sarah walked away. She waited until reaching the door then turned. 'Oh, and Miss Wells?'

'DI Quinn?' Reaching for the Black Magic.

'We've got a sweepstake running at work.' She tapped the side of her nose. 'Was he pissed that night? Jas Ram?' The line was a less than subtle message: don't underestimate me. She'd couched it as a joke to add shock factor. Maybe catch Wells on the hop, force an indiscretion? She also saw it as lobbing a brick into a stagnant pond, you never knew what slime might surface.

It landed a brittle laugh and a pointed finger of mock

censure: 'Client confidentiality, DI Quinn.' Smiling, she popped a chocolate in her mouth. Too canny to take the bait? Not on-the-ball enough to recognise it? Or simply playing along?

She offered another cue. 'A nod's as good as a wink?'

'That would be telling, wouldn't it, inspector? Surely you don't expect help cheating?'

She'd been unsure what to expect. But certainly nothing could camouflage the horror, however fleeting, Sarah had seen race across Caroline's face. Her reaction on hearing Ram's name had to be genuine because given a choice she'd not let anything slip, her defences were tighter than the Old Bailey during a terrorist trial.

'Everything OK, Caroline?' Sarah asked casually. 'Something coming back to you?'

'Let's think.' She flashed a fake smile, flopped back, arms folded. 'My face looks like mouldy pizza, my house's been burgled, my laptop's been nicked, I've lost years of work, and I'm stuck here in hospital with you asking daft questions. Life really couldn't get any peachier, could it?'

Brilliant smokescreen. Total bullshit. Sarah knew what she'd seen. Hearing Ram's name had sparked the reaction, something in the exchange had definitely registered with King. She'd give a lot to know what. The throwaway line had been a shot in the dark. Seemed to Sarah it had set a big cat among the proverbial pigeons.

THIRTY-SEVEN

'I hate to say it but the DI was right.' Ruby Wells poured water into a tumbler, handed it over with a smile. 'You looked as if you'd seen a ghost.'

Caroline gave a distracted nod. With her face a bloody mess, she no longer felt threatened by Ruby's good looks. Besides, as she'd discovered, the lawyer was warm, witty, with a cracking sense of humour. What was the saying? Looks aren't everything. As lessons in priorities went, it had hit home. But nowhere near as hard as Quinn's almost parting shot.

'Any better now?' Ruby asked.

She shook her head. She'd not puked in the bathroom, but her stomach still churned and her mouth felt like the Sahara in the dry season. Staring ahead, she took a few sips, rolled the lukewarm liquid round her tongue, picturing not a ghost, hearing a disembodied voice: Quinn's. *Was he pissed that night? Jas Ram?*

Ruby perched on the edge of the bed. 'Was it another flashback?'

'No. Not that.' What Caroline visualised had more substance than four youths dressed in black, scarves round their faces. And they weren't on her mind now. She closed her eyes. *Was he pissed that night?* Ruby had to have been acting for Ram, or Quinn wouldn't have asked the question. Ruby's comeback about client confidentiality had clinched it. The knowledge lit a visual blue touch paper sparking a series of images in Caroline's head: Ram sitting opposite her in San Luigi's, the seemingly harmless flirting, pathetic jokes about bus passes and the cost of travel cards because *a little bird* had revealed Ram's spot of bother with the law. How had he put it? *A little bird with a big mouth.* It hadn't occurred to Caroline for an instant that in Ram's mind there could be only one contender for the canary title. She groaned as her mental romcom turned into a black and white still straight from Hitchcock: a dead crow, its mangled carcass splayed across a windscreen.

'You're blatantly knackered, Caroline. I'm gonna let you get some rest.' The reporter felt a slight draught, caught a waft of Ruby's Chanel No. 5 as she rose. She watched her reach for her bag, pointing at the box of Black Magic. 'And lay off the chocolates, put some behind your ear for later.' They'd joked earlier about Ruby almost scoffing the lot even though she'd brought them as a gift. Caroline reckoned that in a minute or two the lawyer wouldn't give her the time of day.

'Sit down, Ruby, please. I'm not tired. I have to tell you something. God, I feel sick.' She had to spit it out though; that her glib blather had provoked Ram's petty act of revenge and a potentially ongoing threat. How many dirty tricks were still hidden up his designer sleeve?

Ruby smiled uncertainly as she again perched on the bed. 'I told you to lay off the chocs.'

The light hearted quip made it worse somehow. Caroline felt they'd really hit it off over the last hour or so. Chat had flowed freely, personal and professional: childhood, cars, careers. Ruby had waxed lyrical about helping kids who'd had a shit start in life. Charity began at home for Caroline but she respected Ruby's stance. She ran a hand through her hair. 'I wish it was that simple.'

'Hey, come on. I'm sure it's nothing that can't be fixed. It's not the laptop, is it?'

'God. No. Everything's backed up. Two memory sticks.' One of which would be in the vanity case.

'So what is it?'

'Jas Ram.' Ruby listened in silence as Caroline related the story. She tried reading the lawyer's face, reckoned it would be a hell of a long time before Ruby needed Botox. Caroline sighed as she wrapped it up. 'So the crow shit was all down to me and my big mouth. I'm really gutted, Ruby.'

'At least you've made a clean breast of it now. God. How crap was that?' She winked, flashed a grin. 'Look Caroline, it's done. Over. Spilt milk and water bridge. Fact is I'm grateful.' She'd harboured suspicions anyway, she said, had arranged a date to sound Ram out. 'I probably won't bother meeting the bastard now. All he needs know is I've marked his card.'

'Not *probably*, Ruby. Steer clear. He's poison.' Christ, she'd started sounding like the Ice Queen.

'You can talk, Mother. You're still meeting him even after all this.' She swept the room with a glance.

Caroline nodded. She'd finally told Ruby that Ram was definitely among the key players she'd interview for the book. Seemed the decent thing after all the lawyer had done for her. As for Ram, Caroline was almost certain he had nothing to do with her attack. Either way, she had to talk to him and if it emerged he was less than lily white – he'd pay for it. 'I know the score, Ruby. Dealing with scum like Ram's what I do. The sort of people journalists chase, punters generally cross the road to avoid.'

'I'm a lawyer, Caroline.' She bristled a touch. 'The courts are full of lowlifes and losers.'

'I know, sorry.' She smiled. 'But Ram's up for seeing me 'cause he thinks there's something in it for him. Whereas, I'm the one stands to gain. And don't forget, I've done nothing to piss him off.'

'As it happens . . .' She raised a wry eyebrow.

'I know, I know.' Neither had Ruby. The fact she was erroneously in Ram's sights was down to Caroline. 'Look, when I talk to him I'll set the record straight, make sure he knows you're discretion on legs.'

'No body parts, Caroline.' She curled a lip. 'For God's sake don't talk body parts to the slime ball.' She reached a hand for her coat. 'I'm off now. I said I'd meet a couple of mates for a drink. If you ask me, they just want some free legal advice.'

'Are they in trouble?'

'No, but their boyfriends are.' She sneaked another chocolate. 'Yummy. Need anything before I go?'

'Apart from more chocs?' Caroline smiled. 'Actually, can you pass the case?' It might perk her up if she put her face on. The fact that one of the doctors bore more than a passing resemblance to Ryan Gosling had absolutely nothing to do with her decision.

THIRTY-EIGHT

'**A**re you questioning the call, Quinn?' Baker leaned back in his chair, legs crossed, ankle swinging. She'd made good time from the hospital. Hence the pre-brief confab with the chief. She'd been summoned to the sanctum even before making it to her office. And now wished traffic had been snarled. She knew full well what Baker really meant: was she questioning *his* call. He wanted to charge Zach Wilde and Leroy Brody with murder.

She smoothed the still tight bun. 'It might be a touch premature is all I'm saying.'

Baker laced podgy fingers across his paunch, gave her a
fulsome and totally fake smile. 'And why, pray tell, does the
mighty Quinn think we should hang fire? Would she perhaps
prefer a signed confession – in blood?'

She'd not say no to blood test results but it was more than
that. 'Now we know Foster's sleazy history, a bit of extra
digging wouldn't do any harm, chief.'

A tiny muscle clenched at the side of his jaw. 'We've been
told he's a kiddie fiddler. We've not substantiated it yet and
there's nothing on record.' Thanks to Patricia Malone keeping
fucking mum all those years. 'What's your point?'

'Motive. What if offing him was payback time? Wilde and
Brody swear they've never set eyes on him.'

'Cash back more like. To tossers like Wilde and Brody he
was a walking dispenser. They were after his money. Bread.
Dough. Drug habits need feeding, Quinn.'

She shrugged. 'I'm not disagreeing. But what about the
Chambers Row victim? Where's he fit in?'

'Oh yeah. Looks as if we might have a name.' Straightening,
he shuffled a few papers on his desk. *Why the hell hadn't she
been told?* 'It's not long come in.' They'd had it several days
in fact: Frank Gibbs. Potential confirmation was what the chief
meant. He told her uniform had checked out the address
provided by the credit card company. Gibbs lived alone in a
shabby maisonette in Small Heath. Neighbours hadn't seen
him for days, he was quiet, kept himself to himself. *Blah blah,
don't they all?* But not so much that he didn't leave a key
with an elderly woman two doors away. Officers entered,
discovered no sign of life – or rotting body. They also found
a pile of post on the doormat and an old address book by the
phone. A couple of detectives would be working through
the entries any time soon.

She turned her mouth down. 'Is it not worth seeing what they
come up with?'

He waved an airy hand. 'Why prolong the agony?'

Whose? She studied Baker's still-bruised face as he gathered
his bits for the brief, recalled the theory he'd mooted in the

early days of the inquiry, saw him standing in front of the
whiteboards gazing at photographs of the victims' injuries.
What was it he'd said? *Three mugs left looking like raw mince.*
He'd thrown out a question to the squad. Why batter someone
so viciously? And he'd provided an answer. 'Point taken, chief,
but not so long back you were the one reckoned the violence
had to be personal.'

'I can change my mind, can't I? Or is that a woman's
prerogative? You coming or what?' At least he held the door
for her. Squeezing past, she again clocked the fading bruise
near his eye inflicted by Wilde. *As long as you have changed
your mind chief; as long as personal doesn't come into it.*

It wasn't Baker's management style to ask for a show of hands.
He was too confident to seek anyone's approval. But observing
squad reactions to his thinking on why Wilde and Brody should
be charged with murder, Sarah reckoned the result would be
the same as asking turkeys to vote for a moratorium on
Christmas. Bring it on. Looking round at the twenty or so
detectives present, there was none of the backslapping and
high-fiving that usually coincided with nearing the conclusion
of a case. Low key was Sarah's assessment. More as if the
squad was relieved to see the back of Operation Steel. Cops
were only human – some inquiries had more going for them
than others. This one had been a tough hard slog: lots of shoe
leather worn out mostly on plod work.

Perched on a desk at the front, she watched Baker roll a
shirtsleeve. She couldn't deny the chief's arguments had
come across as sound: the youths admitted attacking Duncan
Agnew, they had no alibis for the other attacks, stolen
property had been squirrelled away at the squat, bloodstained
clothing found, apparently prior to being burned. Cases
had been built with less evidence. So why was she sitting
on the fence?

'OK, chaps, chapesses, you know the state of play.' Baker
rolled the other sleeve. 'Let's have a show of hands.' She
tightened her lips. Well, well. What did she know? 'Who
reckons we throw Brody and Wilde some reading matter?' As
in the book.

'Sooner the better, guv.' Propped against his wall space, Twig gave a thumb's up.

'*Encyclopaedia Britannica*,' Hunt drawled. 'From a great height.'

Someone at the back hummed a few bars of *Why are we waiting?*

Sarah cast the squad a glance, didn't bother counting: only Dave's hand was still down. He gave her an encouraging nod from his customary front row seat.

'Well, Quinn.' Baker smiled. 'You appear to be in a minority of one.' In the chief's eyes, Harries obviously didn't count.

'Actually, sir,' Dave piped up. 'I think—'

'I didn't ask you, lad. So do you want to share the benefit of your superior wisdom, inspector?'

'I'm not saying we don't charge them, chief. I'm questioning the timing.' Baker knew her thinking on it. Why belittle her? She brushed imaginary crumbs from her lap.

Harries raised more than a hand this time, he stood. Sarah watched his colour rise, too. 'As a member of the squad, I think I have a right to say what I think. Sir.'

'Do you now, Davy?' Baker smiled, slipped a hand in his pocket.

'Way I see it, DI Quinn's point's valid.' She winced mentally.

'Do go on.' The smile broadened. Her wince deepened. Baker was at his most dangerous when he played nice. Sarah pictured a cat and a baby mouse. The squad scented blood too; its posture sharpened in the newly charged – or not yet charged – air. As long as someone else was on the receiving end, Baker baiting a junior officer was a spectator sport.

'Given what we unearthed this afternoon about Foster, surely we need to explore motive a bit more? I mean what if this guy Frank Gibbs turns out to be some sort of perv as well?'

'You tell me, Davy.' Baker stroked an apparently pensive chin.

She knew the arguments, could barely bring herself to watch. Dave's white knight act was big of him but she'd not asked for help and any intervention from her now would only make matters worse. It was almost a relief when she felt her phone vibrate in a pocket. The text was from Ben Cooper. He'd heard back from the labs, knew she was desperate for a heads-up. *Get on with it . . .* She scrolled down. Shee-ite.

'Well, it raises all sorts of questions, sir. Maybe—'

'Chief.' Her gaze was still on the screen.

'And you're paid to fucking answer them.' Baker jabbed a finger at Harries. 'I'm not interested in your what-ifs and maybes. Bring me facts and definites, lad.'

'Chief.' She glanced up. *Hello?*

'What do you think I'm doing? It takes time. Sir.'

'And as of now, detective, yours is fucking borrowed.'

'Listen up, both of you.' It was like a frigging school playground. 'The blood samples? There's a match.' She heard the sound of splintering wood as she fell off the fence. 'Go ahead and charge them, chief.'

THIRTY-NINE

'Have they been charged yet?' Ruby Wells reached for the wine. She'd hooked up with Michelle and Lily in their local. The Lamb wouldn't win any Michelin stars any time soon. Unless they started dishing them out for tacky lino and cracked burnt orange banquettes. The young women had bagged a booth at the back. It looked to Ruby as if they'd been there a while, there were half a dozen dead WKD bottles on the table as well as the Soave.

'Dunno.' Michelle swirled her glass. 'Cops didn't say anything about that.' She'd ditched the customary Day-Glo gear for dark trousers, brown buttoned-up top. Her mood seemed subdued, too. 'Will you talk to them for us, Ruby?'

'I suppose.' If she'd known earlier she could've grabbed a word with Quinn at the hospital. 'It's easy enough for you to pick up the phone, though, Mitch.'

She shrugged. 'More up your street, innit? 'Sides, less I have to do with the fuzz the more I like it. They're not exactly my cuppa tea.'

'Oh yeah?' Lily snorted. Her long white dress could double

as a nightie. 'What about dishy DC Dave? You told me he could take your . . . particulars . . . down any time.'

'Yeah, smart-arse, but it's not me he's gagging for, is it?'

'I can't help it, dahlink. Men just fall at my feet.' A pouting Lily tossed her head, sent blonde locks flying. Ruby masked a smile. The jokey femme fatale display put her in mind of a Mae West mini-me. The gesture caught the appreciative eye of a couple of long-haired student types at the bar. One aped the hair flicking, probably hoping to catch Lily's attention.

It didn't.

'Not you, dumbo.' Michelle chucked a beer mat at Lily. 'Didn't you clock him ogling his boss lady? Talk about fancying the pants.'

'Yeah but who'd wear the trousers?' They both got the wine giggles.

'Zip it, you pair.' Ruby wasn't in the mood, the hospital visit had left her feeling sick, too much food – for thought. She checked her watch: half seven. If Charlie and Shannon didn't show soon, she'd push off anyway.

'Zip. Trousers. Nice one, Rube.' Lily smirked.

She batted a hand. 'Come on, stop messing round. How did you leave it with the police? You went in yesterday, was it?'

'Today. First thing. We had to look at a coupla hoodies.' Michelle frowned. 'You look hacked off, Ruby. You OK?'

'I'll live.' She gave a thin smile. 'Come on, what's the score?' All she really knew was that two youths the girls hung out with were in custody in connection with street violence. Sipping wine, she listened as Michelle talked her through the visit from the cops, the fact they'd been unable to confirm alibis and that they'd recognised police exhibits as their now ex-boyfriends' gear. Ruby interpreted the fact they'd not lied to the cops as a good sign. Last thing they'd want is to land themselves in trouble: kids who'd been through the care system were invariably wary of the law, weren't good with authority full stop.

Michelle tucked a strand of hair behind her ear. 'Being honest, Ruby, dobbing in Zach and Leroy was a pisser. But we didn't look to get dragged in to any of this. And we can live without it.' So the downbeat mood was down to guilt?

Resentment? Ruby reckoned they needed to move on, however bad it felt, distancing themselves from lawbreakers had to be good.

'Plus, they said they did it.' Lily ran a finger round the rim of her glass. 'If they hadn't, it might've been a different story. We'd have given them the benefit of the doubt and all that. But what they done's wrong, Ruby.'

She nodded. 'What do you want me to have a word about?' If the police had evidence, the youths would be charged. End of. The girls exchanged glances. Both took a sip of wine rather than answer. 'What is it?' Ruby asked. 'Are you afraid of reprisals?'

'Of what?' Lily frowned.

She managed to stem an eye roll. 'Are you scared if they're released they'll come after you?'

'Nah. Safety in numbers.' Lily sniffed. 'We can take care of ourselves.' Ruby wondered if it was big talk. 'Besides they're not gonna get out, are they?'

'Will we have to go to court, give evidence and that, Ruby?'

'Yeah, and when's it going to come to trial?'

Ruby reckoned they were after reassurance rather than legal advice. 'Hey, it's no big deal. I'll check state of play in the morning, get back to you.'

'What is this – a wake?' Charlie breezed in, bringing a blast of cold air. Shannon was just visible behind Charlie's bulk. 'Cheer up, you lot. I told Amy she'd be in for a fun night.' Charlie stepped aside, ushered the newcomer forward.

'Amy, hi.' Ruby smiled, happy to see they'd taken the Hemming girl under their collective wing. 'Want to get a round in, Charlie?' She handed her a twenty, patted the space next to her. 'Come and sit down, Amy. I hear you talked to Caroline King last night.'

Head down, Amy stared at her hands. 'Yeah.' *Was that it?*

Ruby tried again. 'She reckons you're going to cooperate with her on the book?'

'I said I would. We'll see how it goes.' She gave a shy smile.

'What book?' Lily sat up straight, all ears. 'What gives? Come on, babe, share.'

As Amy explained, Ruby lounged back and listened to the excited banter. She clocked the hair flicking guy weave his way towards them, Charlie and Shannon just behind bearing more bottles and a can of coke. The guy leaned on the table, lowered his head towards Lily. 'Hey babe, can I get you a drink?' Bad move.

'No you fucking can't,' Charlie hissed, elbowed him in the ribs. 'Beat it.'

Eyes blazing, the youth spun round. 'Want to make something of it?'

'Love to.' She grabbed his jacket, hauled him close, faces almost touched. 'What do you suggest?'

'Charlie.' Ruby cautioned. The altercation was attracting unwanted attention from the regulars. The face-off lasted only seconds. Charlie's expression must have made him think twice. He raised a palm. 'No offence, mate.'

'Wrong. Dickhead. You're offending my friend. Piss off.'

He staggered slightly when she released the lapels. Punters resumed card games, domino matches, conversations.

'Can't take you anywhere, can we, Lil?' Smiling, Charlie ruffled Lily's hair before sinking onto the bench 'Come on everyone. Lighten up.'

Ruby tightened her lips. Charlie's protectiveness was touching, but not everyone would regard it that way. If she didn't watch it, one day someone would stand up to her. Even her mates seemed ill at ease. Lily eventually broke the silence. 'This book then. What d'you think, Ruby? Is it worth Amy helping? What's the King woman like?'

'Far as I can tell, she's straight, should do a good job.' Ruby paused a few seconds, looked at Amy. 'Did you hear what happened after you met?' The girl shook her head, took a swig of coke. Ruby told them about the attack, that she'd visited Caroline in hospital.

'That's a pisser,' Amy said. 'What about the cops? They got any leads?'

'Not that I know of.'

'She a journo, isn't she?' Michelle asked. 'Isn't she meant to notice things? What do they call them – trained observers?'

'True. But you have to remember things first.' She started

explaining about the memory loss, the occasional hazy flashback but she sensed fading interest. Charlie and Shannon joked around, and Michelle read the label on the wine bottle.

'Hey, Rube.' Charlie perked up a bit. 'You never said . . . did you find out about the crow? Who it was down to and that?'

'Today, as it happens.' She raised her glass. 'Trust me. There won't be any more trouble.'

'Aw, come on, Ruby, you can't just leave it like that,' Charlie moaned.

Should she tell them? She'd already decided to ignore Caroline's warnings and take the bastard to task. Mind, it would be on her terms and her turf. Maybe a bit of covert back-up wouldn't hurt? She might run it past them. 'Let's just say Amy knows the guy responsible.' No one named Ram. No one needed to.

'Why'd the bastard do it?' Lily asked.

'He cocked up. Got the wrong target.'

'Mistaken identity then?' Michelle.

Ruby nodded. 'That's one way of putting it.'

FORTY

Putting it to someone that they may have had a pervy past was a tough job but someone had to do it. For someone, read Sarah. The DI was at the QE anyway and had volunteered to drop by and question Duncan Agnew. Prior checks on the sex offenders' register and criminal records had revealed nothing and ditto emerged during a seriously painful interview. Agnew had been prickly to say the least, but if cops worried about pissing people off, they'd never get out of bed. Given Agnew's criminal clean sheet, Sarah's payback-as-motive theory was looking flimsy. Make that flimsier. They now knew the blood on Wilde and Brody's hoodies correlated not just to Foster but also to Tattoo Man. The youths had been charged with murder and would be up before magistrates first thing.

Leaning against a custard coloured wall in the hospital cafeteria, Sarah finished the worst coffee she'd drunk in years and slung the styrofoam cup in a bin. She'd felt in need of sustenance before confronting King again, and a five-minute break to try and get her thoughts together. She'd have preferred a slug of scotch to the shot of caffeine. Doubtless Baker and his band of merry men had sunk a few single malts by now – when she'd left the nick most of the squad had been making for the Queen's Head. Celebrating.

Would she have joined them if she could? Yes. No. Maybe. She'd little doubt Wilde and Brody were partially guilty, but felt there was more story to emerge. There was a saying about chickens and counting. Sarah saw too many unhatched eggs.

'Give it back and we'll say no more about it.' Still propped up in bed, Caroline King held out a palm, lips pursed tighter than Scrooge's wallet. Sarah found something faintly comical about the cartoon stance. On a more serious level, she was dead on her feet and could live without the ridiculous posturing. 'That the royal we, is it?'

'That's so not funny.'

'I'm sure you're right, dear.' Sarah stifled a yawn, flopped into a chair. Hospitals were always too hot, the room felt like a sauna. Mind that could be down to King's hot air.

'Just hand it over.'

'Get over yourself, Caroline,' she snapped. The arsy-ness no longer amused. 'Just what's your problem?'

'The memory stick? In my vanity case?' She glared. 'Only it's not.'

Sarah narrowed her eyes, counted to five. Then ten. The fucking nerve. 'What are you saying. Exactly?' The voice was clipped, curt. 'You don't for one instant seriously—?'

'I'm sorry, Sarah.' King put a hand to her mouth. 'You wouldn't. I know that. I'm just so bloody . . . Forget I said anything.' She clearly knew a line had been long-jumped. Sarah had little doubt the remorse was genuine, or she'd have walked, tasked a junior officer with the interview.

The apology was still too late. 'When did you see it last and what's on the frigging thing?'

'Yesterday afternoon.' She always kept it with her make up, apparently. Sarah was tempted to crack a line about vanity publishing but decided on balance it wouldn't go down well. 'As to what's on it . . . what isn't?' King ran both hands through her hair. 'The opening of the book, research notes, interview transcripts.' No prevarication. No hedge betting. That more than anything confirmed Sarah's belief the reporter regretted the slur.

'Interviews with . . .?' Circling an ankle.

'A couple of victims from London, Amy Hemming's mother, social workers, child protection officers, a woman from CROP . . . the Campaign for the Removal of Pimping?'

She gave a brisk nod, knew what CROP was for God's sake.

'The book's structure's on there, contents' table, publicity ideas, promotional stuff.'

My word. She had been a busy queen bee. It struck Sarah there was a big hole in the work load. 'What about Jas Ram? Have you interviewed him?'

'Not in depth. Not yet.' Slight hesitation. 'Why?'

She shrugged. 'I can see why he might want to get his hands on the material.' Ram was an arrogant shit with a sadistic streak and then some. He'd revel in knowing what people were saying about him. And if he didn't like it – which he wouldn't – Sarah could see him making sure they'd think twice about opening their mouth again.

King frowned, thought it through. 'But he's agreed to talk. Why would he try and sabotage what I'm working on?' Not that he had. King apparently had a second memory stick which she kept in a wall safe. Ram didn't know that though; wouldn't know either existed. Sarah turned her mouth down.

King caught up. 'You're not talking sticks, are you? You think he broke into my place, nicked the laptop, the recorder?' Sarah nodded. *Ram or one of his sheep.* 'I still don't see why – not when he's agreed to an interview?'

'Words are cheap. And we all know Ram's a man of his word, don't we? Were you paying him?'

King sighed and closed her eyes. Said it all really. And Sarah reckoned it was a damn sight more than anything Ram would have disclosed. Knowing what she did of the gobshite, he'd either have spun tales of pure – make that sick – fantasy. Or stonewalled every question. Either way he'd have taken the money and run. She almost felt sorry for King. She must have been so desperate to secure the groomer's input, she'd allowed her bullshit alert to go on the blink. She gave the reporter a short time to reflect then asked if she'd noticed anything suspicious in the days leading up to the burglary, strangers hanging round the property, unknown cars parked in the road, anything out of the ordinary. They were stock questions, and got stock replies: no, nada, niente. Big surprise. Criminals who know what they're doing don't generally sneak round wearing Dick Turpin masks and carrying swag bags. Shame, Sarah thought. *Could save me a bunch of time.*

She checked her watch. Nearly eight. She'd already decided to draw a veil over Nat Hardy's pathetic display. If he wanted to tell King about it – that was fine. She was here primarily to discuss the attack and it hadn't even had a mention yet. 'Caroline. Can we cut to the chase? What happened last night? Who were you meeting? What can you remember?' Probably not a lot. Sarah had sought out a medico who'd confirmed King's blood contained traces of Rohypnol.

'Four questions and a cliché? She raised an eyebrow. 'You'll never make a journo, DI Quinn.'

'Thank God for small mercies. Come on, give.' She'd hooked up with Amy Hemming, she said. It only took ten minutes or so to persuade the girl to agree to record an interview at a later date.

Sarah frowned. That was a turn up for the grooming book. 'You definitely had no arrangement to see Ram?' King looked down at her hands. 'Tell me straight, Caroline.'

'He cried off. We'd been due to meet at nine. He called around six, said he couldn't make it. No reason. No apology. Said he'd reschedule. To be honest, I thought he was just dicking me around, showing who was in control, you know?'

Could be. Or he was just keeping tabs. 'OK, back to Amy. What happened once you'd agreed terms?'

'As far as I was concerned, it was a result. I left on a high – and in a hurry 'cause I was keen not to keep you waiting. I'm walking across the park then – bam. It's a blank.'

Sarah's glance fell on the still unopened Chablis on the locker. She'd run out of wine, made a mental note to buy a bottle on the way home. Shame this wasn't a social call.

'Help yourself.' King smiled, clearly didn't miss much. 'Whoops. Better not. You being on duty and all.'

She twisted her mouth. 'The shadowy figures you mentioned this morning?'

'I'm pretty sure there were four youths.'

'Male? Female? Both?'

'Male, of course. Dark hoodies, jeans, scarves, then the shapes just dissolve. Next minute I think it's my mind playing tricks.'

She tapped a finger against her lips. King must've read the scepticism.

'Honest to God, Sarah. I'd tell you if I could. I want whoever did this locked up.' She was pointing at her face; the make-up wasn't helping much.

She nodded. 'What about sounds? Or smells?' Clearly not. No clue either as to what happened in the four hours between leaving Amy in Harborne and being dumped in Edgbaston. Where the hell had she been – and who with? 'Have you any idea how the Rohypnol got in your system?'

'What?' Deep frown lines appeared. Maybe the results hadn't long come through because it was clearly news to King. 'Jesus wept. No wonder I can't remember a frigging thing.' She reached for a glass, took a few sips of water. 'I don't believe it. I just can't get my head round it.'

'Round what?'

'What do you think? The Rohypnol. It's a shock.'

She could see that. 'So, any ideas?' King gave several slow shakes of the head. 'What about before you met the girl? Did you go in a pub? A wine bar? Did someone buy you a drink? Did you leave a glass unattended?' She narrowed her eyes: surely, it meant King had been targeted? *Was that how the mugging gang operated?* Select a victim, slip in a roofie? Shadow the prey? *And is that a clutched straw I see before me?* She sighed. Even if she was on the money, it was way too late to test Foster and Tattoo Man. King still hadn't responded. Sarah could almost hear the cogs ticking. 'Well?'

More head shaking. 'I'm trying to think, Sarah.'

'I can't help if you hold things back.'

'I need more time.' *I bet you do.* And she'd stake a King's ransom on something having just registered. She held Sarah's gaze. 'If and when anything comes to me – you'll be the second to know. I promise you that.'

Sarah tightened her lips. It wasn't worth arguing the toss, short of thumbscrews she'd get no further tonight. Besides, she was so knackered she almost felt like shoving King out of bed. 'Are they still letting you out tomorrow?' The reporter nodded. 'Give me a bell. Let me know when.' She reached for her bag, headed towards the door.

Last thing she wanted was a wasted journey. Another wasted journey.

'Sarah. I'm on the wagon. Painkillers and all that.' Smiling, she took the bottle off the locker, proffered it to the DI. 'Call it a peace offering?'

'What?' Sarah's lip twitched. 'A peace offering from Ruby Wells?'

'Ruby won't mind. She's a mate.' The smile faded. 'I've done far worse to her, believe me.'

Getting into the Audi a few minutes later, Sarah wondered if King had had it in mind to tell her about the windscreen incident all along. The reporter clearly felt responsible for drawing Wells into Jas Ram's line of fire. Ruby apparently had no intention of reporting the threats to the police. Maybe mentioning it to Sarah was King's subtle way of suggesting the cops keep an eye on the lawyer. *Subtle as a dead crow.*

And peace offering as sweetener? She glanced at the Chablis on the passenger seat, gave a wry smile. She'd happily accepted it. Then handed over a twenty. Given the priceless expression on King's face, it had been worth every penny.

FORTY-ONE

The early brief had been exactly that – done and dusted by 08.30. In her office now, Sarah was reading over-nights, writing reports, responding to emails et al. So flaked by the time she got home last night, she'd slung the Chablis into the fridge. Just as well, or she might have ended up looking as seriously hung-over as one or two of the squad. The party had decamped to a curry house, according to Dave; celebrations continued into the small hours though he'd bowed out after a swift pint. Baker hadn't shown this morning, called in to say he was heading straight out to some police authority meeting. He'd probably lost interest, thought Operation Steel all over bar the shouting. She sighed, sipped coffee. Maybe he was right. In less than an hour, Brody and Wilde would be up before the magistrates. They'd doubtless plead not guilty, equally predictably they'd be remanded in custody.

Even so, additional evidence had to be collected, efforts made to trace more witnesses, sharpen statements already taken. The case had to be as tight as they could make it. So why did she still see unhatched chickens? The thought that other gang members were at large continued to bug her. Eggs could land on faces, couldn't they?

The phone derailed her train of thought. 'DI Quinn.'

'Ma'am. DC Lally here.'

'Beth.' She put a warmish smile in her voice, compensation for the shit straw dished out earlier. She'd despatched Lally and Jed Holmes to Harborne park – again. 'Any joy?' She thought she caught a murmured 'boundless' from Beth, but let it go. Ferreting round bins when it was below freezing was never going to be a career highlight.

'Two bags full, ma'am.' Even if the comeback hadn't been intentionally humorous, Sarah's lip twitched. 'Both bin liners are in the boot. Empty cans, mostly, fair few bottles. Strongbow, Red Stripe, Coke, Fanta, Seven Up, Rio, Peps—'

'I get the picture, Beth. Thanks.' Whether it would illustrate part of the puzzle, Sarah had only a vague hope. What was it No Shit's namesake had said? Something about eliminating the impossible and whatever was left – however improbable – had to be the truth. Sounded classy even if it proved total tosh. The notion had struck Sarah around three a.m.; insomnia had to have some benefits. Until then, she'd thought it inconceivable that Amy Hemming had spiked a drink, given it to the reporter. Seeing the girl having means and opportunity was no problem. But, motive? If King had been telling the truth, Amy had been happy to comply with an interview. So why would she try and put King out of action? And what then? How had King ended up in Edgbaston? If Amy had been involved in that, too, she couldn't have done it on her own.

'Where'd you want them putting. Ma'am?' The pause was pushing it.

Don't tempt me. 'Back here, thanks.' A safe berth would do for the time being. She knew it was the longest of shots, but not all the containers would have to go to the labs for testing. She'd ordered a wide sweep to be on the safe side, but there'd be judicious filtering after she'd grabbed a word with King. Surely the reporter had entertained similar thoughts, arrived at similar suspicions. Was that why she'd gone AWOL? So she wasn't on hand to answer further questions – because she was busy chasing the answers herself?

'You still there, ma'am?'

'Sure. Fire away, Beth.' She reached for her coffee.

'As well as wading through all the crap . . .' *Yada yada. Get used to it.* '. . . we might've struck witness gold. A woman who lives across from the park? She reckons she saw four youths hanging round the swings just before it went dark.'

'It was a while later when King was there, Beth.' She took a sip, grimaced. Cold and stewed.

'Yeah. But this woman's big in Neighbourhood Watch. She didn't like the look of them, so she took some pics.'

'And?'

'She spotted them again just before seven. Three of them actually.' Under streetlights presumably. 'Walking down the road heading back to the park.'

'The pics?'

'Jed's about to email them.'

'Great. Well done . . .' Dialling tone. She pulled a face. Had Beth hung up? It rang so quickly, for a second she thought it was Beth again.

'Boss?' One word and it told her Dave was dying to share. She curved a lip. Apt phrase given where she'd sent him.

'How's it going?' Tapping a key, glancing at her in-box.

'I'm still at the mortuary. The murder victim's definitely Frank Gibbs, boss. His brother's here with me now.' Stewart Gibbs had come up on the train first thing from Coventry. All she knew was that he taught maths at secondary school. Harries had traced him via Gibbs' address book. 'And?'

'He'd like a word, boss.'

'Mr Gibbs? DI—'

'I'm sorry he's dead and all that but I don't want my name coming out.'

Hello to you, too. Frowning, she tapped her pen on the desk. He wanted a word – why wait for a prompt. 'And why would it, Mr Gibbs?'

'Always a risk, isn't it?' Voice sounded middle-aged, posh, petulant. 'And people knowing I'm his brother wouldn't do *my* reputation any good. Indeed quite the reverse.' *Bad then?*

Sarah's pen stilled. An adverse impact on his reputation? And Stewart Gibbs worked with kids. Was that what the pompous twat was circling round? 'And why's that, Mr Gibbs?' She heard an impatient sigh, as if she was a particularly dense pupil.

'Granted it never got to court—'

'What didn't?' She kept her voice even, felt tiny hairs rise on the back of her neck.

'But if it's all resurrected again . . . I have my good name to—'

'What didn't?' Keeping her voice level was an effort.

'We're going back six or seven years, I suppose.' And he'd tell it in his own good time. She suppressed a sigh, not easy with bated breath. 'He worked in the kitchen at a children's home. Some youngsters made accusations of . . . inappropriate behaviour.' *Yes.* She punched the air. Despite the weasel words, it was a link. Abuse was the correct term and both Gibbs and Foster had committed it.

'As I say, it wouldn't do any good if it got out.' *Quite the reverse.* She closed her eyes. *Damn damn buggery damn. Why hadn't she seen it before?* The inked letters on Gibbs' arm hadn't read BOD, for Christ's sake. He'd been marked – branded if you like – by someone who knew him. She hit a key, brought up on screen the picture from the pathologist, Richard Patten. Saw it immediately this time. BAD. *The same word Wilde had tattooed across his knuckles.*

'Tell me more, Mr Gibbs.' She wrote *BAD* on a notepad, underscored it so viciously, the pen tore the paper. There'd been a police inquiry, he said, but no action taken. Insufficient evidence apparently. Even so, Stewart Gibbs had severed all connections with his brother. 'No smoke without fire. And mud sticks, doesn't it? We were never close anyway, you understand? Every family has its black sheep, I suppose.' She rolled her eyes. *Thank God, Mr Cliché didn't teach English.* 'Anyway, I'm not my brother's keeper.'

'Indeed not, Mr Gibbs. Thanks for your help. Can you put DC Harries on now, please?' Anything to get the sanctimonious git off the line. 'We'll need detail, Dave. You know the drill.' Shit. The cliché thing must be catching.

'What do you reckon, boss? It's a link, isn't it?'

'Oh yes.' *And not the only one. First, Foster and Gibbs had both abused kids. Second, they'd both got away with it. Until now. It looked to Sarah as if their past had caught up.*

'Dave. While you're there . . .'

There was one more thing she wanted him to do.

Caroline soaked in a hot deep claw bath at the Radisson hotel in town. She sniffed her hair again, convinced she could still smell hospital. She'd discharged herself first thing, been in no rush to get home. Felt in need of time out, personal space and a bolt-hole – preferably one that hadn't been broken into.

The ivory and gold fittings were barely visible through the steam cloud. She used her toes to turn the hot tap again. Despite the heat, she shivered: fear, anger, outrage at having been so royally set-up. Stitched like a tapestry kipper. Scalding tears ran down her still swollen painful cheeks. The double-dealing had been breathtaking. What had she said to Sarah Quinn? The Rohypnol had come as a shock. She screwed her mouth. *Understatement of the frigging year.* Even then, the greater bombshell was realising where it must have come from. Make that, who. Had Amy Hemming been carrying the drug on the off-chance opportunity arose? What would she have done if Caroline hadn't innocently obliged by providing the means? Would Amy have suggested they go for a drink, tried giving it another way? *Give?*

'Don't make me fucking laugh,' she cried out loud. She wasn't laughing, not even close, her voice had cracked. People Caroline knew gave presents, not slipped banned substances into drink cans. Had Amy been so brutalised by Jas Ram and his cronies that she felt spiking a drink to get a journalist off her back was fair game? For the life of her, she could see no other motive. But what if Caroline hadn't happily downed the coke? Would Amy have just walked away, resigned to her cheap vindictive little trick bombing?

She drew a shuddering breath. It all depended whether Amy was a lone wolf, or acting as part of the pack. Because a gang had been involved. Caroline had no doubt now, she'd been set on by four youths as she crossed the park. Odd snatches kept coming back like blurry clips from silent movies. Eyes screwed tight, she willed herself to recall more. She'd said last night if anything occurred to her, Sarah would be the second to know. Caroline needed more answers first. Question exercising her the most? Had Amy been in on it? Colluded by administering the drug as precursor to a planned assault. Or was the attack random? The youths happened to be hanging round and had struck lucky? Struck lucky? She gave a brittle laugh.

The odds the incidents weren't related were infinitesimal. She so wanted to believe in Amy's innocence, knew it was almost certainly wishful thinking. She feared the girl had lost her innocence along with everything else the day she stepped into Jas Ram's grooming parlour.

FORTY-TWO

The image on Sarah's monitor wouldn't win any awards but she needed as clean a version as possible. It was the best of three JPEGs Jed Holmes had emailed from Harborne. 'Can you tart it up a bit, Ben?'

Standing behind, one hand pressed on the desk, Ben Cooper studied the shot over her shoulder. The FSI manager's presence was fortuitous. For an hour or so she'd been toying with forwarding the image to one of his juniors; the quality so poor, it hardly seemed worth the effort. Ben had popped his head round the door to drop off a report. His timing was perfect. Unlike the pic.

The woman who'd snapped it might be the Mrs Big of Neighbourhood Watch but she was short on camera skills. Scratch that, Sarah thought, it was hardly fair. At least she'd had a go, shown a bit of community gumption. Most people sensing trouble these days looked the other way, not focused a lens on its potential source. The term focus had been used loosely. The shot had been taken in poor light from some distance, it was soft, grainy and underexposed. But apart from that . . .

It showed four youths in street gear: black hoodies, black combats, dark trainers. Two slouched on swings, the others lolled against the metal frame. Whether by accident, design, or fashion statement their faces were partially covered by scarves.

Sarah took a sip of water as Ben continued casting a professional eye. Like all forensic investigators, he was trained in photography, stills and video. From what she'd heard, he was pretty damn good too, wags in the unit called him Rankin. 'I have to say, there's not a lot to go on, Sarah. I'm not sure I can do much with it.'

'Every little helps.' Smiling, she turned her head. His face was close. A touch too close perhaps.

'I'll give it a whirl, get back, how's that?' His teeth were perfect. She could smell peppermint on his breath.

'That's good. That's very—'

'Boss.' Harries stormed in, short of breath, glance cutting between Sarah and Ben.

'How many fucking times do I have to tell you to knock, Harries.'

'Sorry. I didn't realise you were so . . . busy. A man's body's been found. Saint Chad's Church. Small Heath. I'll see you out there, shall I?'

'It's not what it looked, Dave.' Sarah had to lengthen her stride to catch Harries as he strode across the car park.

'Nothing to do with me, ma'am.' He aimed the fob at an unmarked Astra. 'You making your own way?'

The cold air hit, she fumbled with the buttons on her coat. 'No. We need to talk.'

'That we do.' The car was in second gear before she'd fastened her seat belt. 'You were on the money about Foster, ma'am.' She'd asked Dave to get a technician at the morgue to let him view Foster's body, thinking – though not expecting – it just might carry the same bad mark.

She smiled. *Top notch.* 'Really?' Cut a glance at his stony profile.

'No I made it up. Of course really.' He papped the horn at a death wish cyclist, muttered. 'Sodding lycra lout.'

'Go on.'

'I'm about to.' Mr Snappy. Boy, was he pissed off. 'It was on his chest. BAD. Blue ink. Just like Gibbs.'

Foster had been in hospital, how long? Christ he'd been in cold store for two days. 'Why the hell did no one think to mention it?' They might have put two and two together a bit sooner.

'You have to really look for it. Tiny letters. Lots of chest hair.' He'd not even glanced at her.

Deliberately concealed again? 'Well done, Dave.' God that sounded patronizing.

'It's what I'm paid for, ma'am.'

She tightened her lips. No call to be childish, churlish, whatever. So why did she feel in the wrong? Because, she realised, she valued his good opinion and normally unswerving support. She cast a covert glance. He stared ahead, face in neutral now, unlike the speeding motor which any passing traffic cop would pull over.

'The body's not going anywhere, Dave.' *Suit yourself.* She turned, gazed through the window. Car slowed anyway as they hit the main drag through Small Heath. This section of the Coventry Road was a mishmash of small shops, rundown businesses, greengrocers, greasy caffs, electrical repairs, beauty parlour, launderette, off-licence. The area was poor, big families, low budgets, mostly via benefits. How traders kept going was a mystery to Sarah. She sighed. The in-car silence getting to her.

'Look. I don't know what you thought you saw back there . . . but there's nothing going on between me and Ben Cooper.' Talk about adding two and two? The hurt look on Dave's face when he burst into the office told her his maths was way out. And though he was being an idiot, she actually minded. They'd had odd crossed words before but nothing like this.

'Know something? It's not always about you, DI Quinn. You and Henry can elope for all I care.'

He so did. Didn't he? 'Come on Dave, you've got the wrong end—'

'And d'you know something else? We're at work. Let's concentrate on the job shall we, ma'am?'

FORTY-THREE

S et back just off the main road, Saint Chad's had long since seen its Gothic heyday. God knew – well he would – what the stonework's original shade had been, by now it was blackened slime-green down to centuries and strata of moss, lichen, industrial pollution. Smashed windows and rusted barbed wire didn't help its grimy appearance. Sarah, suited and booted, gazed up at the façade from the street. She'd asked Harries to have a nose round the locale, knock doors, talk to traders. As she entered the grounds,

she smelled dog shit, decaying vegetation, caught sight of
a church notice board lying rotting in the unkempt yellow
grass. She could just make out the faded lettering: Jesus
Saves. *Tell that to the victim.*

The uniform posted outside the porch greeted her by name.
She frowned slightly. Not only couldn't she recall his, but it
was a sobering thought when even to a cop, police officers
were beginning to look young. 'Hi, sorry, I . . .'

'PC Floyd, ma'am. Wayne.' He tapped his helmet. 'The
gaffer's inside if you want a word. Inspector Lewis.'

Bet he took a bit of stick from Morse fans. 'Thanks.
Forensics here?'

'Half an hour.' He jabbed a thumb over his shoulder. 'Spooky
innit? It's been decommissioned years, mind.'

'Deconsecrated actually.'

He shrugged. 'Whatevs.'

She masked a wry smile. Wasn't her then, he didn't just
look young.

The body was white, middle-aged, male, clothed in cheap
grubby charity shop garb. It lay in the foetal position on the
filthy remains of the pitted stone altar. In the gloom and from
a distance, the man could almost be sleeping it off. Cans of
strong cider scattered around added to the illusion, as did
greasy chip wrappings, KFC cartons, balled newspapers, fag
ends. The illusion shattered as Sarah padded down the hastily
laid forensic corridor. She couldn't tell how badly he'd been
beaten, wasn't best qualified to distinguish between lividity
and bruising. But even a child would be able to see the torn
skin and the teeth marks in the lardy mottled flesh.

'Rats, most like.' A man's voice from behind made her
jump, she spun round, exacerbating her gut's queasy churning.

'Inspector Lewis?' With the curling grey hair, piercing eyes,
he looked more like his namesake's boss. She swallowed,
tasted bile.

'Charlie.' He gave a curt nod. 'Dog found it. Owner's walking
through the graveyard, lets it off the lead. Dumb mutt scarpers
round the back. Door's off its hinges. Dog shoots through. Won't
budge. Barking to high heaven. Owner clambers in, shits herself.

Not literally, you understand? Calls us. And here we are. Aren't we the lucky ones?' He rocked on his feet, his smarmy smirk revealed a gold filling and halitosis.

His attitude stank too. 'Where's she now?'

'I let her go.' He interpreted her look. 'Calm down. The old dear's late eighties, arthritic, asthmatic, weighs less than a sparrow on a diet.' He tilted his head towards the body. 'That's not down to her, DI . . .?'

'Quinn. Sarah.' Shivering, she pulled her coat closer, wished the pathologist would get a move on.

'Yeah, it's like a morgue in here.' Lewis sniffed. 'Ice box. Fridge freezer. Cold store, call it what you will. And it's kinda lucky. Any warmer and there'd be even less body left. Doc reckons it's been here a fortnight or more. Mind, if it had started rotting the smell would've tipped us off sooner.'

'Christ's sake,' she snapped. 'Show some respect, man.'

'Don't rightly have much, Detective Inspector Quinn. And if you knew who it was – I doubt you would either. Are you listening?'

Pointing, she creased her eyes. 'Have you seen that?' A forensic guy was indicating what looked like a tattoo on the victim's hand. She'd bet her pension it had been inked post mortem.

Lewis gave a heavy sigh, followed her gaze. 'Bad? Yeah well that says it all.'

'So you think this guy, Barry . . .?'

'Barry Lingham. He's the first victim, Dave. He has to be. Lewis helped send him down. Said it was a travesty he only got eighteen months.' Hunched over the table, keen gaze searching his face, she willed Dave to see it, too. Stuff the Ice Queen persona, no way could she hide the passion on this. Charlie Lewis had told her he suspected Lingham of getting away with abusing kids for years. He'd apparently worked in three or four care homes round the Midlands but the crime only came to light when one of his victims attempted suicide. The girl was persuaded to give evidence and Lingham finally sentenced. Looked to Sarah like Lewis wasn't the only person who didn't rate the just desserts.

'Lingham was out on licence.' Shuffling forward, she lowered her voice. 'His parole officer hadn't seen him for three weeks. And I tell you this, Dave . . . Lingham's been dead longer than a few days.' She rattled off the names simultaneously lining up the salt shaker, vinegar bottle and ketchup. 'Foster. Frank Gibbs. Barry Lingham. They're child molesters, deviants and they've been targeted and taken out.'

He nodded, but the downturned mouth suggested two minds. 'And Duncan Agnew?'

'I know, I know.' Agnew didn't fit the pattern. She flopped back in the cheap vinyl chair, pushed the bowl to one side. The caff down the road from the church was convenient not haute cuisine. She'd not even tasted the vegetable soup. She was too wired, too edgy, sensed the case could be about to break wide open. Richard Patten was still at the crime scene, she'd left after wresting a promise he'd do the PM soon as. Given the body's state, he wouldn't speculate on the cause of death. Forget *her* pension, she'd bet Baker's it wasn't natural. The chief? She blew her cheeks out on a sigh. He was up to speed, just not on the same page. She'd put in a call but whether what she said actually got through was debatable. He couldn't see how the development affected Wayne and Brody's position. Way she saw it the robbery motive was shot to shit.

She glanced across the table. Dave was shovelling in double egg and chips. No appetite loss there. Neither had mentioned the earlier spat and he'd dropped the ma'am business. He was too good a cop to let personal stuff get in the way. They both were. Fact he wasn't jumping up and down, sharing her conviction wasn't a problem. A yes man was the last thing she needed. He was more than a sounding board, she valued his take.

'Thing is, Dave, we know Brody and Wilde were in care but they swear blind no one ever laid a finger on them. Why would they be wasting paedos?'

He paused, fork halfway to mouth. 'Maybe they were acting for kids they were in the system with? Y'know, younger kids. Victims who wouldn't or couldn't fight back?'

She cocked a scathing eyebrow. 'What? Like caped crusaders. Balsall Heath's answer to Batman and Robin?'

'Yeah, OK.' He curved a lip. 'Now you come to mention it.'

Two cerebrally-challenged losers like Wilde and Brody couldn't orchestrate something so complex. And as for altruism, they wouldn't know how to spell it let alone show it. 'No. My head tells me it's personal. It has to be.' She'd called the incident room already, half the squad was now working the angle, interviewing staff at the homes, chasing kids who'd spent time there, personnel who'd moved on. 'They're marking out the bad guys, Dave, branding them.'

'Yeah, boss. But who's "they"?'

FORTY-FOUR

Post late brief, they were no nearer an answer to Dave's question. The task of tracing people with links to five children's homes over a ten-year period made Hercules' labours look like a Saturday job in a sweet shop. The squad had barely scratched the surface. Even when inquiries were completed, there was no guarantee they'd uncover the full picture.

The more Sarah thought about it the more convinced she was that Brody and Wilde were only part of it. That they couldn't have acted alone. The youths' mugshots lay on her desk. Holding one in each hand, she studied them closer. In her view they just didn't have the mental capacity to plan serial attacks, execute them, maybe. They could certainly provide the brawn. But where was the brain?

And why was she still here? She'd only dropped by to collect her bag and coat, half an hour later she was still collecting thoughts. Straightening, she rolled her shoulders, her neck muscles were in knots. If Dave had taken up her offer of a swift half, they'd be relaxing in the pub by now, could've gone on somewhere to eat. Last she'd seen he was bashing phones in the squad room. She sighed. Maybe she'd pissed him off more than she realised. It wasn't like the guy to play hard to get. She tightened her mouth. Caroline King on the other hand . . .

She'd lost count of the calls she'd put through to the reporter, not to mention texts and a couple of voice mails. Two bin liners full of empty cans and bottles were sitting round taking up valuable space in the exhibits room. How were the cops supposed to investigate an attack when the prime witness had gone to ground? King had better not be playing detective, it could be a dangerous game.

Caroline wasn't playing anything – she'd worked it out. Or thought she had. She needed to talk to Ruby Wells, reckoned the lawyer could help provide a few answers. Keeping a low profile, Caroline was slumped in the driving seat of a rental car four doors down from the lawyer's house. The property was in darkness, the paltry street lighting supplemented by a full moon that did nothing for the ball-freezing temperature. It was gone seven and Ruby hadn't got in from work. Caroline hadn't phoned ahead. Forewarned was tipped-off.

She was pretty sure Ruby wasn't personally involved, but after hours spent piecing together snatches of memory she was ninety-nine per cent certain the four shadowy figures that night had been female. She'd dismissed the possibility out of hand when Sarah mooted it at the hospital, the way she saw it now Ruby, probably in all innocence, had pointed Amy in Caroline's direction. But the lawyer also played mother hen to a group of girls she felt sorry for because of their crap start in life. Amy's life hadn't exactly been a breeze. What if they'd hooked up, swapped stories? Then ganged up. Not just to protect Amy from Caroline's advances, but because they couldn't countenance the reporter giving Ram a voice. Maybe they were so incensed at the prospect of Ram strutting his verbal stuff, that they viewed Caroline as fair game, that smacking her round the face was somehow acceptable. Because given the size of one of those shadows, a hell of a lot more damage could have been inflicted.

Lights dazzled as a car pulled up behind. Caroline checked the mirror, watched a woman get out, walk up the road. She relaxed. The glimpse of her own face confirmed her thinking that the attack was warning shot rather than full-on barrage, punches had definitely been pulled. Not that she wasn't effing furious. But she could see a way of using it to her advantage. It was a bargaining chip, wasn't it? *Hi Ruby, tell Amy if she plays nice, I won't bring in the cops.* Like hell.

Course, she could have it all wrong. She'd just have to play it by ear.

Sarah was almost out of the office when the email alert pinged. She fumbled one-handed for the phone in her coat pocket. *Hi Sarah, Best I can do, Ben.* Retracing her steps, she dumped bag and briefcase, rebooted the computer. If the picture wasn't much cop there was no point viewing it on a small screen. Eyes lit by the monitor, she pursed her lips as she studied the image. *Not bad.* He hadn't worked miracles, only sharpened it a touch, lifted the light a little. It was definitely worth letting King take a look. Just seeing the group shot might spark a few synapses in King's brain, get the thought juices flowing. She forwarded it, added a line: 'call me asap'. Should she give Ben a call? No. Email would do. *Thanks, Ben. Your best's not bad. Not bad at all.*

The quality was crap but Caroline's hand trembled round the phone, the picture sent a shiver down her spine. The faces were all but obscured but without a shadow of doubt she knew it was her attackers. Ironic but the shadows actually gave it away. When she'd been set on, she'd spied the same four silhouettes out of the corner of her eye. Four shadows, one much bigger than the others. She heard footfalls, almost dropped the phone. Glanced in the mirror. Froze. Four girls, arms linked, strutted towards the car. The big one kicked a can, sent it skittering along the pavement. The big one. Even without the dark gear, the macho swagger, it had to be them, didn't it? Back for another go at her? How did they know she was here? Lifting her collar, she slumped further into the seat. In the wing mirror she watched them hive off laughing, letting themselves into Ruby's house. How cosy. All girls together. Caroline clenched a fist. That was a hell of a lot more than she'd bargained for. Maybe seeing the little shits again brought it all back. She looked at the picture on the screen, read Sarah's message.

* * *

The call came just as Sarah unlocked the Audi. Clocking caller ID, she smiled. Maybe he'd changed his mind about that drink.

'Where are you, boss?' Maybe not. He sounded dead sober.

'In the car park. Why?'

'You might want to head back. I'm in the squad room.'

'I'm listening.' And heading back.

'Lingham's victim? The girl who tried to top herself?'

'Tracey Maxwell?' The name had come up at the late brief. She was one of the zillion people on the squad's chase list.

'I got on to Charlie Lewis asked if there was a pic on file.'

'And?'

'I'm looking at it now. She calls herself something different these days, boss.'

Caroline flung the phone on the passenger seat. Half a dozen times she'd got the engaged signal. Whoever Sarah Quinn was talking to, it couldn't be more important than what King had to tell her. There was quite a party going on at Wells' Towers. The girls were still in there and Ruby had turned up five minutes ago with Jas Ram in tow. With the red hair glinting under the streetlight and Ruby laughing and flirting away, bold as brass incarnate wasn't in it. Caroline was no detective, she hadn't a clue what was going on but as journo she was desperate to find out.

Sarah, chin resting in hand, stood in front of Dave's computer screen. The blonde hair was shorter, the face fuller, but there was no mistake. 'Lily Maitland. My God.'

'There's more, boss.' Harries tapped a few keys, ran his finger down the list that appeared. 'These were the kids resident at Grange Manor in 2007.'

'Michelle Keating.'

Harries gazed up at Sarah. 'They were in it with their boyfriends, boss.'

Maybe. Her thoughts raced. 'What about the others?' Charlie and Shannon.

'Huntie's checking now.' John Hunt sat at a desk near the window, phone clamped to his ear. 'It's got to be that though, boss.'

She frowned, not convinced. 'I don't see it that way, Dave. What if they set the youths up, used them as fall guys? Their testimony's why Wilde and Brody are facing murder charges.'

'The girls planned it? They were the brains? Is that what you're saying?'

The brains – and the brawn. 'Remember Charlotte. The other housemate Shannon? I bet they were victims too and I bet the four of them set out to wreak revenge on men who'd abused them. They didn't need Wilde and Brody's muscle. They had enough of their own.'

'That your phone, boss?'

She batted a hand. 'Let's think it through . . . Wilde and Brody definitely beat up Duncan Agnew. We know that, and so did the girls. Say they piggybacked the crime? Copied it when they attacked Foster, Gibbs, Lingham so Wilde and Brody got the blame.'

'They went a hell of a lot further, boss.' He tilted his head at the whiteboards, the barely recognisable faces, the virtually obliterated features.

'Yes. 'Cause it was personal.' Baker had been right all along about that. She'd better call him.

'Bloody clever, too.' Befriending a couple of youths who'd already been in and out of trouble with the law.

'And callous.' Positioning themselves so they had access to Wilde and Brody's clothing; wearing the hoodies when they attacked Foster and Gibbs; planting stolen property at the squat and when push came to shove pointing the finger at their so-called boyfriends. The youths had been a perfect foil. 'We need to bring them in for questioning, Dave. Like now.'

'Do you want to get your phone, boss?'

Grimacing, she snatched the handset from her pocket. 'I'm up against it, Caroline. Make it quick.'

'The attackers are girls. And I know where they are. That quick enough?'

Sarah drove. Bat out of hell on speed mode. Dave was on the car phone liaising with back-up. The DI's initial confusion had cleared within seconds. She'd assumed Caroline was talking about the BAD attacks. Almost immediately it clicked that King meant hers. And that the attacks were down to the same girls. She recalled the picture of the gang. Her thanks to Ben: *Not bad. Not bad at all.* How wrong could she have been?

And now Lily, Michelle, Charlotte and Shannon were ensconced in Ruby Wells' house with Jas Ram. Who had to be the biggest bad man of them all.

'They won't do anything stupid will they, boss?'

Sarah checked the mirror. 'Depends on your definition of stupid, Dave.'

FORTY-FIVE

R uby, smiling, trailed her fingers along the back of the settee. 'I'll get the light. Take a seat.'

'I know what I'd rather take.' Jas Ram paused, casual hand in pocket, a smile playing across his lips.

Charlie landed the first blow. Her huge fist slammed into the back of his head. He staggered forward, stumbled over trip wire, crashed onto his knees. Michelle's kick sent him reeling. He scrabbled frantic to get up, gain some sort of purchase. Shannon just behind now whacked a baseball bat into the side of his face. The crunch could've been bone or teeth.

'Not too hard, babe,' Lily admonished softly. 'We need him talking.' Soft light fell on the room as she flicked a switch, glinted off knives wielded by Michelle and Shannon.

Ram cowered, snot, tears, blood trailed down cheeks, chin. 'Who are you? What—?'

'Shut it, dickhead.' Lily nodded. Charlie grabbed his hair, yanked his head back. Michelle grasped his hands, Shannon cuffed the wrists.

'On your belly. Now.'

'Look, let's—'

Charlie kneed his spine, sent him sprawling. Kicking. Flailing. 'Keep the fuck still.' The serrated blade an inch from his face had more effect than Michelle's words. 'Get his kit off, Shan.'

'Please. No.' Struggling, panic in his voice.

'Move one inch – I'll take an eye out.'

Shannon knelt, dragged down Ram's black linen pants, silk boxers.

'Please . . . let's just . . . talk.'

'Get him in the chair.'

The upright near the fireplace had rope, leather straps readied. Charlie bound his upper body, ankles. Ram's whimpering ragged breaths, Lily's soft humming the only sounds in the room.

'Cold in here,' Michelle said. 'Light it, Shannon.'

She struck a match, waved it close to Ram's face, the flame glinted in his dark eyes. A film of sweat oozed over his top lip. 'Who are you? What do you want?'

As Shannon knelt to light the fire, Lily pranced across the room, sat cross-legged at Ram's feet, placed a recorder in her lap. 'We're babes. Against dickheads.' Head cocked, she smiled. 'And we want a little fireside story, Mr Dickhead.'

'You're fucking doolally that's what you are, love.'

Lily crooked her finger. Charlie shambled over, drew back her arm, hammered her fist into Ram's face.

'Girls.' Ruby stood in the doorway, arms folded. 'A little gentle persuasion. That's what we agreed.'

'Best you go now, Rubes,' Michelle said. 'Slip out the back, eh?'

'This story.' Faux pensive, Lily tapped a finger against her mouth. 'Once upon a time . . . Jas Ram raped, buggered, battered and abused.' She switched on the tape. 'From the top. Who. What. Why. Where. When. Full confession, Mr Dickhead. Then we'll let you go. The end.'

'Tell me this is a joke?'

'Yeah. Dead funny, innit? How's it going, Shan?'

'Not far off, Lil.' Twisting the poker, she rammed it further into the flames. 'Five mins or so?'

'Where've you been?' King held the door as Sarah got out of the motor. 'You took your time.'

Sarah batted a hand, her gaze trained on the house. 'How long they been in there?' She registered the police transit further down the street. No blues. No sirens.

'The girls – an hour. Thirty, thirty-five minutes since Ruby and Ram arrived.' King hugged herself, shifted her weight from foot to foot.

'And you've heard nothing?' Stupid question; she'd have said.

'I've not had my ear pressed to the door, I can tell you that.' Not since hearing the girls were dangerous, had killed already and if panicked, had nothing left to lose.

'Stay here, Caroline. Don't move.'

Sarah and Harries approached the house in step. A low-key strategy had been hammered out on the phone with Baker. She'd try talking first. If that didn't work . . . half a dozen officers in full protective gear were primed, ready to go in, the same number positioned round the back.

'What the hell are they doing in there, boss?'

She shook her head. 'You tell me.'

'You said you'd let me go if I told you. End of.' Sweat ran down Ram's face, dripped from his chin.

'Yes.' Lily smiled that angelic smile. 'You've been a very good boy.' She pressed rewind, made sure his voice was on tape, the whole sordid story on record. 'But.' She stopped the playback, tapped the recorder with a finger. 'You've also been a very bad boy, haven't you? What do you think, girls?'

Lined up on the settee Michelle, Charlie and Shannon gave sage nods, chorused: 'Very bad.'

'Still, who are we to judge?' Lily played a strand of hair between her fingers. 'Come in, babe. What do you reckon?'

Amy Hemming, standing just outside the door, had heard every word. White-faced, cheeks moist with tears, she headed straight for Ram, spat in his face. He jerked back, almost toppled the chair. Sighing, Charlie got to her feet, positioned herself behind, provided ample ballast. Amy lashed out again and again, slapping, kicking.

'Are we good to go, Shan?' Lily cut a glance at the fire. The poker, unused, glowed in the flames.

'Please . . . you . . .'

'What's that noise?' Michelle cupped an ear. 'Someone left a tap on?'

'Yuk!' Lily shuffled backwards. 'Don't shit yourself as well, dickhead.'

Laughing with the others, Shannon knelt at the fire, ignored the poker, picked up tongs, parted the nearest coals to locate the three metal shapes placed underneath. A warm smile lit her plain features as she plucked out the first glowing red letter.

'You can do the honours, Amy.' Lily rose. A low desperate keening came from Ram as she smoothed back his long fringe. 'B is for . . .'

The first ear-splitting scream sounded before Sarah knocked. Heart racing, she pounded the door. Scream after piercing scream filled the air. Harries whacked the wood with his fist. 'Police. Open up.'

'They'll not hear us, Dave. Come on, out the way.' She beckoned at the guys behind. A uniformed officer took a run at the door with a battering ram; wood splintered, didn't give. *Again, man, again.* The screams were incessant, like an animal in pain. Sarah shuddered, realised now the meaning of blood-curdling. 'Christ, Dave, if we don't get in soon . . .'

Charlie's hands clamped Ram's head in place. Lily nodded encouragement. 'Well done, Amy. Almost there.'

'Cops are here,' Michelle said. No panic. No surprise. Like they'd been expecting a visit. 'Best get a move on.'

Amy picked up the third letter, advanced on Ram with the tongs. The screams reached a new pitch. Then stopped. He slumped in the chair; broken face battered and bleeding. The smell of faeces and burnt flesh hung in the air.

Sarah burst into the room. Froze, eyes wide. Harries and two uniforms stared over her shoulder.

'You're too late,' Lily said.

Sarah rushed forward, pushed the girl roughly aside, felt for a pulse. 'Ambulance. Now. He's alive.'

'Shame,' Lily said. 'Still, good work, Amy. He won't fuck up anyone else in a hurry.'

The word 'bad' branded across Ram's forehead formed a life sentence of sorts.

Two Days Later

Friday night and Sarah sat in the Queen's Head, two glasses and a half empty bottle of Sauvignon Blanc on the table. Another time and she might have regarded it as half-full. Eliciting the girls' back stories over the last couple of days had taken its toll, would emotionally scar her for life. In her mind's eye she saw the physical scars inflicted on Ram. She took another slug of wine, fully intended getting smashed – transport home already laid on.

Baker left Twig and Huntie at the bar, sauntered over, pint in hand. 'Cruise cried off again, Quinn?'

'Not funny first time round, chief.'

'Join you?' *Why bother asking?* 'No point dwelling on it, Quinn.' He crossed his legs, took a slurp of beer. What? Failure? Fuck up? Fact that five damaged young women, let down by the system, wanted justice so badly they wreaked it personally and now faced years behind bars. 'They're devious little bints, Quinn. Mad, bad, dangerous to know. Not your fault you didn't pick up on it sooner.'

My fault? 'Pur-lease, chief. Those "bints" ran rings round us, served up Wilde and Brody on a plate. Only thing missing was mint sauce.' They still were running rings. They refused point blank to incriminate Ruby Wells and if the lawyer continued denying knowledge of what they had planned, she might just get away with it. Detectives had been excavating her back story like there was no tomorrow. They'd established that both parents had died fourteen years ago and that a younger daughter had ended up in care and hanged herself. Had she been abused? Was Ruby ridden with guilt and remorse for failing to save her sister? Was it this force that had driven her to form such strong bonds with the girls? She refuted every suggestion; said she'd been estranged from her family, knew nothing of the events. Sarah didn't believe a word, found Wells' innocence-slash-ignorance inconceivable. On the other hand, she was pretty convinced Amy Hemming had only acted against Ram. *Only?* Branding 'bad' across a man's forehead . . . Sarah closed her eyes briefly. She'd asked herself a million times if they could have prevented it, acted sooner. She'd seen Ram in hospital. So not a pretty sight.

'Could've been worse you know, Quinn.' The chief pointed towards his crotch. 'Imagine if they'd gone for his—'

'Mr Baker.' Beaming smile. The DI's drinking partner back from nose-powdering. Must be costing King a fortune in concealer. 'Super to see you again.'

'Ditto.' His smile was less certain. Probably thought she was taking the piss. Sarah sipped wine as King and Baker swapped small talk. The meet had been King's call; she'd wanted a word prior to heading back to London. Before nipping to the loo, she'd come out with words like respect, admiration, how Sarah faced danger head-on while she only wrote about it later. Sarah had almost asked how strong her medication was. As for reporting, King had rarely been off screen all week.

'You still working on this book, then, Kingie?' *Kingie?* Christ, Caroline would be calling him Fred next.

'I certainly am.' Head cocked, she leaned towards the chief. 'How about giving me the police perspective? Top cop tells all.' Sarah twisted her mouth. If flirting was an Olympic sport, King would be wreathed in gold. Jas Ram had certainly given his exclusive. The DI shuddered as she recalled the guy's faltering voice on tape. And the unearthly screams. Talk about forced confessions.

Not a word would be admissible. But, then, Ram's disfigurement was worse than any sentence a court could hand down. Turned out the recorder was King's property, it would be returned eventually. The girls knew who nicked it, no one was naming names. As for the memory stick, King reckoned Wells had lifted it during the hospital visit. There'd been a five-minute window apparently when Caroline left the room.

Sarah sat back, swirled the wine in her glass, shame it wasn't tea and she could read the leaves. Not that she needed special powers to divine the girls' guilt: it was as good as written on the wall. The murder weapons – hammer and knife – had been found hidden at the Sparkbrook house. Doubtless further evidence would emerge during the months of hard graft that lay ahead before the case got anywhere near a jury. Sarah drew her lips together. It seemed to her the young women were proud of taking the law into their own hands. She wondered if the wrongdoings would split public opinion in the way they'd polarised the squad's thinking. All five had suffered appalling abuse for years at the hands of predatory men. Mitigating circumstances don't come much stronger but was it ever right to act as judge and executioner?

'What do you think?' King's catlike gaze was on Sarah.

'Say again?'

'Ruby Wells? I was just saying to the chief, she must've supplied the girls with some of the info: where the men lived, what they were up to – that kind of stuff?'

As a lawyer, she couldn't be better placed. 'You tell me, Caroline. We're still working on it.' Digging away with a fleet of JCBs, but if the gang kept shtum, the squad might never unearth the full picture. Like they'd never traced Blue Eyes, the girl who'd visited the nick to talk about Ram but left without a word. In more than one sense, Sarah saw Slip Girl as the one who got away. Ram certainly wouldn't be troubling her again.

'See, that's another thing.' King tapped a finger against her pout. 'I can't be doing with loose ends. Give me a beginning, middle and end any day.' She'd certainly helped piece together her part of the story: vague memories of hearing piano music convinced Caroline she'd been held in Amy's home before the girls had bundled her into a car. Forensics had lifted confirmatory hairs and fibres from Alice Hemming's Volvo. Not that Amy's mother was involved; alibi evidence proved she'd been out that night.

Sarah gave a tired smile. 'I think you'll find that only happens in fiction, Caroline.'

'Davy.' It was Harries' turn to get the full beam treatment. 'How you doing?'

Baker was half out of his seat. 'My shout, lad.'

He nodded at King, gave Sarah a warm smile. 'No thanks, sir. I'm on taxi duty. I've only dropped by to pick up the boss.'

And the boss had a bottle of Chablis chilling in the fridge. Plus a case of champagne from a still mortified Nat Hardy. He'd dropped it off at the nick two days ago, note attached telling Sarah he'd joined the AA. She assumed he didn't mean the breakdown service. Caroline cut a speculative glance between Sarah and Harries. 'Where are you two lovebirds off to then?' The hand pressed to her mouth didn't quite hide the innocent smirk. 'Whoops. Sorry. Just slipped out.'

'No worries. Facts were never your strong point.' The wink took the edge off her jibe. They'd never be besties, but recent events meant they'd reached a sort of understanding. Harries held Sarah's coat. Returning his smile, she reached her arms into the sleeves. 'I'll look out for the book, Caroline. Has it got a name yet?'

'I've got a good one, Kingie. How's about . . . Ram to the Slaughter?' Talk about tasteless. Blank faces greeted the unbelievably piss-poor offering. The chief raised both palms, even managed to look a little sheepish. 'Sorry guys – bad gag.'

'Close, Mr B.' With an innocent twinkle in her eye, Caroline tilted her glass towards him. 'I'm calling it *Bad Men*.'